THE SMOOTH FACE OF EVIL

On Wednesday afternoon, two boys who had spent most of the day paddling about on the dark waters of the old gravel pit pulled in to the side to refresh themselves with Mars Bars and crisps. They made landfall at a slightly different spot from where they had put their canoe into the water that morning, which explained why they had missed it then.

They saw the pale white hand of a dead man, partially screened by a bush that overhung the black water of the artificial lake, breaking the surface.

Also in Arrow by Margaret Yorke

MARGARET YORKE

The Smooth Face
of Evil

Mysterious Press Books (UK) are published
in association with Arrow Books Limited
62-65 Chandos Place, London WC2N 4NW

An imprint of Century Hutchinson Limited

London Melbourne Sydney Auckland
Johannesburg and agencies throughout
the world

First published by Hutchinson & Co. Ltd 1984
Arrow edition 1985
Mysterious Press edition 1989

Printed and bound in Great Britain by
Courier International Ltd, Tiptree, Essex

ISBN 0 09 944200 0

1

The lonely ones were settling down for the night.

In high-rise apartment blocks and thin-walled cell-like bed-sitters; in cottages nestling in dark hamlets and in terraced houses; in bungalows and suburban villas; in mansions and even, perhaps, in a palace or two; in cities, towns and villages, inland and on the coast, the nightly rituals of the solitary were performed.

Some people put out the cat; others gave the dog a last run. Many checked bolts on doors and windows after leaving the milkman's instructions on the step. Some made cups of tea or malted milk; others poured tots of whisky. Some swallowed pills; some read; some listened to music. The lucky ones fell asleep quickly; others fretted restlessly, suffering old wounds again.

Terry Brett, at the moment without a regular source of income, was walking through the quiet streets of Westborough. An occasional car drove past as he paused to look at the lighted display in a radio and television shop whose window was protected by strong metal mesh. Some months before, bricks had been hurled at the plate glass windows of one of Westborough's supermarkets, breaking them; three boys had made off with bottles of liquor, and more had been broken and spilled. The culprits had never been caught.

Such actions were not Terry's style at all. Violence was crude, uncivilized, and unnecessary. He picked things up by other means – articles left in unlocked cars; or cars themselves, locked or unlocked, parked in quiet streets. Over the years he'd built up a useful collection of keys from various sources – garages, scrap merchants, junk shops – and when funds were low could always dispose of a newly acquired car to a workshop where, in a few hours, it would be resprayed, given new number plates and sent on its way to a buyer. Because of his skill in lifting cars he'd been approached, after his jail sentence, by more than one gang planning a robbery to find them a getaway car, but always he had turned such suggestions down. They might carry guns. They'd be ready for violence. He wasn't.

There were so many opportunities for someone alert. Women laid their handbags, often unzipped, on benches beside them in cafés and snack bars, never suspecting the nicely dressed young man who looked like a bank clerk or an insurance salesman, sitting nearby, when later they found their purses had gone. He'd worked as a barman, a waiter, as a door-to-door salesman, as a market researcher and in a department store. Despite his lack of the correct papers – lost, he always explained, in a fire – he was given jobs ahead of other applicants because of his good appearance, his clean fingernails and his respectful manner. His door-to-door selling experience had led to more; he'd bought damaged prints cheap after a warehouse was flooded and had gone round a housing estate with them. In this way, he had met more than one discontented middle-aged housewife and had become her lover. The grateful women paid well for silence when, later, Terry explained that unfortunately he would have to speak to their husbands unless they could help him clear up some outstanding debts.

The women all paid, always with tears and never with anger. Terry was good at selecting them. He was their benefactor, leaving them precious memories to nurture through the ensuing arid years of their dead marriages. He guaranteed satisfaction until the moment was reached, in every affair, when the level of boredom and the cloying devotion became nauseating. Then it was time to present his account and depart. They were so silly, the women: so soft and so greedy. They were as demanding and stupid as kids would be if given the freedom of a sweetshop.

Terry had just ended such a relationship and had five hundred pounds in hand. The silly cow hadn't been able to raise any more cash, but she'd given him her engagement ring and a locket that had belonged to her grandmother. The ring was quite nice; he'd sell it somewhere well away from where she lived. He'd say it was the sad result of a broken engagement. Terry knew that the jeweller would believe him; he'd done it before.

His parents thought Terry worked in computers. He'd had a spell abroad, they told their friends in Woking, where they lived. Terry didn't keep in touch as much as he might, they lamented, but young people were often thoughtless. They had no idea that while they imagined him in Germany, Terry was in prison. Terry's father was a minor civil servant who travelled to London each day, spending a fortune on fares; his mother was a soft, faded woman not unlike those he now exploited. Terry had a married sister who was a librarian, and a brother who had followed their father into the civil service. Terry himself moved about the country taking a room in whatever town he was working. Now and then, if his papers were up to date, he registered for unemployment benefit, even working for a while if a job was offered; it might lead to a crock of gold; you never knew.

He picked male victims sometimes. He found them in bars. They paid exceedingly well, especially the married ones, and he controlled what happened. There were depths to which Terry was not prepared to go.

Now, Terry felt like tackling something new. He had come to Westborough because he had never operated there and he wanted to look around. It was time to leave Swindon while wounds there healed. So far, none of his victims had met one another and he must take care to keep things that way.

Terry walked past the Rigby Arms, a timbered hotel in the main street of Westborough. He saw a blue Rover 3500 parked outside with a briefcase on the back seat but it was too near the street light to touch. There was a white Porsche, too. He sauntered on, then turned back. It was past closing time, too late to go prospecting in the hotel bar.

A man and a woman came out of the Rigby Arms and went up to the Rover. The man unlocked it and opened the passenger door for the woman to get in: so they weren't married, thought Terry, watching from the shadows. The woman was young, the man much older. Terry made a mental note of the car's number before moving on; he often did things like that; you never knew what information might come in useful.

He walked on through the cold streets, looking at every car, for it was time to go home.

He found an old Marina with the key in the ignition. What fools people were! Terry drove it back to Swindon, leaving it in a street a mile from his digs.

His landlady never heard him enter the house. He was always so quiet and thoughtful; she liked young Mr Terence Brett, who paid his rent regularly and was always polite.

While Terry Brett was prowling the streets of Westborough, six miles away in her granny flat at Harcombe House, Alice Armitage was removing her cosmetic armour of beige foundation, coral lipstick, plenty of eyeshadow and mascara with which, with a touch of Je Reviens, stud earrings, artificial pearls and several bracelets, she daily faced her foes: isolation; ennui; the rudeness of shop assistants. She creamed her papery skin and brushed her thinning hair which was tinted honey-blonde and permed in a frizz round her small head. Before getting into bed she crossed the narrow landing and entered the living-room of her tiny apartment, going to the window and drawing back the curtain to look at the wintry landscape. Because the trees were bare she could see the lodge, where a glow of light showed at the curtained windows. The outside light was on, so Sue wasn't back yet. It was her late week. Sue was a receptionist at the Rigby Arms in Westborough. Jonathan would have gone to fetch her, wouldn't he? For a moment Alice experienced a faint unease. Before now, Sue had been brought home by Alice's son Giles, who had begun to spend too much time in bars. Still, if he happened to be in the Rigby when Sue's shift was over, it was only neighbourly to give her a lift, Alice rationalized.

Thinking thus, she saw the white beam of a car's headlights at the gate, then the bright circles as it turned in. Jonathan in his beige Granada, or Giles in his Rover? Alice waited to see.

The car stopped at the lodge, and a figure got out. Then Giles, in his blue Rover 3500, drove on to the barn which was used as a garage for their four cars – the Rover, the Granada, Alice's Metro and Helen's Volvo. Helen was Giles's wife and it was because of her, and her aspirations, that Alice had thrown in her lot with her family after her husband died. By

10

selling Windlea, her home on the outskirts of Bournemouth, and adding the money to theirs, Alice had enabled her son and his wife to buy Harcombe House, on which Helen had set her heart.

'It's the sensible thing to do, Alice,' her daughter-in-law had said, when Walter had died suddenly after a minor operation. She'd said nothing about wanting to have her with them, Alice had often remembered since.

Harcombe House was a large granite mansion built by a Victorian tycoon. It had barns and outbuildings, and, at the end of the short drive, a small lodge with a high gabled roof. When the Armitages moved in it had been empty for some time, and needed a thorough renovation. Much had been done: the kitchen was modernized; the main rooms papered and painted; but the antiquated heating system still remained. There were heavy, old-fashioned radiators in Alice's rooms but the warmth never reached that far, and Helen decreed that using electric convector fires was far too extravagant. Besides, the aged wiring might not stand the load.

The parts that showed downstairs had been made pleasant and comfortable, and some of Alice's own furniture had been used in the drawing-room. Helen was developing the scope of the interior decorating business she had begun a few years before. Then, she had merely advised on curtains, covers, lampshades and so on; now, she undertook an entire house, including buying the furniture. She wanted to make her own home a shop-window for her skills and she was striving to build up a circle of acquaintances – whom she called friends – who would recommend her because they had seen her taste reflected here at Harcombe. When money was easier, plumbing, heating and draught-proofing would be tackled; meanwhile, a swimming-pool had been built in the grounds, and the old hard tennis-court rescued and re-surfaced. There were eight acres of land with the house, part meadow, where now Dawn and Amanda, Alice's grand-daughters, kept ponies. Giles, helped by a jobbing gardener, was slowly reducing the jungle growth that had swallowed the flower beds.

'She's set her heart on the house,' Giles had said to Alice, explaining that the sale of their house in Pinner would not begin to cover the cost. Even with her contribution the mortgage was vast and terrifying.

'Couldn't Helen's father – ?' Alice had hazarded, when Helen was out of the room helping Alice's Mrs Bennett wash up after the cold meal they'd had when they returned from the crematorium.

'Not again,' said Giles. 'I'm beholden enough as it is.'

Giles worked for his father-in-law in a firm that made plastic casings for other industrial users. It was a sound business, but its profits had dropped in recent years and a takeover bid was in the air; Giles saw no point in telling Alice this. Helen's father had given them their first small house when they married, taking Giles into the firm with a higher salary than he had received as an accountant and promising him a place on the board before long. Giles had his director-ship now, but to justify it he laboured long and hard, and at home spent hours poring over sales figures and production statistics.

Alice and Walter had loved their only son and delighted in his modest youthful successes. When he first brought Helen home, they were overjoyed. She was a fair, pretty girl just back from a year abroad. There was no sign, then, of her driving ambition, but Alice and Walter had seen its birth. They had worried together, knowing that Giles lacked what-ever was needed to keep her content. What would Walter have advised, Alice had wondered, faced with Helen's scheme?

Before going into hospital, Walter had explained that if anything went wrong Alice would have the house and a good pension, but she had barely listened. Soon he would be home, able to enjoy car outings, bowls with his friends, their weekly theatre trips. Since his retirement they had drawn closer together – a surprise for Alice, who had seen her friends irritated at having their husbands about the place all day, requiring lunch. But Walter had had a heart attack after his operation and died without regaining conscious-ness; their new joy had been wiped out. That was a week ago, and now here were Giles and Helen offering her a chance to share their home.

Alice hadn't needed a lot of persuading. Windlea was too big for her alone, as Helen had pointed out. Vague thoughts of a bungalow somewhere near drifted through Alice's mind but she dismissed the idea. She'd be alone. Of course, she'd be alone in her flat at Harcombe House, too, but the family would be in the main part of the house and she'd make friends in the village.

'Mrs Bennett – 'Alice had said. Mrs Bennett, who had cleaned and polished Windlea twice a week for the last twenty years was a friend; she it was who had dried Alice's tears when she came back from that last hospital visit and had had to telephone Giles.

'There'll be someone like her,' Giles had reassured her. 'Helen will need help. There's a lodge. We'll put a couple in there to work the place.'

But they hadn't. Helen had found Mrs Wood, who came five days a week from her house in the village and seldom had time to do any work for Alice because of all that Helen required her to do. And the lodge had been let.

When Jonathan and Sue had moved in, the lodge had been screened from Alice's dormer window by the huge beech tree that spread wide, shady boughs over the gravel sweep in front of the house and the barn, and which, in autumn, cast its leaves like copper filings on the ground. They weren't married, but Alice felt sure that they would be, soon. There was some hitch about a divorce; Helen had not realized this when she arranged the lease and was annoyed; she did not like any sort of messiness. Sue was so friendly; Alice thought she must be well suited to her hotel work. Jonathan seemed quiet and calm; he must have been sadly provoked to have left his wife and children, Alice felt. He often looked rather sad. But the two were obviously so much in love that Alice was enchanted with them. She hoped that it would last. Things didn't, always.

Now, Jonathan would be welcoming Sue home from work. Alice imagined them together and felt happier. She watched Giles walk from the barn across the gravel sweep to his own front door. His tread was heavy; odd to think that he was well into middle age. When he had gone, Alice drew the curtains across the window, turned out the light and walked across the landing to her small bedroom which was almost totally filled by the big bed she had shared with Walter. Helen had wanted her to have a small divan which would take up far less space, but Alice had refused to do so. Now, she drew the covers around her and tried to pretend that Walter's large, friendly bulk was at her back.

In the night, she woke from a frightening dream. It concerned Giles. She'd been running to warn him of some impending danger, but her legs were slow and heavy, as if stuck in treacle, and she could not move them fast enough. She'd been calling and shouting to him: then she woke.

Alice sat up in bed, hands to her thin chest that was covered by a printed viyella nightgown and a knitted bedjacket.

The dream faded, as dreams so often do when the dreamer wakes. Alice sipped water from the glass at her bedside and lay down again. The room was chilly. It was a long time before she slept.

2

Alice's first weeks at Harcombe had been spent in a haze of misery. It was summer, and the overgrown garden was full of roses, many of them old-fashioned scented varieties. On fine days, bees hummed among the twiggy overgrown lavender, and at weekends, when Giles cut the grass, sitting on a large mower which left huge stripes across the lawn, the sweet smell of the fresh-mown grass reminded Alice of Windlea, where Walter had cut their lawn with a Suffolk Colt and where the scent was the same. Alice, sitting with her library book on the terrace if Helen was out, or round the side of the house out of sight if she were at home, tried not to weep as she mourned the loss of a companion who had never been exciting but who had been gently amiable and always dependable for the greater part of her life, even during the war, for his job with the ministry was a reserved occupation.

Alice had expected to see much more of her grand-daughters after the move, but they were sent to boarding-school, and as soon as term ended in July the family went to Corfu for a fortnight, leaving Alice alone. They'd booked their villa before Walter died, and it was not large enough for her to go too, Helen had stated.

'Couldn't I – ?' Alice began.

'Couldn't you what?' Helen asked sharply.

Alice had been going to suggest that she might stay in a hotel near their villa, but she saw how Helen would respond to that idea and changed direction.

'I might pop back to Bournemouth, just for a few days,' she said. 'See my friends, and so on.'

'I hope you won't,' said Helen. 'Go when we return, by all means, if you must, but I'd been counting on you to keep an eye on things here. With a house this size, if one's away, thieves get in, but if someone's about they're discouraged. Besides, the workmen are still around.'

The surround to the swimming-pool hadn't been finished. During her lonely days Alice had liked going out to talk to the men making the pool, which had been done very quickly once the hole was dug and the container dropped into the cavity.

She gave in.

'Well, of course I'll be glad to be useful,' she said.

Alice's sense of isolation, during the fortnight, was almost more than she could endure. She recalled Helen's words and often woke in the night imagining that she heard intruders. She would get up, and with a large torch held before her would patrol the house, which was always empty. When Mrs Wood arrived, Alice would invent reasons for pottering about the main part of the house. She would perch in Helen's own sitting-room, which faced south-west and on fine days was full of sun, when Mrs Wood was busy elsewhere, guiltily enjoying the light airy room which was such a contrast to her own dim, north-facing attic.

'Shame they didn't find you a better part of the house, Mrs Armitage, dear,' Mrs Wood said once, catching her there as she read the paper. 'It's big enough, lord knows.'

'We all value our privacy,' said Alice repressively. 'It

wouldn't do if I were on top of them.' She folded her paper and left the room, giving Mrs Wood the impression that she was, after all, a stuck-up old biddy, which until then she had not appeared to be. After that Mrs Wood made still less effort to clean Alice's rooms, but they didn't need it; Alice was quite able to clean and polish her tiny apartment.

Mrs Wood did not come on Fridays. By Saturday evening Alice had not spoken to a soul for two days, nor seen another human. Sue was on day shift, and Jonathan had gone to see his children. His wife insisted that he took them to his parents' house in Kent; she did not want them meeting Sue.

In desperation, on Sunday, Alice went to church. She had learned from Mrs Wood that there was no vicar in Harcombe; a roving one came twice a month to take services, which were not well attended, and Alice found herself one of a congregation of five, three other women and an old man. She sat at the back, stood, knelt, mouthed hymns and responses and fled from the building without speaking to anyone. Religion had played no great part in her life with Walter; they'd gone to church at Christmas and Easter; that was all.

That evening, when she turned on the television, Alice began to talk to the announcer, just to see if she could still converse.

She'd imagined a populous village, before she came, with the big house at its centre, but Harcombe was only a hamlet, a single road ending at the church, with two or three large cottages – tasteful conversions of former labourers' dwellings – a few smaller ones and some bungalows bordering it. Some council houses had been built after the war, but there was no recent development. The school had been closed; there was no pub; and the single small shop only succeeded because it was also a sub-post office. That was now under threat of closure, and pensioners would have to go to Great Minton to draw their money. Most of Harcombe's residents shopped in Westborough; there was no bus service through the village, but by walking a mile you could catch the bus on the main road. A fish van came every Wednesday afternoon and parked for an hour outside the shop, and a butcher from Great Minton delivered once a week. The village shop sold mass-produced bread.

Alice, when she first arrived, had explored by car. She saw few people about, and no one had come to call. People didn't, these days. One of her duties was to visit the fish van each week for Helen. She would buy herself a small trout, if the fishmonger had one, as a treat. A few faces grew familiar from these excursions; there might be a nod and perhaps a smile, but no one spoke to Alice, though they all knew each other. She was too shy to break in to their talk and introduce herself. Why should they want to bother with her? She took to going further afield in her Metro – to Westborough, where there were several inns and cafés in which by turns she had lunch, and where there were, as in most towns, Boots, two supermarkets, a good dress shop, and, down a side street with plenty of room to park, the public library. Alice joined it, but found that she could not concentrate on the books she brought home; she would turn the pages, her eyes moving over the print, and at the end be unaware of what she had supposedly read. This worried her and she went to the doctor in Great Minton; he thought her predicament natural after bereavement and a removal, prescribing Mogadon but only when really needed. She'd soon settle down, he declared.

Alice, already thin, had lost seven pounds when Giles and his family returned from Corfu, but because make-up hid her pallor, and she looked, as always, elegant, in a long-sleeved cotton dress and her pearls and bracelets, he did not notice.

Giles, Alice thought, looked better after his holiday; a tan was superimposed over his heavy, florid features. They'd all swum a lot, and he and the girls had enjoyed using the boat which went with the house. Helen had made friends with some people in a neighbouring villa and had thus acquired potential clients, since they were moving into an old house in Wiltshire quite soon and were faced with a big renovation programme. He'd had to admire the subtle way in which she had found out all this and made apparent her own ability to lift the burden of selection from her new friends. She had all the ruthlessness he lacked; in his job, she would have reached the top, family firm or not, whereas Giles himself laboured away to earn a salary that was far higher than he merited. He was always tired, and often had a pain in his stomach which he feared was an ulcer, if nothing worse. Sometimes, when he read of men struck down by heart attacks in their prime, Giles wished it could happen to him; it would solve all the problems he could not handle.

Giles had begun calling at the Rigby Arms rather by chance, though he often stopped somewhere for a bracer or two on the way home. The first time he went there after the holiday was the day the girls went back to school. He would miss them. Things were better at home when they were there; there was the illusion of contented family life at meal times, and Amanda's infatuation with her pony, Mr Jinks, was an enchantment. But tonight there would be just Helen. She would have plans to draw, patterns to choose. She worked most evenings now.

He'd forgotten about Sue until he went through the swing doors of the Rigby Arms and saw her in the foyer.

He did not stay long that first time, but soon, when she was on the late shift, he began to stay on for a meal. It seemed only sensible, then, to suggest that he should take her home to save Jonathan turning out. Sometimes, on such nights, alone in his bedroom at the further end of the passage from Helen's, Giles would have sensational dreams.

Alice noticed the poster about the coffee morning when she went to the shop for a tin of soup. In aid of the NSPCC, a cause all must approve, it was to be held at Meadow Cottage.

She would go to it, Alice resolved. She would meet people there, some of the women she saw in the fish queue, no doubt. They were probably pleasant when you became acquainted. She asked the dour woman who ran the shop where Meadow Cottage was, and on the appointed day set forth, inwardly quaking. She'd taken pains with her appearance and wore a fawn woollen two-piece and smart patent shoes.

The poster had advertised the time as ten-thirty; Alice arrived at ten forty-five to find several cars outside Meadow Cottage, and, as she turned off the Metro's engine, she could hear a loud hum of talk coming from the open windows. She almost turned back, but forced herself on.

At the door, a girl in jeans and a loose pink sweater smiled as she accepted Alice's entrance fee.

'Coffee's through there,' she said, pointing to an open door.

Alice's head was swimming slightly as she walked into a sitting-room which seemed filled with women all on the most intimate terms with each other. It was several minutes before someone offered her a cup of coffee and a bourbon biscuit. There was no spare seat, so she took her cup to a corner of the room and shrank against the wall. Her hand shook, the metal spoon chinking in the saucer.

She was far too smartly dressed, she saw, glancing round. The younger women were all in jeans or cotton skirts, the older ones in tweeds. Alice possessed no such clothes. Walter had always liked her to look smart, and she owed it to him, she felt, to keep her standards up.

At last someone spoke directly to her, but only to ask her to buy a raffle ticket. She was a large woman with big bosoms billowing softly beneath a pale cream sweater, and wide hips covered in muted checks.

'Will you be here for the draw?' this woman asked, tearing off Alice's tickets, five for a pound, the least you could decently buy, Alice inferred.

How could she stay? At that moment Alice, her ears buzzing with the unaccustomed high-pitched chatter, thought she might not last out another five minutes.

'No – I have to go,' she said. Her voice sounded harsh even to herself.

'Ah – well, tell me your name,' said the woman, grasping the ballpoint pen which hung on a string round her neck.

'Armitage,' Alice croaked. 'Alice Armitage.'

'Oh – so that's who you are!' the woman exclaimed, in booming tones, and beamed at her through her spectacles. 'From the house?'

Barbara Duncan knew everything that went on in the village, and almost everyone who lived there. Her cleaning woman brought her a good deal of news, and her early walks with her elderly spaniel took her past most of the houses, so that she kept abreast of change, but though she often passed the gates of Harcombe House, she had not met the Armitages.

She knew that the husband worked in Slough, and that the wife ran her own business – wallpapers, went the rumour, not altogether incorrectly although Barbara had pictured a do-it-yourself shop of some kind. The two girls had been briefly descried on their ponies. There was an old lady, people knew, but Alice Armitage, standing here and recognizable as someone occasionally seen at the shop, was not aged; merely fragile, and somewhat over-dressed.

Barbara now took her round the room, briskly introducing her to everyone present. Most of the younger women lived in Great Minton.

'Come to sherry on Sunday,' Barbara instructed. 'At noon. I lived at the Old Vicarage, just by the church – you can't miss it.' She swept on, allowing no time for Alice to refuse.

The following Sunday, Alice set off in some agitation. It was raining, so she went by car – she would have, anyway, whatever the weather: she felt safe in her little red box on wheels. She wore the black and white suit she had bought after Walter died. He'd liked to see her in pastels, like the Queen Mother, but she no longer felt like dressing in pink or yellow.

Two cars were parked outside the square brick house. Alice reversed hers neatly in beside them and walked up to the front door which opened as she reached it. Her hostess had seen her arrive and had been impressed with her skilful parking.

Today, Barbara Duncan wore a grey flannel skirt with two sharp box pleats front and back, and a pale blue sweater. Among her pearls rested spectacles on a gilt chain.

Alice was introduced to two elderly couples whose names she didn't take in – one was Colonel something – and two women who had been at the coffee party. After a while, Alice sorted out their names – Violet Hedges and Nancy Wilson. She drank two glasses of medium dry sherry and was talked to kindly by everyone present. The colonel and his wife came from Great Minton, the other couple from another village further away. It seemed obvious that Barbara was a widow, but what a much more capable one than herself, Alice reflected. The colonel poured out the sherry and the other man proffered peanuts and crisps. They all asked Alice how she liked the village and if she was settling in, and Alice replied, 'Very well, thank you,' to both questions, the blackest lies she had uttered in her life.

Harcombe was quiet, they told her, and she agreed. There'd been more going on in Bournemouth, where she'd come from. It was beautiful here, though, she said; the views from the house were lovely, but she missed the sea.

After a while it was time to leave.

She'd forgotten about lunch, and had to scramble an egg. She rarely had lunch with Helen and Giles; Helen had soon killed any idea of that as routine. They often had guests who would bore Alice, she said, making it clear that she really meant Alice would bore the guests.

The following Tuesday evening, Alice's telephone rang.

Giles and Helen must both be out, she thought. There was one line to the house; by day it was switched through to her, and she took messages for Helen, but the rest of the time the caller was connected to the main part of the house.

But the call was for her. It was Barbara Duncan. She and three other women – two of them Violet Hedges and Nancy Wilson, whom Alice had met on Sunday – had tickets for a matinée in London the next day. The fourth woman had severe bronchitis and couldn't go. Would Alice take her place? Barbara would collect her in the morning and drive her to Westborough station in time for the nine-forty train. They liked to shop or go to an exhibition on days when they made these trips, which Alice now learned were regular events.

She answered evasively, taken by surprise.

'What else are you doing tomorrow?' asked Barbara, who in her time had been head girl of her school, a junior commander in the ATS, the wife of a brigadier, and was now chairman of the women's branch of the British Legion and the local Conservative Association. She was also the mother of three sons and had four grandsons, was unused to female competition and accustomed to getting her own way.

Alice had no plans beyond going to the library. Despite cuts in its budget, there were still periodicals there, and she liked sitting comfortably in the reading area leafing through them.

'Well – ' she admitted. 'Nothing important.'

'Good. Then you'll come,' stated Barbara. 'Could you be at the gate if it isn't raining? I'll be there sharp at nine.'

So Alice went to London, and had her first happy day since Walter's death.

There was a routine about these trips, Alice saw, as she sat quietly in the train listening to the other three women's talk. Each had her own theatre ticket, in case they failed to meet for lunch in the coffee shop at the Strand Palace Hotel, which was close to the theatre. All could act freely if detained in any of the various ways they intended to spend the morning.

At Paddington, Barbara Duncan plunged down the stairs to the tube while Violet and Nancy set forth towards the hotel, bound for the ladies' cloakroom.

'Much nicer than the one on the station,' said Nancy, neat in her brown tweed suit and <u>fawn</u> polo sweater.

Alice followed them up a flight of stairs. How should she occupy the morning? She was unused to visiting London: she and Walter had seldom been there, for Bournemouth had so much to offer. She wondered how to fill the time as she patted powder on to her short, already matt nose. Violet and Nancy were going shopping. Alice went into the tube with them but when they got off at Oxford Circus, she stayed on. At Piccadilly she changed trains and returned to Paddington, where she spent the morning in the hotel lounge reading *Homes and Garden*, which she had bought on the station concourse. She had lunch at the hotel, too; you could get a nice snack, she found. She felt safer doing that than facing the Strand Palace alone, or feeling herself an intruder among the others who had known each other for years. After another visit to the cloakroom she went into the tube again, this time with confidence, and travelled to Charing Cross with ease. She walked from there to the theatre, in her smart black shoes which pinched her toes a little. She was in her seat when the others arrived, Nancy and Violet with carrier bags from Selfridge's and Marks and Spencer, Barbara with two from Harrods. No one commented on Alice's lack of shopping, merely asking if she'd had a nice morning and enjoyed her lunch, which she had.

It was in this way that Alice formed her attachment to Paddington Station and its hotel. She went there often, whenever she was overburdened by her solitude. At first she had hoped that the other women might invite her to join their regular excursions, but then she remembered that she had been a stopgap because of the fourth person's illness. Four was a good number; four filled the car. She must not expect admission to this group.

Sometimes she had lunch in the hotel restaurant, where, from a small carvery, you could choose your cut of meat or poultry. There was often a great piece of beef such as no family, now, would buy except for a special party. Greedily, Alice would eat her large helping, with roast potatoes, vegetables, and a glass of red wine. Flushed and warm with food and drink, sometimes she went on to a matinée, as on that first occasion, sometimes to a cinema, but as the days shortened she caught an early train home because of the dark drive back through the lanes to the village. The flat would be cold when she got in. To supplement the ineffective radiators, Alice had a fan heater she had bought herself, and a two-bar electric fire which Giles had secretly brought her after Helen had refused, because it would be extravagant, to let her borrow a convector heater. With both of these full on, and wearing her overcoat, she would drink coffee laced with brandy as she waited for the room to warm up.

It was when she was bound for the station one day that she met Terence Brett.

3

Giles had something important to say to his wife. He must do it today – he'd been putting it off ever since he'd made it necessary, two nights ago, when he last brought Sue home from the Rigby Arms.

Breakfast – always a silent meal in the big kitchen where, expensively and, in Giles's opinion unnecessarily, Helen had

had a ceramic floor laid over the stone flags so that now they walked on Italian tiles – was over, and Helen was stacking the crockery in the dishwasher. Guests were expected for drinks, as was usual most Sunday mornings unless the Armitages were going out themselves.

'I've invited Jonathan and Sue round this morning,' he plunged.

'Whatever for?' asked Helen.

'I thought it would be friendly,' said Giles. 'We've let them use the pool but we've never asked them in.'

'They're our tenants, not our friends,' said Helen.

'Why shouldn't they be both?' asked Giles boldly. 'Don't you like them?'

Helen had found them as tenants, after all. She had met Jonathan Cooper in the estate agent's office where she had gone to put the lodge on the books. Jonathan was there seeking somewhere to rent because he had left his wife and was living with Sue, whom he'd met when he stayed at the Rigby Arms. He was an agent for a firm selling chemicals and called regularly on various factories in a wide area.

'She's such a common little thing,' said Helen. 'I can't think what he sees in her.'

Giles found Helen's remark offensive.

'She's not common,' he snapped. 'Though it's true that she hasn't been to school in Switzerland. She's had a rough time.' Sue had married young, she had told him; she had had a miscarriage, and after that her husband had left her. She'd used money from their settlement to train for her present post.

'Oh, sorry, sorry,' said Helen in a caustic tone. 'I didn't know you had a lech for her. By all means ask her in, if it will give you a kick.'

'I haven't – ' Giles began. But he had. 'I just thought it would be friendly,' he repeated, sulkily, his small burst of rebellion dying.

'She's hardly likely to return your interest,' Helen said. 'Even if she is on the make.'

'Helen, why must you talk like that?' Giles asked. 'I only invited them because they're our neighbours. We've had no one here from the village.'

'There's no one to interest us here,' said Helen.

That might be true of herself, but what about his mother? Giles knew that they should cultivate local acquaintances for her, although there had been no overtures made towards them from the village. Whose fault was that? Helen bought nothing from the shop. They were all registered with the doctor in Great Minton, but otherwise, apart from Mrs Wood and the gardener, they had no contact with the locals. His mother seemed to go out in her car quite a lot, though from the mileage clocked up, which he glanced at now and then, she never went far. He assumed she found things to do; he must ask her.

'I haven't time to argue now, Giles,' said Helen. 'And since you've asked them, I suppose it can't be helped today, but please don't do it again.'

Why not, Giles fumed, when this is supposed to be my home and my mother has sunk all her capital in it? But he said nothing aloud. He went to see to the drinks. This was always his job, while Helen thawed canapés she bought from a girl who undertook to stock your freezer or cope with your party. With what she bought from her and the cooking done by Mrs Wood, Helen spent very little time in the kitchen herself. Mrs Wood herself refused to come in on Sundays, but her two schoolgirl daughters were glad to wash up the glasses; they were pleased with the money they earned and found it a bit of a giggle.

This weekend, Alice had done the flowers. Like buying the fish every week, it was one of the tasks Helen often delegated. Giles always recognized his mother's free, light, airy arrangements. Helen arranged flowers well, but she regimented the blooms into stiff, massed displays, often with bold and effective colour combinations that his mother would not attempt. Her style reflected her, Giles thought: she was brilliant in appearance, always dressed in strong colours and made up rather more vividly than seemed current fashion, with a lot of eyeshadow and her hair a brassy gold. He was constantly astonished at finding himself sharing a house with someone who looked like an exotic butterfly and was just as restless. Dawn, their elder daughter, was heading the same way already but Amanda was more like him – slow, cautious, plodding. Giles knew he was dull. He had few thoughts, now, outside his work, for if he let his mind stray he became very depressed. He lived with a stranger, and an unfriendly stranger, at that. Had he ever known her at all? Could she really have changed so much? What had he expected from her, and she from him, when they were young?

He'd wanted a wife, of course; in those days young men got married and young girls wanted husbands and families; people didn't just live together freely, as now. Helen had been pretty and lively. He'd felt lively himself, in her company, and had been proud to be seen with her, heads turning as she passed by. He'd wanted, he thought now, gratification of his lust, all the while telling himself that this was love – as it could have become, if she had been gentle and he less complaisant. She had always run their lives on her terms, chosen the girls' schools, picked their holidays, consulted him about nothing. It was difficult, now, to remember how things had been at first. All Giles could recall with clarity was the pressure he had been under, since joining his father-in-law's firm, to keep up with the demands of his job, which exceeded his capabilities.

There had been moments of joy with the girls when they were small. He'd liked reading to them and playing with them. He still enjoyed their company on the rare occasions when he was with them. He played tennis with them, and romped in the pool, but Dawn, he sensed, had, like her mother, already begun to despise him. Things hadn't changed, with the move. They were simply happening in nicer, more spacious surroundings, at greater expense.

He liked the ponies. They were new. Before, the girls had hired ponies from a riding-school. Now, in the field, there were Trixie and Mr Jinks, whom Giles looked after in term-time. The ponies had soft whiskered muzzles, and whickered to him when he went out with their hay. He'd had nothing at all to do with horses before this, but Helen had known what was required, as she knew what was needed for so much. She'd given him the necessary instructions. He was glad to do it; it was a way to be busy and useful, and he enjoyed it much more than the parties.

How Helen loved entertaining! Vivid in a bright dress, she would circle about, admired by all the men – lusted after, no doubt, Giles thought. If only they knew!

He didn't think about that so much now. It was probably all his fault. He had been inexperienced when they married, and he was inexperienced still. Sometimes it amazed him that they had ever had the girls.

Naively, he now saw, he had expected, when Helen suggested that Alice should throw her lot in with theirs, that his mother would join them for meals, be part of the household, a true member of an extended family. He'd been grateful, at first, for what had seemed a real kindness on Helen's part. Then he'd learned the extent of his mother's welcome.

'It'll save trouble as she gets older. You won't have to keep going to see her. We needn't bother a lot about her – old people value their independence and we must respect her privacy. I'm sure she won't try to intrude upon us. She can live an entirely separate life,' Helen had said.

Giles had dreaded the interview in which he must explain Helen's attitude to his mother, but it never became necessary. Alice seemed to divine the position without explanation. He never knew that Helen had made things clear.

Now, as Giles lit the big fire in the drawing-room and piled it with logs, he found the party preparations bearable, for today would be different: Sue would be there. He hummed under his breath as he took bottles from cartons and set them out. What a lot these things cost: why couldn't Helen pay for them out of her business turnover? They were her guests.

Helen's friends were never punctual. None of them ever came before half-past twelve, though invited for noon, and they rarely left before two. Sunday lunch was always eaten during the afternoon. In the school holidays, Dawn and Amanda staved off starvation with crisps, but Giles thought the whole thing a waste not only of money but also of time. It happened too often.

At last the bell rang. The first arrivals were a computer analyst and his architect wife. Then came a television announcer. Giles had met none of them before. Where did Helen find them? He knew she hoped to win work by showing them her own gracious life style. Giles moved about pouring gins and tonics, vodka, campari, his mind switched off except for a tiny part that was watching for Sue.

She and Jonathan came at ten minutes to one, both flushed and smiling. They'd only got out of bed half an hour before. How happy they looked, Giles thought, handing Sue her vodka and tonic. She glowed, standing there in a scarlet dress, her long dark hair drawn softly back from her face and into a ponytail. She wore it up at work, and it gave her an austere look, but now she seemed, to Giles's fanciful eye, like a foreign princess. How thin her little neck was, he thought: like Mary, Queen of Scots. He pulled his wandering mind together. He must attempt to introduce the two to some of the other guests; Helen wouldn't. The trouble was that Giles could recall none of their names.

But meanwhile Sue was looking around.

'Isn't your mother here, Giles?' she asked.

'No,' said Giles. Some explanation seemed to be required, so he added, 'It would be too noisy for her.'

'Oh – I'd have thought she'd enjoy it,' said Sue. 'She's ever so sweet, Giles. She gives me a lift to work when she sees me at the bus stop.'

'Oh!' Giles was surprised, but why not? It would be natural for his mother to pick up someone she knew.

'I don't see a lot of her,' Sue went on. 'But then I'm not around all that much. I'm either at work or with Jonathan. He likes your mother. He gave her some dahlias, once.'

'Did he? But there are –' Giles had been about to say that there were plenty of dahlias in the garden. Then he realized that his mother might not want to pick them without Helen's consent and might not want to ask permission. But she should feel free to help herself to anything; the place was as much hers as his and Helen's. Giles vowed to sort this out later, then put it to the back of his mind, where it remained interred.

'I think that Helen's really mean,' said Sue, when she and Jonathan returned to the lodge after the party.

'She's a hard piece,' said Jonathan. 'But why is she mean?'

'The old lady wasn't there. I bet Giles wanted her asked,' said Sue.

'Maybe she doesn't like Helen's parties,' said Jonathan.

'My guess is she hasn't tried one,' said Sue. 'She's quite lively for her age, after all. Nicely dressed and all that – hasn't let herself go.'

'I'm not sure that it's a very good idea to pluck up old ladies and plant them in new areas,' said Jonathan. 'They're like trees – they need established roots.'

'Makes sense, though, doesn't it?' said Sue. 'What if she's ill?'

'Well, there's no one to look after her,' Jonathan said. 'Helen's out all day.'

'She goes out a lot in her car,' Sue said. 'She's been in to the Rigby for lunch. I don't think she liked it much. She told me she'd been to lots of places and some weren't nice to be in on your own. I can imagine that, at her age.'

'Poor old thing,' said Jonathan, who thought this a bleak life style for Mrs Armitage to pursue. 'There must be some other old ladies in the village, surely?'

'Maybe, but she may not like to ask them round,' said Sue. 'That flat of hers is tiny, and bitterly cold. I carried up some shopping for her once and I thought she'd ask me to stay, but she didn't – pushed me off as fast as she could before my teeth began to chatter.'

Sue knew a lot about physical deprivation. After her father abandoned her mother, sister and brother, they often had no money for fuel and shivered indoors in threadbare, outgrown coats bought at jumble sales. There was no more violence; no more punch-ups between her parents on Friday and Saturday nights after her father came back from the pub; no more cuts, bruises and black eyes and screaming matches; but there was hunger. Sue had resolved to escape from all that as soon as she could. She had rushed into an early marriage at the first opportunity; then, pregnant, she had seen her new, precarious security threatened: with a baby, money would be short. She had had an abortion. As soon as he discovered what she had done, her husband had left her.

Jonathan knew only Sue's tailored version of this, but hearing her talk about Alice and theorize about her made him uneasy. He knew that her imagination sometimes carried her away into fantasies about wonderful holidays they would have, which there wasn't a chance they would ever afford with the payments he made to his wife. She would talk about what she would buy one day 'When I'm rich' – not 'When we're rich', he'd noticed.

He knew that Sue had had several affairs between the breakup of her marriage and meeting him. He excused her in his mind; she had been young and inexperienced; people had taken advantage of her. With him, she had found the stability she needed; in time, Jonathan thought, she would give up her dreams of the unattainable and settle, as most people had to, for what was possible.

There was no question of marriage for them yet. Jonathan's wife was holding out for all sorts of things before she would divorce him. But Sue was only twenty-three and one experience of marriage had shown her its restrictions. She might not stay with Jonathan, if someone with more to offer her came along. Like Giles. She'd got Jonathan away from his wife; she could do it again.

Sue liked older men. She had met plenty at the hotel, and several times had been to their rooms, though if the manager had ever found out, she'd have lost her job at once. Older men were grateful. Some were so ignorant: it was fun, teaching them things: like Jonathan. Maybe Giles needed that sort of schooling, too. Sue thought Helen was just the sort to short-change him, but he wouldn't know any better.

At that stage, the idea was just a fancy to Sue, an amusing notion to think about when she was bored.

4

Helen loved skiing, and after spending a year at school in Switzerland, was good at it. Every winter, when the works closed for Christmas and remained shut until after New Year's Day, she and Giles and the girls went for a winter holiday to the Alps. Giles, a poor performer on skis, thought the three females would enjoy themselves as much – more, even – without him, but he had no excuse for remaining behind.

Alice had shared their Christmas dinner. Everyone had dressed up, the girls in pretty long dresses, Alice in a sweeping black velvet skirt and silk blouse. She'd worn a wool vest and her mink stole, for although the heating worked in the downstairs rooms, the house was draughty. Helen, in dark green, had looked magnificent; she also looked austere and remote. The dinner was delicious. Amanda supervised the turkey; the pudding had been made by the caterer Helen often used.

Two days later the family departed and Alice was left alone, feeling very forlorn.

The sky was grey and lowering. If it snowed – Alice didn't think it was cold enough, and the sky wasn't yellow – she would be quite cut off. She took the car out for a spin in case, in the days that followed, the roads grew too icy and she became a prisoner. Helen had given her what was left of the turkey, and returned some of the mince pies which Alice had made as a contribution to the meal, so she decided not to stay out to lunch. In any case, with so many people on holiday, the cafés and pubs would be full and therefore alarming.

Presents were so difficult. She'd given Helen bath oil, done up in a gift box with soap and bath powder, the same as last year.

They'd given her a bottle of port. She and Walter had liked a glass of port after dinner. Amanda had knitted her a pair of gloves. Dawn gave her a box of notelets, sold in aid of a charity.

When Alice came back from her drive, she parked her Metro next to Helen's Volvo. The family had gone to the airport in the Rover. Jonathan's car was out; he and Sue must be off somewhere together, Alice decided, forgetting that Sue would be on duty for part of the day. This was a busy time at the hotel.

Alice had brought a pile of novels back from the library. She was concentrating better now, but only on things that were easy to read. She'd found an M. M. Kaye she had not read, and three family sagas, and after lunch began one of them. It was heavily romantic, and the tender passages brought tears to her eyes so she skipped those bits, paying attention to the background detail, which was about mill workers during the industrial revolution.

Love worried Alice. She had loved Walter – quietly, grate-fully; and he had loved her – she had never doubted it. But once, before they met, Alice had loved someone else in a wilder way. He had died of pneumonia, as people did then, before the discovery of antibiotics. Alice still thought of him sometimes, and remembered the very different form of that love. It might not have lasted – might have burnt itself out with their youth. The feeling between her and Walter was more like a fire that glowed – was tended and fed, and burned steadily on. She often wondered about Giles and Helen. She supposed there was love between them. Cer-tainly, when they married, Giles had been infatuated with Helen. It had worried his mother. It had seemed too febrile an emotion to last, and she had seen no answering excite-ment in Helen. Alice had noticed Helen look at Giles cal-culatingly, as if weighing up the prospects for their future. Walter had had reservations about her, but he could not say what it was that made him uneasy. She certainly had both looks and brains. Alice hoped it was all right. To think otherwise was too frightening, but she wished her son looked happier, and now there was Sue, on the doorstep, a threat if he were unsettled. But Sue wasn't a danger, Alice told herself. Sue and Jonathan were close; otherwise they wouldn't be living together in what used to be called sin. And Giles had most of the things that money could buy and some that it couldn't, such as his daughters. Alice had loved her rare moments in their company when they were small, but she and Walter had seen them only for fleeting visits. She still didn't really know them, she felt sadly. She could discuss few of their interests for she knew nothing about horses and hated pop music. At first the girls had never come to her flat without being asked. Helen had told them not to bother her, Alice discovered. Now, Amanda often came up to watch television when Dawn wanted a different programme on the set in the girls' sitting-room. But often was a relative word; the girls were away at school for most of the year.

Alice decided to go to London the following day. She wouldn't go far. The sales were on so the shops would be crowded; she'd settle for just lunch at the Paddington Hotel, then back again. She'd stick to that plan, unless it snowed.

Rain wouldn't put her off, for she'd be back before it was really dark. The day after that she'd go somewhere else. She'd make an excursion every day and soon the fortnight would end. Then she'd ring Audrey, who'd urged her to come back to Bournemouth and stay, asking if she might visit after the family returned.

When she went round drawing the curtains, the lodge was in darkness. Time switches turned lights on in the main house, and Alice always drew the curtains. That was wise. Prowlers would think someone was in, with the lights on and the curtains closed.

As she went back to her own apartment, Alice heard the timbers in the house creak, as if it stretched itself in sleep. Sometimes she wondered if the ghost of Mr Goring, the previous owner, who had died there aged nearly ninety, stalked the dark passages.

She made herself keep busy for the next hour, washing out underclothes, sorting what she would wear the next day, ironing a blouse. Then she did her nails, filing them carefully, painting on pale varnish. She polished her smart boots with their low heels, and put out a new pair of stockings. Alice had never taken to tights; though she was thin, she liked the support of her girdle.

There was a film on television which looked as if it might be worth watching; it would certainly pass the evening. Before switching it on, Alice drew the curtain aside at her attic window and looked out at the lodge. She was just in time to see Jonathan return from wherever he had been in his Granada. He drove it into the barn. Alice watched him close the big heavy door, dropping the bar that latched it into position, and then, in the light cast by the exterior lamp which was fixed to the barn wall, walk over to the lodge. As he did so, the porch light there came on. That was good. His princess was inside, waiting for him, Alice thought, smiling as she turned away from the window. She felt happier, thinking of them there together.

In the morning it was raining and Alice's resolution faltered. Propped up in bed with her morning tea, and the electric fire taking the worst of the chill off the room, she wondered about going to London. It would be so much easier to give up – she could even spend the day in bed. With the fan heater and the fire, the room would soon warm up.

'No, Alice,' she admonished herself aloud. 'You're to go. You're quite well. It's raining, not snowing. If you don't go out and see some human faces, you'll rot.'

The sound of her own voice, speaking so sternly, made her giggle nervously. Was she going potty, talking to herself? She drank her tea, and then got out of bed. Soon she was dressed, and had made up her face ready for the day. She added her bracelets and pearls, and fastened stud earrings in place. Then she put on her boots, her lined raincoat with the fur collar, her brown felt hat with the feather, took up her umbrella, and set out to the barn.

It was always difficult for Alice to open the door. Struggling with the heavy bar, she looked round once, wistfully, at the lodge, hoping that Jonathan might be a witness to her difficulties and help her, but he didn't come. Perhaps he'd gone back to work, she thought. Not everyone ceased until the New Year, and when at last she got the door open, she saw that, indeed, his car had gone.

Alice got into her Metro and turned the key to start it.

Nothing happened. She turned it again, fiddled with it, took the key out and reinserted it, but the car was completely dead. Not a sound came from beneath the bonnet.

She almost wept with frustration. Indeed, she laid her head down on her folded hands which rested on the steering wheel for a few despairing minutes. Then she tried the key again. Nothing.

You could put the car in gear and rock it. Sometimes that worked. Alice engaged first gear, got out, went to the front of the car and pushed as hard as she could, then climbed back into the driver's seat and tried again. Nothing happened.

So she couldn't go to London after all. Now, after her earlier reluctance, the disappointment seemed, paradoxically, hard to bear. She could telephone the garage, but they would be unlikely to get out to Harcombe and fix the car in time for her to reach London for lunch.

Slowly, Alice got out of the Metro. The burden of the day's isolation pressed upon her; even Mrs Wood was absent, still revelling with her family. With the young people at the lodge gone for the day she was all alone. What if she had an accident – burnt herself – had a fall? It would have to be bad to prevent her from reaching the telephone, Alice thought, trying to calm herself down. Meanwhile, the whole house was hers to use: she could light the drawing-room fire, watch Helen's television set which was so much bigger than her own.

Why not take Helen's car?

Alice looked at the blue Volvo parked in the space beside her Metro. Surely she could drive it? During the war she had driven a canteen van; she had regularly driven the Peugeot they'd had until Walter died, when Giles had persuaded her to exchange it for a smaller car which had been wise advice. The Metro was economical and easy to park, and hitherto had whizzed along in lively fashion. She was only going to Westborough station where the car would be safely parked all day; she would make sure to return before dark. Why not? No one would ever know.

Dare she? The idea was rather exciting!

Alice knew she should change her plans. She'd no commitment, no one to meet in London, but she'd made up her mind to escape.

She knew where the Volvo keys were kept – on a hook in the lobby by the kitchen.

She went back to the house, through the back door, her normal entrance. There were the keys. She took them down and went out again, locking the back door once more.

Alice padded back to the barn and got into the Volvo, which wasn't locked. None of them locked their cars in the barn. Helen was tall, and Alice had to pull the seat right forward before she could reach the controls with comfort. She inserted the key, checked that the car was in neutral and made sure she could find all the gears. Then she started the engine. It fired at once, running smoothly. Alice's heart beat fast with excitement as she reversed slowly out of the barn, past her silent Metro, slipping the clutch. She stopped outside the barn, putting on the brake and leaving the engine running while she closed the heavy doors, which she wouldn't have done if she'd taken her own car, though who should query the Volvo's absence she didn't know. Jonathan was out, and wherever he was – at work or with his children – he'd be unlikely to return before she did.

Before moving off, Alice made sure she could find the switches for the indicators and the windscreen wipers. Everything was straightforward. It was exciting, driving away in this larger, lively car. She would go slowly. Even with the delay, she had plenty of time as she always allowed more than was necessary.

Alice set forth down the lane, the windscreen wipers swishing to and fro to clear away the drizzle, elated by her own daring.

5

Terry Brett had been home for Christmas. He'd given his mother a bottle of scent and his father a bottle of whisky, one lifted from a department store and the other from a supermarket. His parents were pleased to see him and his father had given him a cheque for fifty pounds. His mother had given him a sweater which he was wearing under his smart car coat as he drove into Westborough. The previous day he had told his parents he was getting a lift from a friend he'd arranged to meet at a roadhouse half a mile from where they lived. There, he had picked up a Ford Escort parked in the yard with the key in the ignition. He grinned to himself as he drove off, imagining the horror his parents would feel if they could have witnessed his action. They thought it was time he had a car of his own instead of depending on lifts. Surely he could afford one? He'd promised to think about it.

They'd seemed sorry to see him leave, but forty-eight hours was all he could stand of the family scene. His sister and her husband and children were due to call on their way back from spending Christmas with his parents in Leeds. Terry's brother, who had been at home too, had already left for a walking holiday in the Fells, an odd thing to do in winter, in Terry's opinion.

He dumped the Escort on the outskirts of Swindon. It didn't do to borrow a car long unless you changed the plates; the police were pretty quick off the mark if you parked in a prohibited spot or committed any sort of misdemeanour, and with the strict rules about tyres, it might be that the owner hadn't kept things up to scratch and you'd be nicked for a fault of his, which would be very unfair. Terry never borrowed a car that did not display a valid road fund licence on the windscreen.

Next morning, he lifted a pale green Vauxhall from the station. Among his selection of keys was a good variety of Vauxhall keys which he'd got after a chance visit to a dealer one evening when there'd been just a single attendant on the pump. Terry had been able to amble in and help himself while apparently waiting to find out about new models. It was amazing what you could pick up while seeming to be on innocent business if you had nimble wits, quick fingers, sharp eyes and the nerve.

Terry had nerve for most things. In Westborough, which he'd reconnoitred just before Christmas, he intended to call on a woman he'd met soon after he'd grabbed the scent for his mother. He'd knocked into her, apologizing effusively as he helped her collect the packages he had caused her to drop. Then he'd offered to carry them to her car for her. He had stolen nothing from her. His success as an operator depended on knowing when to yield to temptation and when to resist for greater gain in the long term. Virtue was rewarded when he was able to read the address on an envelope which fell from her unfastened handbag. He memorized it. She'd been reasonably nice-looking, about forty or so. He wouldn't mind earning his keep with her for a bit. Her clothes had been expensive and she had a well-kept look, a promising target. He had an excuse for calling on her: he would show her a silver propelling pencil he'd acquired and say he had found it after she'd left the car park that day and wondered if it was hers. She might be alone in the house, though that wasn't likely in this holiday period, but in any case she'd be sure to invite him in, and he'd have a chance to survey the prospects – maybe the husband, too. If she wanted to know how he knew where she lived, he would tell her the truth. She'd be flattered, and might offer him a meal.

Thinking of food reminded Terry that he'd had no breakfast apart from a cup of coffee. He'd forgotten to take some supplies from his parents' larder, and the sliced loaf he'd left in the cupboard had grown mould. He'd have a snack now, then wash and brush up before calling upon his prey.

Terry saw a space in the main street of Westborough and slid the Vauxhall neatly against the kerb. He felt safe with this car; its owner had left it while he went off for the day, for certain, for the bonnet was warm to the touch when Terry took it. He'd return in it to Swindon tonight, and leave it somewhere not far from the station, he planned, with seasonal generosity. Terry whistled under his breath as he walked round to the Coffee Pot, which he had noticed on his earlier visit to the town. There, he had coffee and hot buttered toast. In the cloakroom he ran a comb through his springy curls, and checked his appearance in the mirror. He looked, he decided, like a schoolmaster or an insurance salesman on holiday: reassuringly relaxed. Then he went back to the car, thinking, as he started it, that if the woman was out he would pursue some other plan so as not to waste the day. Something was sure to turn up, he knew; it always did. He was always stimulated by the challenge of fast thinking; people were easily led by the nose and deserved all they got for being so foolish. Still pondering, Terry rested his right foot on the accelerator pedal while slipping the clutch with his left, the car in first gear ready to move. He turned the wheel to the right and edged forward clearing the car in front, then paused to let a stream of traffic pass. The road was busy; you'd think they'd have built a by-pass by now, Terry thought. He took out his comb again and ran it once more through his curls, which had got damp as he walked back to the car through the drizzling rain. While he did this, he watched in the mirror for a chance to slip out. Ah – now there'd be a gap, after this blue Volvo.

Terry revved the engine, eager to thrust the Vauxhall into the road as soon as the Volvo, which was moving slowly, passed.

'Come on, come on,' said Terry.

The bonnet of the Volvo drew level – went by. Terry had

time to notice a woman driver, wearing a hat, before his foot, the smooth sole wet from walking on the rain-soaked pavement, slipped on the clutch and the car bounded out from the kerb sooner than he had intended. The Volvo was almost past, but the Vauxhall's bumper caught its rear wing a glancing blow.

Alice felt this as a severe bang on the side of the Volvo. She had been driving very carefully, attending to the rear view mirror, and she knew there was no one close behind her. She stopped almost at once, her legs turned to jelly by the shock of the jolting collision. She'd seen the wing of the other car edged out from the kerb, but she, on the main road, had the right of way so it must wait. Suddenly there was this dreadful crumping noise.

Alice switched off the engine and levered herself out of the car to examine the damage. She was trembling.

Terry was about to pull out and pass, anxious to get away fast before a copper came along and found the Vauxhall didn't belong to him, when Alice, wavering slightly, blocked his way. Had anyone seen what had happened? Was there a policeman in sight? He glanced round. There were a few pedestrians, but now the rain was falling heavily and each was intent on hurrying on to his destination, head down, ignoring what went on around them. Although the sound of the crash had seemed loud to the two participants, in fact it had not made much noise and had attracted no attention. The following traffic was pulling out to pass the Volvo, now seemingly double-parked, not yet causing an obstruction.

The rear wing of the Volvo was badly scraped and slightly dented.

Fright and anger gave Alice the strength to advance towards Terry, who now could not get past her because of the overtaking cars pinning him in. Young fool, she thought, remembering that you must never admit blame in the case of an accident, even if it was your fault, and in this case it most definitely wasn't hers.

'What did you think you were doing, young man?' she demanded, peering in at Terry's window, trying to control her quavering voice and trembling limbs. One part of her was relieved to see that the offender looked conventionally neat, a collar and tie revealed in the vee-neck of the sweater he wore, his curly hair not too long.

Terry got out of the Vauxhall. He'd try to persuade her back into the Volvo and away from the scene quickly, before any nosy bobbies turned up, but if he couldn't manage it, he'd be able to leave the stolen Vauxhall himself, escaping on his feet. He was wearing gloves. He always wore gloves when driving. He never took chances.

'The insurance,' Alice was insisting. 'Your name and address.'

'There's no damage, is there?' asked Terry, with his most winning smile. He walked round to the Volvo. 'Ah yes – I see there is,' he said, thinking quickly. 'Are you hurt?' He saw that she was quite old – older than he'd thought at first. If she was injured he'd take to his heels at once and get away from the district as fast as he could. Too bad, but there it was.

'No, I'm not,' said Alice. 'Just shocked.'

He seemed a nice young man, and he looked concerned.

'Good – then let's move our cars out of the way and talk things over, shall we?' Already he was beginning to see that if he played it right, he might win advantage from what had happened. He glanced down the road and saw a big space by the kerb ahead. Taking a chance, he said, 'I'm very sorry. Look, you put your car down there, and I'll park mine and join you. Can you manage?'

Alice wasn't sure that she could, but she got into the Volvo. His suggestion was sound. The last thing she wanted was for a policeman to come and find she was driving her daughter-in-law's car without permission. Her legs still felt weak, but she managed to drive the car to the end of the line of parked vehicles and park. Terry, meanwhile, reversed into the space from which he had so recently and so disastrously emerged. He could disown the Vauxhall from this instant, he thought, jingling his collection of keys in his pocket as he walked towards the Volvo.

Having parked, Alice studied the damage again.

It was Helen's car, and look what had happened to it! Tears of fright and shock filled her eyes, and Terry saw them.

'How soon will I be able to get it repaired?' she asked in

quavering tones, instead of demanding more personal details from Terry, as he had expected.

'Right away, I should think,' said Terry. 'There's plenty of body repairers about. Depends how busy they are.' He glanced at her warily. 'But if it's an insurance job, you'd have to wait some time, till it's been inspected.'

She was really swaying now, and he saw that beneath the thick layer of make-up she wore she had lost all natural colour. He put his hand on her elbow.

'What about a cup of tea to get over the shock?' he suggested. 'While we decide what to do?' He could still walk out – take her to a café and leave her there – in fact, it might be the best thing to do, then she wouldn't fall down in a faint in the road, which would be sure to cause trouble.

Giving her no time to refuse and still holding her elbow, Terry led Alice along the road to the Coffee Pot, which he'd only just left. He settled her into a corner seat and went over to a waitress, the one who had served him earlier and with whom he'd exchanged some badinage.

'What – back so soon?' she asked, grinning.

'Couldn't keep away,' he said, and then leaned forward confidentially. 'See the old girl in the corner? She felt a bit giddy outside and I brought her in for a cup of tea to settle her nerves. Bring us one each love, and plenty of sugar. Quick as you can.'

'Seeing it's you,' said the girl, 'I might,' and she turned back to the service area with a flourish of her short green overall skirt.

Terry walked back to Alice, who was struggling to regain her self-control. She had removed her gloves and he noticed her ring at once, an emerald surrounded by diamonds on her wedding finger.

'Would you like to take your coat off?' he asked. Pearls, he was thinking; she'd have great fat pearls, real ones, with a diamond clasp. Some of these old girls were well heeled – rich men's widows. That car she was driving was not your run-of-the-mill shopping car, either. There would be ways of ingratiating himself into the favours of an old dame like this one, he was sure; it was a whole new area to explore. He'd almost forgotten, by now, what had brought them together. He wondered how old she was. Seventy? More than that? She had brown spots on the backs of her hands – not a lot of them, just faint ones, like his grandmother who could be touched for a fiver easily whenever they met.

Alice declined to remove her coat, but she undid it and loosened the silk scarf she wore. There was no pearl necklace, but a diamond and pearl brooch was pinned to her sweater.

Their tea came.

'I'll be mother,' said Terry, the adrenalin racing around in his system. 'Milk and sugar?' He poured out dextrously, and passed Alice her cup.

'I must get the car mended as soon as possible,' said Alice. 'Do you think it could be done in ten days?'

'Oh – certainly,' said Terry. 'But not,' he repeated, 'if you have to wait for the insurance assessor.' He hesitated, leaning forward and gazing at her with what seemed to Alice to be honest brown eyes. 'Why the hurry? Can't you manage without it?'

'It's not mine,' Alice said. She kept enough control of herself not to tell him everything. 'I – er – a friend lent it to me.'

'Oh jeepers,' said Terry. 'And your friend wants it back in ten days?'

'Yes.'

Terry snapped his fingers.

'Hang on,' he said, and he went to the back of the shop to talk to the waitress again. She soon granted his request, which was to borrow the Yellow Pages of the telephone directory.

Terry took it over to the table where Alice waited. She was feeling deathly tired now and had completely forgotten her plan for the day; her one thought was to undo the damage without being discovered.

Terry, meanwhile, was highly delighted with this turn of events. By now he'd lost all sight of his responsibility for what had happened; his immediate aim was to make what he could of the situation.

'Cars, cars, cars,' he muttered, turning the pages. 'Car accessories – car breakdowns – car and coach – ah, car and coach body builders: that's who we want.' He gazed at a double spread of entries, small itemized ones and large boxed advertisements. Alice could read, upside down, *car body and paint spraying*, *car body repairs*, the information repeated in various forms.

There was one firm in Westborough.

'Let's go there,' said Terry. 'Let's take the car there right away and see what they say.' Before she regained her cool, he thought, before she began laying the blame on him once more. 'Finish your tea, Mrs – er – ?'

'Armitage,' Alice said quietly. 'Mrs Armitage.'

Things were steadying down. The room had stopped swaying around her. She looked up, through her bifocal spectacles, at the young man.

'Drink your tea,' he repeated, using the coaxing tone that worked well in different circumstances with younger women.

Alice obeyed.

'Let's go,' Terry said, and was about to push the bill towards her when he had a new thought: a tiny investment now, the price of their tea, might yield future dividends.

She made no demur at all as he counted out the appropriate money and even added a tip for the obliging waitress. Then he stood behind Alice to pull out her chair as she rose, waited while she buttoned her coat and put her gloves on again, hiding the ring. He took her arm once more as they returned to the Volvo.

Alice looked at the damage. The scrape, like a graze, covered quite a big patch.

'Doesn't look much,' said Terry cheerfully, but he'd seen that there was more than one dent. 'Let's get on with it, shall we?'

Alice went round to the driver's side and began fitting the key into the door. Her hand was shaking.

'Do you know where this place is?' Terry asked. 'Norton Road?'

Alice didn't, but Terry did. He'd spent some time learning the geography of Westborough, on his earlier visit. Knowledge of one-way systems, dead ends and escape routes was very useful.

'Shall I drive?' he suggested.

It didn't occur to Alice until much later that she was taking a great risk in allowing someone who had just, through his own carelessness, crashed into the car she was driving, to take the wheel of it within half an hour. She merely felt unable to do it herself.

'Thank you,' she said, and handed him the keys, primping her lips.

Terry settled her into the passenger's seat, tucking her coat in round her thin legs in their expensive boots. He was whistling under his breath as he walked behind the car to the driver's side. He'd never driven a Volvo. He pulled carefully out from the kerb; it wouldn't do to repeat what had just happened.

Part of Alice's mind knew she should be berating this boy – asking him to face up to what he had done, arranging for his insurance company to pay whatever the repair would cost – but most of her thoughts were concentrated on putting right the damage before she could be found out, like a child who has played with some forbidden object and broken it, and now seeks to remove the evidence before discovery. It wouldn't cost such a lot, she was thinking; you had to pay part of most claims, anyway, didn't you? But not if it wasn't your fault. She'd never made one, though Walter had once had a small contretemps with a milk float in Poole.

Terry drove confidently through Westborough to the end of the main street where there were houses among the shops, and roads radiated out into estates and an occasional factory or warehouse. Down here was Norton Road, where there was a joinery and a printing works as well as the body repairer.

He drove straight through the entrance into a hangar-like building with breeze-block walls, a corrugated iron roof and a concrete floor. Several cars were parked about the place, some with parts missing and one in a devastated condition. A man in brown overalls was working on a dark blue Audi. He did not look up as they drove in.

'I'll find someone,' Terry said. 'You wait here, Mrs Armitage.' Always use their names, he'd found: Jeannie – Diane – Sandra – whatever it was, murmur it, use it a lot: the personal touch. And remember it! Never get careless and use the wrong one! In this case, he must defer to age and status: none of your 'loves' or 'dears' for Mrs Armitage.

He walked over to speak to the man working on the Audi. Alice saw them talking. The man gestured, and Terry went off in the direction he had indicated. Alice got slowly out of the car, moving stiffly, like a really old woman. She seldom thought of herself as old: most of the time she felt, though forlorn without Walter and depressed at her new way of life, much as she had for most of her life; it was only her limbs, which would not move as fast as once they did, and her face, with its lines and pouches, that reminded her of the years. And she tired swiftly: that, too.

There was a strong smell of chemicals in the air of the workshop, and a faint haze in the atmosphere. Alice stood hesitantly beside the car, thinking about money. She must pay whatever price was asked to have it repaired before Helen returned. In her head, in slow motion, she ran a film of what had happened: herself proceeding slowly along past the line of parked cars with the windscreen wipers flicking to and fro; the wing of the green car sticking out from among the others and then the sudden, unbelievable jolt as it drove into the Volvo. The boy's carelessness was incredible: there could have been a serious accident.

Meanwhile, Terry was talking to the body-shop manager.

'I was quite stationary,' he was saying. 'I'd nosed forward a little way, waiting for a gap in the traffic, and along comes this Volvo, much too close to the parked cars. The old lady caught the wing against my bumper. Didn't hurt my car, but it's made a bit of a mess of hers.'

'Is it an insurance job?' asked the manager.

'No,' said Terry. 'Least said soonest mended – her family thinks it's time she gave up driving and she wants to get it fixed without them finding out. And after all, why should I make things difficult for her? My car's not damaged.'

'No one hurt?'

'I had a fright, as you might expect. That's all,' answered Terry, looking at him with frank, honest eyes.

Repairing wrecks was the manager's job, not making judgements. Odd that the rear wing had been damaged, not the front, he thought, and forgot about it.

'Let's have a look at it, then,' he said, setting off briskly towards the spot where Alice stood drooping beside the Volvo.

'Don't say too much to the old girl,' Terry warned. 'She's a bit edgy.'

Terry's words had led the manager to expect an aged crone, not the well-dressed, still pretty, elderly woman, no older than his own mother, whom he now saw.

'Mrs Armitage,' Terry introduced.

'Well now, let's have a look at the trouble,' said the manager in the breezy tone of a doctor cheerily assessing a lesion. He looked carefully at the car, peered underneath, inspected the rear and the door, at last giving his diagnosis. 'About two hundred and fifty,' he said.

'So much?' said Alice, dismayed.

'I understand it's not an insurance job,' said the manager.

'No.' What difference did that make, wondered Alice.

'Might work out a little less, then,' said the manager. 'The paint's expensive, and we have to buy a much bigger quantity than we really need. I've none of that colour in stock. It's new, you see – only about six months old.'

It was true that Helen had not had the car long.

'How quickly can you do it?' asked Alice.

'Hm – let's see. Would you mind coming into the office and I'll look at the book,' said the manager.

The office, heated by a paraffin stove, was small and frowsty. A plump woman with jet black curls sat behind an electric typewriter, a cigarette smouldering in an ashtray beside her. Alice wrinkled her nose. No one smoked at Harcombe House. The manager consulted a large engagement diary on the desk, muttering to himself as he did so.

'If you bring it on Monday, you could have it back on Friday,' he said at last.

'Oh dear, can't you do it at once?' asked Alice. She could not drive it back to the village like this. Anyone might notice the damage – Mrs Wood, for instance, and certainly Jonathan, going daily to the barn. 'I can take a taxi home,' she added.

'Well,' said the manager. 'I can't promise to start on it at once, but as it's urgent, I'll see what I can do.' He noticed

46

that Alice was shaking. Not surprisingly, the accident had shocked her. 'The paint needs time to dry,' he explained. 'Before we spray again, that is. That's why it takes so long.'

'I see,' said Alice. 'You will do your best?'

'Yes,' said the manger.

'I'll pay in advance, if it will help,' Alice offered. Her Barclaycard would see her through this emergency. Silently she blessed Walter for his generous pension arrangements.

'That won't be necessary,' said the manager. It was lucky for her that the other party was being so helpful. She might have hit someone who would have made a real nuisance of himself. 'Mrs Hawkins will make a note of your name and address. Shall we telephone you when it's ready, if we can finish it before Friday of next week?'

It was arranged. The Volvo's registration number was noted, together with Alice's address and telephone number. Terry watched as Mrs Hawkins wrote it all down.

'I'll go and fetch my car to drive you home, Mrs Armitage,' he said solicitously. He looked at the manager. 'Mrs Armitage can wait here, can't she? I won't be long.'

'Yes, of course. Have a seat, Mrs Armitage,' said the manager. He indicated a sagging wooden-armed chair in a corner. 'Mrs Hawkins will make you some coffee.'

Before Terry returned, Mrs Hawkins had led Alice right through the paint-hazed workshop to a squalid washroom at its far end, a trip made necessary by her breakfast coffee and the tea after the accident.

'It's not much,' said Mrs Hawkins, referring to the washroom. 'I'm only part-time, so I don't bother a lot. The men need it, of course.'

The pan was stained. A filthy roller towel hung behind the door. Luckily Alice had an All-Fresh cleansing tissue in her handbag.

There were three men working on car bodies as she followed Mrs Hawkins back to the office. The Volvo had been moved to a bay in a corner, which made her feel it was at least on the way to recovery, a patient awaiting treatment.

'Have you worked here long?' Alice asked, for something to say as they entered the office.

'Twelve years,' said Mrs Hawkins. 'It suits me. I live just

down the road, and I'm my own boss.' She smiled, her ugly face with the mole on the chin lightening. 'I expect it gave you a shock, knocking into that young man.'

'Yes,' Alice agreed. But she hadn't hit the young man: he'd hit her car. Mrs Hawkins had got it wrong. 'I saw his car had edged forward,' she began to explain.

'No one's hurt, that's the main thing,' said Mrs Hawkins. 'And there's no need to report it as you've spoken to the other driver.'

The very thought of the police was enough to make Alice shudder. She'd have no hope of concealing what had happened from Helen if they were involved. The enormity of her own misdemeanour now appalled her.

'I shan't make a fuss,' she said quietly. 'It's better just to pay up and get it done quickly.'

Mrs Armitage looked as if she could pay all right, Mrs Hawkins thought, feeding an invoice form into her typewriter while the kettle boiled.

It did not occur to Alice that Terry might not return to collect her.

6

Terry had no intention of abandoning Mrs Armitage. Not with that ring, her brooch, and the address she had given to the woman in the body repair shop.

The rain had stopped as he strode whistling through the town, along the side streets to the main road. The pavements were crowded, now, with shoppers enjoying a post-Christmas splurge, either changing their presents or looking for bargains in the sales. He felt the excitement that usually lit the first weeks of a new job, as he always thought of them. It was work, after all: he put enough into it, for goodness' sake! All that sweet talk, not to mention the rest of it. He certainly gave full value for the money he extracted when the time for that came. This was a whole new scene, this old woman. He'd have to play it by ear as he went along. He might find milking the elderly a profitable line; on the other hand, they wouldn't be so open to blackmail, not that he called it, even to himself, by so harsh a name. Even Mrs Armitage wasn't a target for that sort of attack; she was just afraid of facing her friend with the damaged car. But wait! Depending on the nature of the friend, he could later threaten to reveal what had happened. If she tried to blame him for the accident, it would be her word against his, and who would believe an old woman who shouldn't be driving at all? She ought to be in a home somewhere, like his grandmother.

If a policeman or a traffic warden were anywhere near the Vauxhall, he'd leave it, he resolved. He'd get a taxi – tell the old girl he hadn't been able to start the car and that it must have got damaged in the collision after all; she'd know no different. She'd pay the taxi. She hadn't uttered a murmur when the price of the repair was mentioned. Of course, Harcombe House, where she lived, might be nothing special; people called even bungalows by such names these days; it might even be an old people's home. But he'd soon see.

As he approached the Vauxhall, Terry looked round. There was no policeman in sight. He'd seen a traffic warden up near the market square as he passed. He didn't know how many of them there were in Westborough – more than one, for sure, but none could be seen from where he stood.

He got into the car, extracted it, this time with extreme care, from its position, and drove back to the body repair shop in Norton Road.

Alice told him which way to go from the town. Four miles beyond Westborough, two miles short of Great Minton, she told him to turn off to the right where a signpost pointed to Harcombe.

'Out in the wilds, isn't it?' he commented, as they made their way along the narrow winding lane. Trimmed stark hedges bordered it, with, beyond, fields given over mainly to sheep, though some were ploughed, showing rich brown soil not yet spiked with young growth. Terry had never lived in the country; it made him uneasy.

'It is quiet,' said Alice. 'Left now.'

They entered the village of Harcombe at a T-junction. On

either side stretched the main street with its row of dwellings, all, at first glance, on a modest scale.

But not Harcombe House. Terry hid his surprise as they turned in through wrought-iron gates past a tiny lodge with a steep gabled roof and went up a short drive to a mansion. It might still be an old folks' home, he reminded himself, swinging round on the gravel sweep in front of the house. At one side was a long low barn, with big oak doors latched across by a wooden bar. On one side of the barn door were more doors. Terry wondered what was behind them. He saw that Harcombe House itself was like a much larger edition of its own lodge – gaunt, grey granite, with high steepling roofs and gabled windows on the top floor. All the windows were densely <u>latticed</u>.

'Nice place you've got here,' he said casually, putting on the handbrake and switching the engine off.

'It's my son's house,' said Alice. 'I have a flat in it.' She reached out to open the door. 'Thank you for bringing me home,' she went on, and added, with an effort at reproof, 'You drove back very nicely, you must be more careful in future. Someone could have been badly hurt.'

'Oh, we've forgotten all about that now,' said Terry. 'That's in the past. And I wouldn't have met you, if you hadn't had an accident.'

Alice hadn't had the accident; it had been his. But before she could point this out, he had got out of the car and was coming round to help her alight, ready to tell a tale to the son if he appeared.

Terry was looking past her at the house. It had the blank look of a place that was empty, though it was so large that there could have been dozens of people in it, at the back or in its inner recesses, whose presence would not show at the front.

'Is everyone out?' he asked.

'They're away,' said Alice. 'Skiing.'

Terry couldn't believe his luck.

'It's your son's car,' he said. 'The Volvo.' The old baggage, telling him such a story.

'It belongs to my daughter-in-law,' said Alice. 'I couldn't start mine.'

'What's the matter with it?' asked Terry.

'I don't know,' said Alice. 'It just wouldn't start when I turned the key. Nothing happened.'

'I'll have a look at it for you,' said Terry. 'I know quite a bit about cars.' One way and the other, he did; he'd picked it up here and there, from casual encounters and in prison. It was useful to know how to get into cars without keys and start them, for instance, and before now he'd made some rewarding contacts helping marooned female drivers with punctures or shattered windscreens, or cars that, like Mrs Armitage's, just wouldn't start. Even if he couldn't get them to go – and mostly he could, or could spot the problem – he could send other help and follow up later with enquiries. He'd met one woman like that who, after three months, he'd forced to come up with a grand: not bad.

'Oh, would you?' said Alice, who felt too frail after her adventures to relish the thought of telephoning the garage that serviced her car to persuade them to come out and mend it.

'Show me where it is,' said Terry.

Alice led him to the barn. Terry opened the door. Within, it was vast; there was space for at least eight cars. The Metro sat there alone. Alice took the key from her bag and gave it to him. He got into the driving seat, inserted the key and turned it. Nothing happened.

Probably the starter had jammed, Terry thought. That was the first thing to try, anyway. He opened the bonnet. He'd had nothing to do with Metros – he liked bigger cars, he liked the sense of power you got, seated behind a long bonnet. But the principle was the same, whatever the car.

'I need a spanner,' he said. 'An adjustable one, for choice.'

The Metro contained nothing suitable, but Alice knew where Giles kept his tools. Terry followed her through the back door and along a passage to a small room at the rear of the house. This was Giles's study, from which another door led to the kitchen. He was relegated to what had once been the servants' hall and it had not yet been re-decorated; it was not even on Helen's agenda. From the floor to about four feet up, a chocolate-brown dado circled the walls, and above that, the rest was painted a drab, yellowy cream. The carpet, bought with the house, was a threadbare brown haircord.

Here, in a big cupboard, were fuses, insulating tape, glue, boxes of screws and nails, and a number of tools.

Terry selected a spanner.

'You wait in the warm,' he said kindly. 'I'll come in when I've done.'

Alice went into the kitchen wondering how to reward the young man for his assistance. She would not offer money; the accident had been his fault, after all, and he wasn't a pauper; he was nicely dressed, well-spoken, and drove a good car himself. But he'd done his best to make amends. Some people in his position would have driven off quickly before they could be faced with the consequences. Perhaps a cup of coffee would do. Not sherry – not when he was driving.

In Helen's kitchen, Alice set the kettle to boil on the Aga. She found cups and saucers and put them on the big marble-effect formica-topped table. Then she sat down to wait for Terry's return. Helen was far away, and Mrs Wood was with her family. Alice stretched out, warm, briefly at home.

Terry soon freed the jammed starter. He enjoyed his tinkering and felt tempted to take the Metro out for a spin, but he resisted the impulse. This was not the right time. The cold barn filled with fumes as he ran the engine. He switched it off, grimacing. You couldn't be too careful about exhaust fumes; he knew they didn't take long to have an effect. Terry closed the barn door and let himself into the house, padding down the passage towards the kitchen soundlessly on his rubber-soled feet. The door was ajar, and through the space he could see Alice sitting at the table. He glanced to right and left. He would dearly love to look round the house, but if she caught him spying her trust in him would be broken. He'd play it straight – get her to show him round. It shouldn't be hard.

Terry entered the kitchen wearing a wide smile.

'There, that's done,' he said.

'Oh, you were quick,' said Alice. 'Thank you.'

'It should be all right now,' said Terry. 'I'll just put the spanner away, shall I? Through there?' and he nodded towards Giles's study.

'Would you? Thank you,' said Alice.

Terry had a quick glance round the study as he replaced

the spanner in the tool-box, but he could hardly open the desk or search the cupboards with the old girl next door. The place looked as if it hadn't been touched this century, with its dark paint and junk furniture. It was not Terry's idea of a gentleman's study, which he imagined as a warm room with book-lined shelves and rich carpeting, a flat desk with leather let into the top, and deep leather armchairs. And brandy in crystal goblets.

Alice made him a cup of coffee with Helen's Gold Blend, adding sugar from an Italian pottery storage jar that was kept on the dresser.

'You're on your own, then, are you?' Terry asked. 'While your family is away?'

'Yes,' said Alice. 'Alone in the house, that is. But there's a couple at the lodge – it's rented. They're nice young people. And a woman comes in to clean.' She didn't mention Mrs Wood's prolonged Christmas break. 'And there's a gardener who comes up to feed the ponies with hay and so on.'

She told it all to him, just like that! Terry was amazed. She couldn't know that he wouldn't tell someone else about it, someone less scrupulous than Terry about what he did, someone who would come into the house one dark night and strip it. It would be dead easy, and Terry knew people who'd pay him to tell them about the place. But this was a plum he meant to keep for himself. This was a rich prize for the plucking.

'Oh yes?' he prompted. 'Ponies?'

'They belong to my grand-daughters,' said Alice.

Terry asked about the girls and soon knew their names, ages and interests. Poor old thing, she's lonely, he thought; it was the same as the women on the housing estates. Give her a bit of his time, listen a while, nod and smile, and she'd eat out of his hand just as they did, and without him having all that other bother which sometimes grew tedious.

'It's a great house,' said Terry. 'Will you show me round? I don't think I've ever been in one this size that was lived in.'

Alice hesitated. She knew she had been talking too much – reaction, probably, to the strain of her morning's adventure – but the young man – culpable though he certainly was – had more than made amends by his kindness after the accident.

'I don't see why not,' she said. No one would know.

She led him along the passage into the dining-room, a big, square room with an oak refectory table in the centre. High-backed Jacobean oak chairs with cane seats were arranged along either side, and there was an old oak dresser against one wall. Alice shuddered to think what Helen had paid for this furniture, which she had bought to set off the room and demonstrate to would-be clients how things should be done. Beyond the dining-room another door led to the hall, where several rugs were laid on the stone-flagged floor, and at the rear a wide staircase led to the first floor. More doors led from the hall. Alice opened one, and went ahead of Terry into the drawing-room.

'Well!' For once Terry was at a loss. This was the life, all right! He stood on the deep pile carpet surveying the velvet upholstery, the brocade curtains, the various ornaments. An artificial Christmas tree, tinsel-branched, decorated with gold and silver baubles, stood in a corner.

Without comment, Alice led him on to Helen's own sitting-room, which overlooked the garden. The walls were ice-blue, the carpet a deeper blue. Two armchairs were covered in chintz with a yellow, lime green and blue design; two others were covered in yellow. There was a bureau against one wall. Here, Helen often worked in the evenings. The room was beautiful, but there was something about it that made Terry almost shiver.

Alice noticed.

'You feel it, too,' she said. 'It's a lovely room but it's somehow cold – though the heating works in here.' She laid her hand on the radiator. The boiler was programmed to run through the twenty-four hours in case of severe frost, though the thermostat was set low. 'The house isn't so warm upstairs,' Alice went on. 'The system needs renewing but they've had such a lot of expense. Things have to be done bit by bit.'

'Yes,' said Terry, nodding gravely. He looked out of the window at the garden which rolled away from the house. There was a wide lawn bordered with shrubs and trees, including, some distance from the house, an immense cedar with great spreading branches.

54

'There's a lot of land,' he said.

'Yes,' agreed Alice. 'Most of it's meadow, though, for the ponies. They're over there.' She waved vaguely. 'You can see them from some of the upstairs windows. Not mine – I overlook the lodge.'

'Maybe you get the morning sun,' Terry said.

'Well – no, it faces north,' said Alice.

She showed him the girls' sitting-room with its television and stereo. From its window he could see a paved path leading down the garden towards the west side of the lawn.

'The pool's down there,' said Alice. 'The girls love that.'

Swimming-pool, she meant.

'I'll bet,' said Terry.

He'd have one too, one day.

Alice knew she must send him on his way and retreat to her own quarters, shoulder her isolation again. She led him back through the house.

Following slowly, Terry paused in the hall to look at the long-case clock which stood there. He knew little about such things but thought it was probably worth a bomb. Breaking in here would be a doddle. If he failed to collect from the old girl, he could always sell his information. It could be useful to see her rooms. She'd show him them if he asked, Terry felt sure; after all, hadn't he gone out of his way to help her when she'd got herself into a right old mess? Borrowing her daughter-in-law's car without asking, indeed!

'How do you get to your flat?' he asked at the foot of the main staircase. 'Up here?'

Alice was about to explain that she used the back stairs when both of them heard a voice calling.

'Mrs Armitage – are you there?' came the question, and Sue appeared from the back of the house. 'The door was open so I walked in and then I heard voices. I could see you had a visitor.'

She turned then, and looked at Terry, who was standing on the lowest tread of the staircase. Her first sight of him gave a false impression of height, but she saw, too, the ingenuous expression, the ready smile, the bright curls framing the round head. His eyes were alert and regarded her with as much attention as she was looking at him.

'Hullo,' said Sue.

'Oh, Sue,' said Alice, and the warmth in her voice was apparent to Terry. Who was this pretty dark girl with the long hair? He had seen her before somewhere.

In all the time that they had spent together, Alice had not learned Terry's name. She looked at him blankly.

'I'm Terry Brett,' he said.

'This is Sue Norris,' said Alice. 'She lives at the lodge.'

'Hullo, Sue,' said Terry, and then he placed her; he'd seen her leaving the Rigby Arms one night and going off with some old guy in a blue Rover 3500.

'Hi,' said Sue, and then turned to Alice. 'I just popped up to see if you were all right, Mrs Armitage, as you're on your own,' she explained. 'Though I could see you had a friend visiting, from the car outside.' Her words hung in the air, waiting for an explanation of the nature of this friendship. Sue had never before known Alice to have a visitor, and she had wondered if the caller was bona fide; you heard of such terrible things these days.

'How kind of you, Sue,' said Alice, and was about to add that Terry had mended her car for her when she realized that this could lead to further explanations which must be avoided if what she had done was to remain undetected. Would Jonathan notice the Volvo had gone? Probably, but would he attach importance to it? The idea of inventing an explanation – saying it was at the garage for service – some lie – filled Alice with dread. She went on quickly, 'What time do you have to be at work?'

'Three o'clock,' said Sue, and turned to Terry. 'I'm a receptionist at the Rigby Arms in Westborough. Know it? It's a nice place. I have to catch the bus at the end of the lane.'

'What – no car?' asked Terry, grinning.

'Not of my own. I don't drive,' said Sue, who meant to get Jonathan to teach her. 'Jonathan takes me when I'm on the early shift, and he comes in to collect me at night when I'm late.'

Unless my son brings you home, Alice thought.

'Jonathan's away at the moment, with his children,' said Sue. 'He's got them with him at his parents' place in Kent. He'll be home tonight.'

'I could give you a lift to Westborough,' said Terry lightly. 'I'm going that way.' He could, easily; Sue was a looker, and besides, she knew what went on here.

'Oh – that'd be great,' said Sue. 'Thanks. When are you leaving?'

'I'm in no hurry,' said Terry slowly, and he held her gaze. 'I've got a few days off, like most people. I've no definite plans.'

Both of the young people had forgotten Alice for a moment. Then, reluctantly turning their eyes away from one another, they glanced at her. She was their link.

'I was going to have a sandwich for lunch,' Sue said. She would have dinner that night at the Rigby, where meals were part of the perks. She looked from Alice to Terry. 'Why don't you both come over and have a sandwich with me?'

'Yes please,' said Terry promptly.

'I don't think I will, thank you, Sue,' said Mrs Armitage. 'I'm not very hungry.'

'Oh, come on,' said Sue. 'You must eat something. Mustn't she?' she appealed to Terry.

Terry had been looking forward to having Sue's company to himself, but he'd be alone with her, after all, driving into Westborough.

'Indeed she must,' said Terry. 'Must keep up your strength, you know.'

Through Alice's head ran thoughts about whether it would be proper for Sue to entertain Terry in the lodge without Jonathan. People did these things these days and thought nothing of it, but looking at Sue and looking at Terry, seeing the glances they exchanged while she hesitated, Alice was reminded of how her own mother had always said one shouldn't put temptation in the path of others. Her presence would ensure the absence of opportunity, at least. She was shocked at the direction of her own thoughts. Terry and Sue had only just met; he'd be leaving soon and that would be the last they'd see of him. And anyway Jonathan and Sue weren't married, though that didn't mean Sue was free to spread her favours about. Alice decided that her experiences this morning had made her light-headed. Sue was a nice, friendly girl who felt lonely when she was at the lodge on her own. Hadn't she come looking for Alice just now from purely neighbourly motives?

She'd been watching too many modern plays on television, Alice reflected – hence, too, her anxiety about Sue and Giles seeing too much of each other. In real life people still had standards and considered how their actions might affect those to whom they had responsibilities. Suppressing her base fears, she nevertheless agreed to go over to the lodge.

Inside it was warm and snug. It was Alice's first visit, and she looked round at the oak-panelled living-room with interest. It was rather dark, for the latticed windows were small, but there was a big log fire, and also, beneath one window, an electric storage heater which Alice noticed with envy. She was installed in a large armchair and given a glass of sherry, and a magazine to read, while Terry and Sue went into the kitchen to make the sandwiches. She heard them laughing as they worked. It was nice to hear people happy.

When they came back with a plate of cheese sandwiches made with Kraft slices and white sliced bread, Sue refilled Alice's glass and asked how long she and Terry had known one another.

Before Alice could answer, Terry had launched into his version of the collision.

'Oh – but it wasn't like that!' Alice tried to interrupt.

Terry swept on.

'She'd borrowed her daughter-in-law's car,' he told Sue. 'Without permission,' and he pretended to frown at Alice.

'You didn't!' exclaimed Sue. 'Why, you mischief!' There was approving admiration in her tone although she accepted Terry's description of the crash.

'You don't mind Sue knowing, do you, Mrs Armitage?' said Terry. 'She's on your side.' He went on to explain that the car would soon be repaired and no one would be any the wiser. 'You're not going to give her away, are you, Sue?' he asked.

'Of course not,' said Sue.

'And – er – ?' What was he called, the fellow she lived with?

'Oh, Jonathan won't, either,' said Sue. 'Don't worry. Lucky you weren't hurt, either of you.' She noticed that Mrs

Armitage was looking very upset. Naturally she wouldn't like people to know that she had boobed. It was lucky for her that Terry was being so easy about it, otherwise she might have been in real trouble, with the police and all that. If Helen found out, she'd be furious. 'Where were you going?' she asked. It must have been important for the old girl to take such a chance.

'Oh – to London,' said Alice. 'I do sometimes.'

'Do you? Good for you,' said Sue warmly. 'Meeting a friend, were you?'

'No – not this time,' said Alice, and thought that she was almost as bad as Terry in letting an implied untruth slip by uncorrected. She met no friends in London.

She was lonely, poor old thing, thought Sue.

'You ought to have a party,' she said. 'This is the time of year for parties.'

'Who would I ask?' said Alice.

'Jonathan and me, for a start,' said Sue. 'And Terry. And haven't you any friends in Harcombe? Haven't you been invited out?'

'I've met a few people,' Alice admitted. She'd finished her second glass of sherry and now Terry filled it again. Alice took a sip. 'I've been to Mrs Duncan's,' she said. 'At the Old Vicarage.'

'Well – there you are. You must ask Mrs Duncan back,' said Sue. 'Have you done that?'

'I can't,' said Alice. 'My room is too small.' And too cold, she thought.

'Why don't we go and have a look at it?' said Terry, whose earlier attempt to inspect it had been foiled by Sue's arrival.

After all that sherry, Alice was unable to protest with any conviction. Sue and Terry took the plates and glasses out to the kitchen and there were more sounds of laughter. Alice, muzzy by now, found herself smiling too. It was a long time since she'd heard laughter like theirs.

Soon they reappeared, ready to escort her back to her flat and examine it before going to Westborough. After Sue had closed the door of the lodge, which locked automatically on the Yale, they walked across to the main house, one on each side of Alice. Terry steadied her as they went up the steps to the back door, which had been unlocked all this time. Alice led the way up the narrow twisting staircase that rose from the back of the house to the attic floor where, years ago, servants had slept.

The top corridor was icy. Alice walked along it to a dingy brown door and opened it to reveal a tiny lobby in which there was not enough room for the three of them to stand together. Doors led to a sitting-room beyond which was a tiny kitchen, to a miniscule bathroom, and to a bedroom almost totally filled by a double bed, Alice, still feeling the effects of the sherry, showed them all round since they seemed so interested.

'Christ, it's cold,' Terry said, in the sitting-room. His breath puffed into a cloud before him.

Sue went to the window and felt the radiator.

'It's stone cold,' she said. 'Isn't the heating on?'

'It doesn't work very well up here,' Alice said. 'I'll get the electric fire from my bedroom.'

'I'll get it.' Sue had noticed a small two-bar fire in the corner.

While she was fetching it, Alice opened a cupboard in the sitting-room and took the fan heater from it, plugging it in. It purred out warmth at once. It was automatic for her, by now, to put it away whenever she went out, in case Helen came snooping and confiscated it, and she did not notice Terry's puzzled expression as he watched what she was doing.

'You need a couple of good convector heaters,' said Terry. 'They'd soon warm you up.'

'Have you only got this one fire?' Sue asked, bringing it in. It had to run from the same plug as the fan heater, using an adaptor, and Terry raised his brows as he noticed this.

'Yes,' said Alice. 'I did think a convector would be better, but how would I get it upstairs? I don't think I could do it myself.'

'The shop would deliver. The guy would carry it up,' said Terry.

'I know.' How could she possibly explain that Helen would ban it?

She didn't have to: Sue understood.

'You don't want Helen to know,' she said. 'And Mrs Wood might tell her.'

Alice's averted gaze and drooping shoulders were her answer.

'I'll bring you two tomorrow,' said Terry. 'One for in here and one for the bedroom. They'll soon warm you up.'

'Yes, but – ' Alice looked wretched. They'd take up space. Where could she hide them if Helen was about?

'You do need them, Mrs Armitage,' said Sue, and added, 'Doesn't Giles realize how cold it is up here?'

'Er – I don't think he does,' Alice said. He so seldom came up. When had they last had a chat? She couldn't remember. It would be lovely to be warm, she thought. Giles would understand and wouldn't be cross if he caught her; hadn't he brought her the fire? She could hide the bedroom heater in her wardrobe if she went out, and push the other one into a corner with the big chair in front of it, in case Helen came in.

She opened her handbag, took out her notecase, and gave Terry seventy pounds, in ten-pound notes.

'Will that be enough to buy them?' she asked. She thought they would cost at least thirty pounds each.

'Should be,' said Terry, who could probably get them at cost from someone he knew. He put the money in his pocket. He knew the old duck was loaded. Of course, she'd been going to London, to splurge at the sales, no doubt; hence her well-filled notecase. 'I'll bring them tomorrow without fail,' he said.

They left Alice there, alone, with the electric fire and the fan heater both on as she sat in her armchair. Replete with sherry and sandwiches, she dozed off, only waking in panic when it grew dark, for something dreadful had happened.

No, it hadn't. To be sure, there'd been the crash, but it had brought her a new friend. Now she had two, for Sue was her friend already, and they were going to help her. Before they left they'd mentioned the party again, saying that she should hold it in the big drawing-room while the others were still away. What an idea, thought Alice drowsily. It was out of the question.

7

As they drove into Westborough that afternoon, Terry discovered from Sue that she would be working the same shift all the week.

'I'll give you a lift in tomorrow, then,' he said. 'After I've fixed the heaters for the old girl.'

'You'll get them, then?' said Sue. 'Buy them, I mean.'

'Of course. She's given me the money, hasn't she?' Terry drove on, his gaze intent on the road ahead; he didn't like these narrow twisting lanes, and he didn't want to run into some idiot belting along towards him not looking where he was going.

'I'd have thought you might be tempted,' said Sue.

'Whatever gave you that idea?' said Terry, but without any hint of affront in his voice. 'I wouldn't take advantage of an old lady.'

'Wouldn't you?' Sue's tone was sceptical. She'd noticed a lot about Terry. His clothes were neat – not trendy, but stylish, and he was driving a fairly new car – but his shoes were shabby – worn, and not polished – which didn't tie in with the rest of his appearance. During her time at the Rigby Arms, Sue had met a lot of people and had learned to interpret certain signs. At first she'd thought Terry was a salesman of some kind. Now she was less sure. There was something about him that excited her, but she wasn't sure what it was. When they met as he stood at the foot of the staircase, she had felt a strange shock – a sense of recognition unlike anything she'd ever experienced before. Here was someone who, underneath the mild surface, was as ruthless as she was; Sue knew it without any doubt.

'What's your job?' she asked him. 'You are working, I suppose?'

'I'm a middle man,' said Terry grandly. 'I supply things that people want. Like convector fires for the old bag,' he added.

'So you will take your cut,' said Sue, turning her head away so that he could not see her smile if he took his eyes from the road. 'I thought there'd be something in it for you.'

'From the dealer, yes,' said Terry. 'All fair and square – cash down.'

'I don't believe you,' said Sue. She snuggled into the seat beside him, a gloriously comfortable sensation stealing over her. In her whole life she never remembered feeling so much at ease with anyone – and she fancied him, too: she liked his eyes and he had a big laughing mouth.

'Why not?' asked Terry. 'Why should I lie?'

'Did Mrs Armitage really drive into you? Your car isn't damaged, is it?' said Sue. 'Surely it would be, if she'd done that?'

'It was just a scrape. She misjudged how close she could go to the line of parked cars,' Terry explained. 'I'd edged forward a little, ready to move out from the kerb.'

Each time Mrs Armitage had given Sue a lift she'd driven in a very capable manner, Sue had thought. She could not drive herself, but she'd been a passenger often enough to be some judge of competence, and she'd been surprised, because until then she'd assessed Mrs Armitage as an ineffectual old woman, someone who was at the mercy of her not-very-thoughtful family, and to be pitied.

'She's a good driver,' said Sue.

'Even good drivers have off moments,' Terry said. 'And she wasn't in her own car. Those Volvos are lively.'

'She'd be being extra careful, driving Helen's car,' said Sue.

'Well, it was raining,' said Terry. 'Maybe she couldn't see properly because of the rain. I don't suppose her eyes are too good, at her age.'

The rain had stopped now, though the sky was still grey and overcast with heavy low clouds.

'Maybe you were in too much of a hurry,' suggested Sue. Her voice was light; she sounded amused, not reproving.

Terry glanced quickly at her. This one was something again, he thought; this was no ordinary sort of girl.

'I wasn't going anywhere special,' he said. 'Why should I be in a hurry?'

'I expect you were looking for the next opportunity,' Sue remarked. Rather as she had been when she met Jonathan. 'Come and have a sandwich tomorrow,' she suggested when he dropped her at the Rigby Arms. 'I won't invite Mrs Armitage to join us.'

Alice woke in the chill dark hours of early morning feeling clammy with fear and shame. Such a terrible thing had happened the previous day. Clutching the bedclothes round her, she remembered what she had done. How could she have been so silly? It was almost wicked, taking Helen's car like that without permission.

Alice reached out to turn on the bedside light, then sat up, the cold striking her through her bedjacket and the warm, high-necked nightdress she wore, with its long sleeves gathered in at the wrists. It was pale pink, printed with tiny, darker pink rosebuds and trimmed with lace frills. At the end of the bed lay her dressing-gown. She put it on, slid her feet into her sheepskin slippers and shuffled into the kitchen to make herself a cup of tea. Then, while the kettle boiled, she went back to her bedroom where she turned on the electric fire and took the now cool rubber hot-water bottle out of her bed to refill it. This was a quite regular routine in the small hours, and so was a feeling of sorrow and loss, but not this panic, the almost heart-stopping terror.

Alice wasn't afraid of burglars breaking in to Harcombe House, or of being coshed while alone there. Harcombe, she thought, was a safe village; there were no gangs of louts parked astride motor cycles in the street, as she'd seen elsewhere, and no great local unemployment problem. As far as she knew, all residents of working age who wanted them had jobs. Several cars left the village when Giles did, he had said, bound for London or places like Swindon or Slough. What did frighten Alice was people: the lack of them, for company and stimulation, and the perilous path she must tread among those who comprised her family. And now she had committed a great folly which could bring immense and deserved trouble down on her head.

She'd never see that boy again, she felt sure. He'd

wriggled out of the consequences of a collision that had been entirely his fault, but she'd been responsible for making what would have been simply a tiresome event, if she had been in her own car, into a catastrophe by her use of Helen's car. To cap all, she'd given the boy a large sum of money to buy her two convector heaters, and she'd never see that again.

She looked out of her window across at the lodge. There it lay, in peaceful darkness, with Jonathan and Sue enjoying their illicit union under its steep grey slate roof. Alice had felt so happy there for that short time, sitting by the fire in a shabby, comfortable chair, not worrying about dropping sandwich crumbs on the worn carpet. Some of the furniture was familiar; it had been at Windlea. There hadn't been space for it in Alice's flat; Helen had used it and her own cast-off pieces to equip the lodge for letting. Alice had thought her surplus things had been sold: she had felt a pang at seeing these old friends again.

Why hadn't they offered her the chance to live in the lodge? Because it could be let for probably quite a large sum, she thought grimly: because the only way Giles could keep Helen content and their marriage together was to gratify her craving to live in this style. Alice moaned to herself, rocking to and fro, keening softly with grief as she recognized that her son was an unhappy failure. If only he'd never met Helen, she thought; if only he'd stayed with his original firm, married a girl with modest tastes, a generous nature and less ambition; avoided putting himself under an obligation to his father-in-law.

What if Helen found out about the car? What would she say? What would she do? Thinking about it, Alice cringed with dread.

The kettle was boiling its head off in the kitchen; something had happened to its ability to switch itself off – another thing she must see to; Walter had been quite clever at simple repairs and would probably have happily bought some part and cured the complaint. Alice made her tea and got back into bed to drink it. The room was warmer now. She left the fire on, a single bar burning, something she never liked to do when she first went to bed, for fear of fire. But now it was nearly morning.

She fell asleep after drinking her tea and did not wake until nine o'clock.

At noon, the back doorbell rang. Both bells were wired so that they pealed in the corridor outside Alice's flat. Before Christmas she'd plodded downstairs several times, summoned by youths selling prints and cards in aid of various charities and by small boys singing carols. But most itinerant callers gave up waiting when their summons was not answered promptly. Harcombe House, and its lodge, which was usually empty, were not worth visiting.

Now, when Alice opened the door, she saw Terry outside. He was grinning, his mop of curls standing out brightly against the pale winter sky. The air was colder today; there had been a frost in the night.

'I got them,' he said. Beside him were two large cardboard cartons. He patted one. 'They're good ones.'

After parting from Sue the previous day, Terry had been to a discount centre. He'd bought the two heaters for less than the price advertised because he found two discontinued models, one with a slight scratch. He got a further reduction for paying cash. He'd found a sharp salesman to deal with; each had respected the other and struck a bargain, a fiver passing from Terry to the other young man. The account had been doctored. On paper, Alice now owed Terry a further eight pounds. But she had a genuine guarantee, if anything should go wrong with either heater, which was most unlikely. Terry had bought plugs, too, and an extension lead. He had decided to make himself essential to Mrs Armitage. In small ways, costing himself minimum effort, he would bring cheer to her life and thus gain acceptance by the whole family as part of the regular scene. He'd have a reason for being about the place, for seeing Sue.

What a girl! She was exciting! She'd kissed him before leaving the car – a warm, quick pressure of soft lips against his, a breath of scent. What a change from the older, dissatisfied housewives who formed his main experience of women. Terry had never had sex with someone his age, whom he'd picked for her looks. He never thought of that intimacy as making love: love was a con; it didn't exist, not really.

But the question is: what was Terry driving?

If ever he did fall in love, it would be with someone like Sue.

Whistling, he carried the heaters, one at a time, up the narrow staircase to Alice's flat. Seated in her armchair, he made quick work of fitting the plugs and he demonstrated the extension lead.

'It could be useful,' he said. 'You shouldn't run too many things from one point, you know. This way, you could run the television on it, wheel it into your bedroom – you can get an aerial extension too, if you need one. You can have the fire on and the iron, for instance. What else would help to make you snug? Mind if I look round when I've fixed this?'

At that moment Alice would have agreed to any suggestion he cared to make. How could she have been so mean and suspicious, she was asking herself, as to doubt his honesty? What did it matter if he'd adjusted the facts about yesterday's accident? He'd probably felt too ashamed to face the truth, just as she was ashamed at the enormity of her escapade. He was only young; he'd learn from this mistake,

Terry felt the change in atmosphere, the dissolution of Alice's reservations. He always knew how to play it, he thought complacently, fitting the brown lead to the positive point in the plug on the extension.

Washing his hands in the bathroom, he saw the rubber hot-water bottle in its knitted cover hanging on the back of the door.

'Haven't you got an electric blanket?' he asked her. 'Or a Teasmade machine? You know – it wakes you up with a cup of tea.'

'No.'

Walter hadn't wanted an electric blanket, and when he was alive, Alice had not needed one. A comforting glow – sometimes, in hot weather, almost too much of one – had emanated from his familiar body curled up alongside her. They didn't sleep entwined, but there he was, pleased if she felt like snuggling up against him, always ready to embrace her. It wasn't sex that she missed; that, in Alice's view, was over-rated, given too much emphasis these days, when friendship was so much more important. It was just the contact that she mourned, the warmth of a human touch.

They'd never gone to sleep without mending any small difference they'd had; it had been a rule.

'My granny's got one,' Terry told her. He didn't know if she had, in that home she was in, but his mother, in her single bed in Woking, certainly had. 'There's two sorts, one for on top, and one for beneath. The top one's best, you can sleep with it on. They're quite safe.'

'Are they?' Alice looked doubtful.

'Oh yes,' said Terry.

'I sometimes get up in the night to refill my bottle,' Alice confessed.

'Well, even if you'd turned your blanket off, you could turn it on then,' said Terry. 'I expect you wake up because you're cold.' Or to pee, he thought, at her age; but better not say so.

'Perhaps I do,' said Alice.

'Well, you won't be cold any more,' said Terry. 'You could run it off the same socket as the bedside lamp. That would be all right.'

'The cost,' worried Alice.

'I think they're about thirty-five pounds,' said Terry, who had looked at the discount store.

'Oh, I didn't mean the blanket,' said Alice. 'I meant the cost of the electricity.'

'They don't use much,' Terry assured her. 'And as for the convectors, once you've got the place warm, the thermostat switches them on and off so they don't use power all the time. They're cheaper to run than that bar fire.'

'I'll get a blanket,' Alice decided. 'I'll buy one this afternoon.'

'I'll get it for you,' said Terry. 'I'll bring it out, fix the plug, make sure it's working all right.'

'Oh, I can't put you to all that trouble,' said Alice.

'It's no trouble,' said Terry. 'I'd like to see you again.'

And she'd like to see him. He throbbed with vitality. Alice felt better just for looking at his bright curly head, let alone his cheerful smile.

'I'll get the blanket. You come and fix the plug,' she said. She hadn't got a grandson. 'How old are you, Terry?' she asked.

'Twenty-two.'

Giles was forty-five. It could have been. Alice smiled.

'You'll be back at work soon,' she said. 'What's your job?'

'Selling,' said Terry promptly. 'This and that. I make my own timetable.'

'Oh,' said Alice, accepting it. Rather like Jonathan but at a much lower level, she supposed. Or perhaps he was one of those moonlighters the papers kept mentioning; it sounded so romantic.

Later, over at the lodge, Terry told Sue about the electric blanket. Alice had rejected his suggestion of a Teasmade. He thought she might change her mind later. After all, it was quite an outlay all at once, and there'd be the bill for the car, too.

'Fancy her taking it,' Sue marvelled. 'Naughty old thing. Like a kid. I hope that Helen doesn't find out. She's a cow. Hard as nails.'

So are you, Terry thought. The women on the estates weren't; that was part of their problem. What a combination he and Sue would make together, with her iron will and his soft talk. They'd be invincible.

Upstairs in the bed that she shared with Jonathan, he said, 'You know that party we talked about? For the old girl?'

'Mm.' Sue was trying to count his ribs. He was lean, not flabby like Jonathan who took no exercise and drank too much beer.

'Let's fix it for her. It'd be great.'

'Might be a giggle,' said Sue. 'Poor old thing, she doesn't have much of a time. She deserves a treat.'

'In the main house,' Terry pressed. 'In that swank room.' Terry would have a room like that one day, though maybe more modern. And here, beside him, was the partner who would help him secure it. The means were at hand. She'd already got in with that geezer with the blue Rover, the old girl's son.

'What if the people who came to it told Helen?' Sue asked. 'She'd be in trouble then.'

'Would they meet? Does Helen know these people? Surely they're old ladies too? You could find out – chat her up about them.'

'Yes.' Anyway, it was a risk worth taking for the fun of it, Sue thought.

Later, nuzzling her shoulder – she smelled good, an odd sort of scent, it fairly turned him on – Terry had another question.

'What about the son?'

'Giles? What about him?'

'What sort of fellow is he? How well do you know him?'

'Drinks a lot,' said Sue. 'I know him well enough.'

'As well as this?' Terry took her hand, kissed the palm and gently nipped the fat pad beneath her thumb with his sharp white teeth. He'd learned that trick from a widow in Barnet.

'Not yet,' said Sue. 'But I will.'

There was no need to say more. They did not have to explain their ideas to each other, not at this stage. Both knew they were going to fly high together, and the manner and speed of that ascent would be dictated by Giles's response to Sue. Sue was confident. She'd already levered herself upwards by throwing her lot in with Jonathan; she'd do better with Giles.

Neither had mentioned Jonathan as someone to be considered or as an obstacle. Terry, coming down on Sue, making her moan, knew that he would not be where he was now if Jonathan were going to be any problem.

8

'Now, about your party, Mrs Armitage,' said Terry. 'When shall it be?'

He'd returned the next day.

'Oh, that was just your joke, Terry,' said Alice. 'I can't really have a party.'

'Yes, you can! Leave it all to Sue and me – we'll fix everything. Who shall we ask?'

He pulled the second chair forward so that their knees almost met in front of the softly glowing convector heater from which warm thermals arose. The room was cosy at last.

Alice hesitated, looking at the smooth, enthusiastic face so close to hers. He had a small pimple on one cheek, and his eyebrows were curly; when he grew old, they'd be bushy, she thought inconsequentially.

'We can't,' she said. 'It's not possible.'

'You owe people, don't you?' Terry said. 'It's rude if you don't ask them back. Let's write their names down.' He got up to look for a piece of paper and found a small pad by the telephone, kept there so that Alice could make an immediate note of messages for Helen. Terry slowly began to write, in uneven script. 'Sue and Jonathan,' he said. 'And me, of course. Who else? Who's asked you?'

'Well, Mrs Duncan. That's all, really,' said Alice. 'But I know Mrs Hedges and Miss Wilson. I've been to a coffee morning at their cottage. But this is just your teasing, Terry. We can't really do it.'

'No, it's not. It's going to happen,' said Terry. 'There's all this big house, going spare. What's it to be? Gin and tonic?'

In their young days, Alice and Walter had given plenty of parties. She had enjoyed most forms of entertaining, but in the last years they'd settled for about eight friends at a time, offering sherry or wine; spirits were so expensive. She'd taken pride in constructing tempting canapés – varied spreads on crisp pastry, and cheese straws. But not now: not here. That was all over.

'No,' she said. 'We can't do it.'

'What's stopping you?' asked Terry, regarding her gravely, his eyes large and apparently innocent. He'd dangled the idea before her again more for his own amusement than anything else, but now the challenge of making her give way to him spurred him on.

'It's not my house,' said Alice.

'Well, you live here. It's your home,' said Terry. 'Surely you can ask a few friends in?'

Alice looked away from that penetrating gaze. What he said should be so, and it was her house – part of it. She was uncertain how much Helen and Giles had paid for the whole estate but eighty thousand pounds had come from the sale of Windlea. Surely that entitled her to more than this tiny allotment of space under the eaves?

'They'll never know,' he prompted. 'Your family.'

'It's true that I owe Mrs Duncan,' said Alice. 'I'd thought

of taking her out to lunch one day – to a pub somewhere.' She hadn't, until this moment, when the notion came to her as inspiration. But hot on its heels came the knowledge that she would find it a huge strain to impose her will over the managing Barbara Duncan, obtain service in the pub, act efficiently as hostess.

'Do that another time,' Terry said. 'When it's your turn again and your family's here.' He drew a line on his piece of paper beneath the names. 'Now, we'll want plenty of drink,' he went on. 'Gin, whisky, vodka.' He wrote them down, one after the other.

'We won't,' said Alice, firmer now. 'If it happens at all, it'll be just sherry.' As she felt herself yielding over the main idea, some instinct warned her not to let Terry have a free hand with spirits. Besides, Barbara Duncan had offered only sherry.

'Sherry, right,' said Terry, crossing out what he had written and printing the word in big letters. 'Tomorrow, then,' he added. 'About six?'

Alice thought of a way of staving it off.

'That's too soon,' she said. 'We must give them some notice. And Sue's on late shift this week. We must have it when she can come.' That would kill the whole idea. By the time Sue was on the early shift, Giles and the family would have come back and the plan would have to be abandoned.

'Next week, then,' said Terry. 'Sue changes rotas then. You're right, we can't have it without her.'

In the following minutes, Alice found herself agreeing to Friday and telephoning the three intended guests, for Terry insisted that she should do it while he was there. She might change her mind, he thought, and he didn't mean to let that happen. By the time the car had been repaired and they'd had the party, he'd have quite a hold over old Mrs Armitage, who wouldn't want her secrets revealed. He didn't know, yet, how he would use this power; time would give him the opportunity, just as time would show what use Sue could make of Giles; quite a lot, he thought, remembering her sharp little teeth, her hands on his back, the rest of her, so soft, warm and moist. He'd never known anything like it, and there'd be more today, quite soon, when he'd got the party set up with the old girl and went over to the lodge.

All the ladies were at home when Alice reluctantly telephoned. They accepted warmly, sounding genuinely pleased, Mrs Hedges speaking for herself and Miss Wilson.

'Like that, is it?' said Terry, learning that they lived together.

'What do you mean?' asked Alice.

'Well – ' Terry shrugged. 'You know – two women – ' he raised his eyebrows with a knowing expression on his unlined face.

'Oh, it's not like that at all,' said Alice, who didn't know whether it was or not. 'People are so unkind,' she went on. 'Why jump to conclusions?'

'Human nature,' said Terry.

'I expect they just want company,' said Alice. 'And it's cheaper for two than separate houses. They're probably old friends. Anyway, what does it matter? It's their business.' She thought it might be rather pleasant to share a cottage with a woman friend: divide the chores and the responsibility: have someone to talk to, to go out with, to take care of you if you were ill. But when you'd been contentedly married for nearly fifty years, you didn't have women friends in quite that way; she'd never felt close to any of the widows among their acquaintance, except Audrey, who, with her husband, had often made up a quartet with Alice and Walter. 'I wish I'd stayed in Bournemouth,' she said suddenly. For she could have drawn closer to some of those women her own age whom she'd known superficially for years. They must be lonely, too. She could have taken up bridge, like some of them, who played three or four times a week and were busy and cheerful.

'That's where you lived?' asked Terry.

'Yes. Then my husband died,' said Alice. 'And my son and his wife asked me to come and live with them. It seemed a good idea at the time.'

'You had a nice place in Bournemouth, did you?'

'Yes. You could see the sea from the garden. Just a bus ride into town if you didn't want to take the car.'

He could see it all. Terry knew what they'd done, the son and his wife: stripped her of what she'd got for the house to help with this place. He'd have done it himself, but he'd have made the old thing comfortable until she had to go into a home.

73

'It's nice when the girls are at home,' Alice went on. 'They come up here sometimes, especially Amanda. We play cards and Scrabble. But they're away at school most of the time. Boarding-school, you know,' she added, to make sure he understood.

'Well, you've got me now,' smiled Terry. 'We're friends now, like as if I was your grandson.'

Though she'd thought of the same thing herself, somehow, when he said it, Alice felt chilled. She looked at him doubtfully. Terry was beaming at her. By the time her son and his family came back, he'd be so much a part of the place that they'd easily accept him, he decided. It was all going splendidly. He'd plan as he went along, as he always did. He was excited by the future and the prospects it held. Who knew where it might lead? The daughter-in-law, Helen, for instance, could be a target for him while Sue got to work on the son. They could bleed this family for thousands, the two of them, make anything he'd done in the past seem like peanuts. Paris, Rome, the South of France, here we come, thought Terry, Sue and me together. She was wasted on that slob Jonathan. Terry hadn't met him yet but he was sure he was a slob. The two of them could conquer the world, and without any violence. There had never been any need for it in his operations; an edge of steel in the voice and glares in place of smiles had been all that was required when he met resistance.

'I'll go and fix things with Sue,' said Terry, eager to get away now. 'Little eats and so on.' But Sue didn't like cooking; he already knew that. 'Maybe she could get them from the hotel, cheap,' he suggested brightly.

'No, I'll see to that,' said Alice, determined at least to set the tone of the party. 'We won't need much, not for so few people.'

'All right. It's your baby,' said Terry.

Alice watched from the window to see him emerge from the house. She was in for it now. At Windlea they'd had their routine; the food had been her department and Walter had dealt with the drinks. It had been team-work. Terry could pour the sherry. He and Jonathan would be the only men present. She saw his curly head below as he walked to the lodge past his parked car. There was something wrong about the car. Alice, about to draw back from the window looked at it again. It was the wrong colour. The Vauxhall he'd been driving that first day was pale green; in her mind's eye she could see it now, its wing jutting forward as she went by. The car parked outside the lodge today was brown.

He said he bought and sold things. Perhaps he dealt in cars. That must be the explanation.

She put it out of her mind.

In order to have a base approved of by Hilary, his wife, where he could see his children, Jonathan had spent part of his Christmas holiday at his parents' house in Kent. He'd fetched the children on Boxing Day and they'd stayed several days. Then he'd taken them back to their mother.

He'd regretted leaving Sue, but it couldn't be helped. She was on duty anyway at the Rigby Arms, doing extra hours, for the hotel was full and had arranged special Christmas festivities. Before they moved in to the lodge together, their meetings had been spiced with the thrill of complicated arrangements. Jonathan, after his wife had found out about his affair with Sue and thrown him out, had moved into a one-roomed flat in the town, and Sue had lived at the hotel, but gradually she'd moved more and more of her belongings, and finally herself, into his flat, which was far too small for two. Used to life in a tall Victorian semi-detached house with lofty rooms and plenty of space spread over three storeys, Jonathan found the discomfort of these cramped conditions hard to bear. He'd snapped at Sue several times when he couldn't find his own things among the jumble of her clothes – she had few other possessions. She was untidy, and not always very particular about washing. At first he had found this intriguing, for his wife had always run things in an orderly way, never behind with her chores, the washing done on time, his shirts ironed and put away, the children taught to keep their rooms tidy. Sue's disorder, combined with a degree of abandonment in bed which Jonathan had only met in his imagination before, had sparked in him a reaction which, most of the time, made him indulgent about the squalor and irritations of their life, but after some weeks of this his tolerance had been strained when he found a white shirt tinged pink from being washed with a red sweater of Sue's. The fact that it had been he who had taken their things to the launderette and failed to realize the peril posed by Sue's garment among the otherwise fast-dyed articles only made him crosser. Hilary would never let such a mistake occur.

But Hilary was dull, he reminded himself. Hilary was bored in bed and interested only in their children, to whom she was a devoted and exemplary mother.

'It might be your fault, you know,' Sue had said, when he had spoken about their problems. He'd felt disloyal, mentioning the lack of rapture in their intimacies as he lay, hot and sticky, his limbs still tangled with Sue's in her attic room at the Rigby Arms. She liked him coming up there. Until Hilary found out about them and turned him out, they had nowhere else to go, and she'd have got into trouble if they'd been caught, although she wasn't the only one who broke the rules about conduct among the staff. It would be fun to bring a case for wrongful dismissal for such a cause, she'd thought, though she doubted if, in fact, the manager would go so far. He'd turn a blind eye. But Jonathan wanted no notoriety, and he didn't want Sue to lose her job, for a love affair was very expensive. It was more so when he had to find a place of his own while still supporting his family.

He'd been chagrined when Sue had suggested that he might be to blame for Hilary's want of ardour. How could that be so, he'd asked.

'Well, you've not had much experience, have you?' Sue had replied.

He'd been married for eight years, Jonathan had said, and he'd got two children.

'Anyone can do that,' said Sue. 'It's more than a tap, you know, to turn on and off.'

In their weeks together, he'd discovered what she meant, but he soon saw that their relationship would not survive if they went on living in such confined quarters. He'd already taken over the cooking. Sue had her main meal at the hotel and saw no need to take trouble preparing one for him. After a day on the road, with a snatched lunch in some bar, Jonathan needed a good dinner in the evening; he was used to it. He was a competent cook, and it saved trouble all round if he prepared food in the tiny recess which contained the twin burner stove and minuscule sink rather than letting Sue loose in there. But they had a sharp row one morning after he'd found a grey grubby bra and an unwashed pair of nylon briefs among his clean shirts, washed and ironed by himself and airing by the radiator.

After that, he saw that if they were to stay together they must find somewhere better to live, and that had led him to the lodge at Harcombe House. It was small, and because it was in the country the rent was reasonable. Sue contributed to that; her salary was adjusted when she moved out of the hotel.

Jonathan was very subdued when he came back after seeing his children. Sue did not ask about them. He hadn't let her go with him when he went to buy their presents; the subject was dangerous ground for her to tread. He'd helped them carry their presents to the door when he took them back to their mother, and had half hoped Hilary would ask him in, but she didn't. She'd closed the front door upon herself and the small boy and girl before he'd got back into the car.

She had found out about Sue in such an unpleasant way. One of Hilary's female friends, so-called, visiting the Rigby on her way to London and stopping off for a meal, had seen them together leaving the hotel, and had put two and two together. Hilary ought to be told, she'd said.

Would the break have come anyway? Jonathan didn't know. Couldn't he have managed to keep on with Sue and stayed a good father and a dutiful, if not a loving husband? He was torn, now, between the new sexual excitement he had discovered and his longing for his children, and the adjustment to life with Sue was not easy after years living with neat Hilary. He had to remind himself that Sue was having to adjust too. Country life was new for her, and getting to and from work, except when he took her to Westborough on the early shift or collected her at night, meant a long walk to or from the bus stop. But he liked the lodge; he liked the small garden, enjoyed weeding and planting, keeping it tidy. He'd missed all that, after leaving home, and wondered how Hilary coped with it on her own: competently, he had no doubt. She was a capable girl.

He and Sue would work things out, he was sure. All partnerships needed time to develop and had to be nourished with care – marriage in particular, he thought, and would not let himself wonder whether he and Hilary could have tended theirs more, and saved it.

He seemed unable to avoid thoughts that were disloyal to one or other of the women. Jonathan, driving home, switched his mind from Hilary back to Sue. Soon he'd be wrapped in her thin arms, smelling again her strange musky smell, lost to everything else.

9

Terry did not visit Alice over the New Year weekend. He'd perfected the technique of making himself an essential part of someone's life and then playing hard to get for a while. His return after an interval was always greeted with rapture; Alice, he was sure, would be no exception to this.

She'd listened for him on Saturday, but no visiting car drove up to the house. Jonathan and Sue went off in the morning; Alice saw the Granada's boot disappearing through the gateway when she looked out of the window. The day, spent in solitude, pressed down on her. She took the Metro out in the afternoon and had a mock Devonshire tea with clotted cream and scones at Pam's Pantry in West-borough. On Sunday she saw Jonathan busy sweeping up sodden dead leaves that had lain around the lodge all winter. Alice put on her coat and boots. She'd go out for a walk; that would give her a chance to talk to him.

She loitered as she passed the lodge and he leaned on his broom to exchange trivialities with her. He saw that she was killing time, and, remembering Sue's remarks, asked her in for coffee.

Alice fluttered a little. She longed to accept but didn't want to be tiresome.

'I was going for a walk,' she said.

'Come in on your way back, then,' said Jonathan, playing along with her.

Alice walked the whole length of the village street, as far as the church, and back again. She saw a few people: a woman with a dog, two boys on cycles – and a number of cars drove past, but no one spoke to her as she stepped along in her fur-collared coat and smart leather boots, and her hat with the feather.

Jonathan had just finished clearing away the leaves and sweeping all the paths round the lodge when she returned. He led her inside, sat her down by the fire and poured her some sherry. Sue was upstairs, having a bath; it was her weekend off, before she changed shifts.

'I know you and Sue are great friends,' he said. 'She's told me about your lunches together.'

Lunches? There'd been only the one. And she saw very little of Sue – just glimpses from the window, unless she noticed the girl at the bus stop and gave her a lift. What did he mean?

Jonathan had come home several times that week to find the debris from two people's snack lunches piled any old how in the kitchen. He had begun to enjoy the evenings when Sue was working the late shift. He would pour himself a beer, and cook himself a chop, or sausages – usually something he'd bought on the way home, for Sue's housekeeping was unplanned and she often forgot to shop for food. He would tidy up whatever mess she had left behind, sighing over it, recognizing she could not change her ways. When he realized that someone had been in the house, he had jokingly asked her if she had been entertaining, and she had told him that Alice was so lonely that she had taken pity on the old woman.

As Alice drank her sherry, he sat facing her on the small sofa that had been in Walter's den at Windlea. It had grown shabby over the years. A new cover would give it a fresh lease of life, Alice thought, before she turned again to Jonathan, who seemed tired. His face was soft-featured, with an indeterminate nose and a small mouth. He had pale straight brows over brown eyes that looked mildly bewildered. It wasn't a strong face. Alice hoped Sue would soon appear as she sought a topic to discuss with this dull but amiable man. Sue didn't come, however, and at last Alice left.

'See you on Friday, Jonathan,' she said. 'At my party.'

This was the first Jonathan had heard of any party. When Sue came downstairs, smelling of bath oil and scent and unusually clean, he asked her what Alice had meant.

'Oh – didn't I say?' Sue smiled at him, her long dark hair hanging down on each side of her face. 'She's got this sort of nephew – well, more like a grandson, in actual fact. Terry's his name. He had the idea of her having a party while she's got the run of the place. It's on Friday.'

'Seems a good idea,' said Jonathan. 'She's breaking out, isn't she – borrowing Helen's car and now this? A bit like a child playing pranks.' He had noticed the Volvo's absence and without mentioning Terry, Sue had described the escapade.

'Well, I expect she's not far off getting senile,' said Sue carelessly, shocking Jonathan. She came out with these callous remarks at times. 'It's not much of a party, really,' Sue went on. 'Just three old girls from the village she's met. To pay back hospitality, you know.'

'And this Terry? He's coming?'

'Oh – him. Yes, he'll be there,' said Sue.

Jonathan imagined a gangling lad of seventeen or so. When he met Terry, and found him to be a confident young man in his early twenties, he was so happy for Mrs Armitage. How nice for her to have this relative, who was being so attentive to her as they made the room ready for the party. Once, he thought he saw Terry wink at Sue, but decided he must have imagined it.

By the night of the party, the Volvo was safely back in the barn. Mrs Hawkins from the body repair shop had telephoned on Thursday morning to say it was ready, and Alice had ordered a taxi to take her to fetch it. She had examined the shining door and wing. Not a trace of what had happened could be seen. She had paid by cheque with her banker's card and had driven away with the greatest care.

Terry was put about, when later he arrived full of plans to collect it the following day, the day of the party, and found himself forestalled. But he rallied when Alice produced her new electric blanket and asked him to fit its plug. She had bought a new electric kettle, too.

Euphoric at having pulled off the small coup of the safe return of the car and the exclusion of Terry from its recovery, Alice found herself easily whisked into a state of some excitement about the party. The guests from the village all arrived together. Barbara Duncan had brought the other two in her white Allegro. All were anxious to see how the interior of Harcombe House had been altered by its new owners.

The Armitages had bought the house from Mr Goring's executors. During his last years, ill-health had turned him into a recluse, and little maintenance had been done to the house. Rather as Alice now dwelt in an attic area, he had existed in a few of the main rooms attended by a resident nurse and a succession of housekeepers. A desperate niece had the task of supervising this menage; she came once a month, dealt with the prevailing crisis, hiring a new nurse or housekeeper when required from the relevant agencies, and departed hoping that all would stay tranquil until her next visit.

When Mr Goring died, the house remained empty for nearly two years after failing to reach its reserve at an auction held just as the property market slumped. From time to time there were various rumours in the village about possible buyers, and occasionally a man from the estate agent's office handling the sale showed people round, but no one displayed real interest until the Armitages offered a price which the niece, the main legatee, decided to take. The village sighed with relief; there were fears that the executors, anxious to wind up Mr Goring's affairs, might let it go to a developer who would tear down the main house and build an estate, thus putting Harcombe on the map. But in the present economic climate there was not enough demand for that sort of housing in the district. By the time the Armitages' furniture vans were seen edging down the lanes, only minor interest was shown in their arrival. The house was so far out of the village, and had been a lost cause for so long, that no one cared any more. Helen Armitage asked in the shop about help in the house, and Mrs Rogers produced her sister-in-law, Mrs Wood, who was glad of the job and the run of the place to herself. She, in turn, sent along her uncle, just made redundant at a Westborough canning factory, when a gardener was required.

Barbara Duncan had not ignored the new arrivals. She had waited for several weeks after they moved in to give them time to settle and also to appear in church, in the pre-war signal that the lady of the house was now ready to receive callers, but no Armitages appeared among the congregation. On the day she went to the house, workmen were papering and painting, but no one else was at home. Mrs Armitage was at her showroom in Newbury, Mr Armitage at his office, and the old lady hadn't yet moved in. Barbara had meant to call again, but one way and another, she hadn't done so. The fact that the younger Armitages were out all day meant they were busy and unlikely to have much in common with her. Their natural friends would be younger people whom they'd meet in due course, though there was little social life in the village since it lacked a community building and rarely set up any fund-raising events of its own. The Armitages would find their friends outside the village, Barbara felt, for their life style was likely to be far in advance of anything anyone else in Harcombe maintained.

There were lights on in the lodge as the three ladies drove by.

'Who's living there now?' asked Nancy Wilson.

'The girl works at the Rigby Arms,' said Barbara, who had learned this from her cleaning woman. 'The young man's a salesman of some kind. They're not married.'

She parked the car beside a blue Ford Escort near the barn and the three got out. It was a fine night, crisp and cold, freezing hard, and Nancy slithered on the icy approach to the front door, above which shone a welcoming light. There was an old-fashioned bell-pull which Barbara tugged, and almost at once a young man with curly hair opened the door to them, beaming.

'Come in, ladies,' he greeted them, ushering them in. 'I'm Terry. Let me take your coats.'

Alice appeared as the three ladies discarded their coats, scarves and gloves, which Terry swept up.

'Oh, Mrs Duncan, how nice that you could come!' Alice was a little flustered. She had had a pre-party glass of sherry, pressed on her by Sue, and so had sustained her mood of excitement. With natural colour glowing in her cheeks beneath her make-up, dressed in a pale grey knitted suit, she looked pretty and elegant. Pity she didn't let her hair go its natural colour, thought Barbara, running a hand over her own iron-grey head in case her set had been disturbed.

While Terry hung the coats in a cupboard, Alice led her guests into the big drawing-room. The tinsel tree – Helen wouldn't have a real fir tree – had gone. Mrs Wood had been detailed to strip it and pack it and the baubles up in their boxes, and this had been done on her only visit since Christmas. But there were chrysanthemums in pottery vases, and the room with its blazing log fire looked warm and inviting. Terry had turned the heating up at the thermostat and the old boiler roared away loudly in the cellar. Terry had gone to look at it and was amazed at its age.

'It's prehistoric,' he'd said.

He could not understand the delay in installing a new heating system. If you lived in a place this size, it meant you had an income that could support it, or limitless credit. Why wait? Why wait for anything, if you could make sure of it now?

'How lovely you've made this room!' exclaimed Nancy Wilson. 'I used to come here to see Mr Goring before he got really ill.'

The old man had admired Nancy and had mildly courted her for years. They both studied the market and gambled a little, he in large amounts and she in small ones. His sound advice had helped her to increase her modest investment income. She'd enjoyed his company, and before he grew too frail to go out, had dined with him in various restaurants once or twice a month. He had left her two thousand pounds in his will, most of which she had spent on a Greek cruise.

Violet, whose own husband had died during this time, had been surprised that Nancy had refused Mr Goring's proposals of marriage.

'I'd only be an unpaid housekeeper-cum-nurse who could never give notice,' Nancy had said. 'I'm not going to marry anyone just for a meal ticket.' The price would have been too great, and when the old man lingered on for another six years, she was thankful she had kept her head – and, indeed, her personal integrity.

She and Violet had known each other since their school days and when Violet moved into Nancy's cottage they had extended it, building on a big new kitchen and a second bathroom so that each had her separate bedroom and bathroom.

'Have you met Sue and Jonathan?' Alice was introducing. 'From the lodge?' She had decided to present the pair in this way, without their surnames, to play down their unmarried status.

Barbara began talking to Sue while Jonathan asked the other two ladies about their garden, and Terry soon appeared with their glasses of sherry. Everyone discussed how they had spent Christmas. Barbara had visited her married son in Dorset and told Terry all about it, including the full tale of her drive each way through fog and frost. Terry listened with earnest attention, but all the time he was assessing her. Oldish, but healthy, he decided, and muscular too. She wore two good rings, and her woollen dress, in which she seemed a cylindrical shape, was expensive. You could always tell.

'And what do you do?' she suddenly asked him. 'Where do you live?'

'Oh, I've a place near Swindon,' said Terry, implying a mansion. 'I do various things – buying and selling. I'm starting a new job soon, in actual fact.' He'd picked this expression up from Sue.

'Where?' asked Barbara.

'Locally. I'll be moving to Westborough,' Terry said, and moved smoothly away to top up the glasses before she could ask any more questions. Nosy old thing, he thought; he was incapable of distinguishing genuine – or at least civil – interest from curiosity.

Jonathan was now discussing roses with Violet; and Sue, who was wearing dark red silk pantaloons and a black velvet top and looking very pretty, helped Alice hand round the tiny patties she had prepared. She had made them in Helen's kitchen, using the Aga. Some were stuffed with prawns, some with chicken, and there were cheese straws, and prunes wrapped in bacon.

'How lovely,' exclaimed Nancy, when these titbits appeared. She'd hoped there'd be something nice to eat, and now she saw that they'd need no supper – perhaps a mug of soup, nothing more. Sometimes this luckily happened when you went out in the evening. She was always cast down at mere peanuts and crisps.

'What relation to you is Terry?' Nancy asked Alice at one point.

'Relation?' Alice was about to deny kinship when Terry himself appeared at her elbow with more prawn patties and broke in.

'How long have you lived in Harcombe, Miss Wilson?' he asked, to learn that it was longer than the extent of his life. Until she retired, Nancy had been an accountant, working for a time in Swindon, and then in Westborough with her own business. By the time they had finished this conversation Nancy had forgotten what she had originally wanted to know, and only remembered later, in bed, thinking about the party.

When the guests had gone, everyone set about clearing up. The women washed up while Terry vacuumed the carpet and Jonathan took the left-over bottles of sherry up to Alice's flat. When these tasks were done, and no trace of the party remained, Alice produced a pie from the Aga's oven, chicken and ham, with potatoes and carrots sliced into it under the crisp crust. There was wine, too – a bottle of burgundy. They sat round the table in Helen's kitchen enjoying this feast, all with good appetites in spite of Alice's cocktail fare. There was fresh pineapple to follow. By the time all this was disposed of and the kitchen cleared, it was half-past ten.

Terry insisted on escorting Alice up to her flat, carrying what was left of the party food to put in her refrigerator. When he left, he managed to take with him, unseen by Alice, two of the bottles of sherry from the carton which Jonathan had taken upstairs.

He'd taken ten pounds from her unattended handbag – an easy thing to do during the day. He knew she would never miss it.

She'd noticed, however, that he was driving yet another car.

10

'How have you been, mother?' asked Giles on the evening of the family's return from the Alps. His conscience had troubled him during the fortnight away, for she would be quite alone most of the time, with not even Mrs Wood coming in to clean. He'd asked Sue to keep an eye on her, fearing that she might fall and break a leg, and no one would notice.

At the prospect of seeing Sue again, Giles's spirits had risen as he sat beside Amanda in the plane coming back. Helen and Dawn were across the aisle, seated near new friends they had made on the ski slopes. Dawn had enjoyed a holiday romance and was engloomed at the prospect of parting from her beloved; Amanda, on the other hand, was looking forward to seeing her dear Mr Jinks again.

As soon as the bags were in the house and the car put away, Giles hurried up to his mother's flat.

Alice had been watching for the Rover and had hurried down to greet them. Then she'd run back again, for perhaps Helen would not want to find her in the main part of the house. She was just about to run downstairs for the second time when she heard Giles's tread on the back stairs. They met on the landing and embraced gingerly. He never held her warmly.

'Safely back, then,' said Alice, ignoring his enquiry about her, wise tactics when anyone asked how one was, for no one really wanted to know. 'Have you had a good time? Was the weather good?' She had received two postcards, one from Giles and one from Amanda, two days earlier, and knew that it had snowed a lot. Amanda had mentioned an avalanche.

'Very pleasant,' said Giles heartily. In spite of three days of heavy snowfall when skiing was restricted and tempers grew strained, he had enjoyed it more than other such holidays. Helen had quickly made friends, so they had seen very little of one another. Giles's skiing had progressed and he had been on some runs with Amanda, who waited patiently for him at the bottom of steep stretches of piste. His life could improve if they stayed friends, but she would develop new interests as she grew older and would even, like her sister, have romances, a thought he found hard to bear. 'And you, mother?' he repeated, peering anxiously at her. The light on the landing was dim. 'You're fit?'

'Yes, dear, thank you,' said Alice. She wanted to hear the girls' tales of prowess, vicariously enjoy some of their pleasures. 'I was coming down to welcome you,' she added.

'No need for that,' Giles said, patting her arm.

Helen had said, as they entered the house, 'For God's sake don't let your mother get under my feet now, Giles. I've got a lot to organize.' She wanted, the next day, to go to her shop where some fabric ordered from France should have arrived. The girls were going to a party across the county and would have to be driven. There would be mail to deal with, enquiries and orders. She knew that Alice and Mrs Wood between them would have obeyed her written instructions about thawing a casserole from the freezer and putting it in the oven for their evening meal.

Alice had delayed boiling her cod in butter sauce in its polythene bag, hoping they would ask her to share the casserole while she heard about the holiday, but now she saw it was not to be.

Giles, who had noticed with relief that his mother looked well, saw the droop of her thin shoulders.

'No problems?' he asked, still in hearty voice.

'None,' said Alice, crossing her fingers at the lie and thinking of the Volvo, safely in its usual place.

'I'll pop up later,' said Giles.

Would he? He might not, and then he'd feel guilty. Alice let him off.

'Don't bother, dear,' she said. 'It's late and you've plenty to do if you're to get off on time in the morning. There are so many letters waiting. Come another time.' She smiled at him brightly, too brightly.

Giles took the raft she had floated towards him.

'Soon, then,' he promised, patted her arm again and lumbered away down the stairs. He was getting so heavy, unlike his father who had kept his trim figure all his life. Alice blinked back tears as she returned to her flat.

Amanda came, however, in her dressing-gown, just as Alice, who in the end had had no appetite for the cod, was drinking some Horlicks.

'Oh good, Gran, I thought you'd be having your night-cap,' said Amanda. 'Can I have some?' She loved Horlicks. Helen did not encourage milky drinks; the extra calories, she said, were bad for the figures of growing girls.

'Of course you can, darling,' said Alice, brightening at once. 'It's only instant. There's not enough milk for ordinary.'

'That's all right,' said Amanda magnanimously.

Alice cheered up as the kettle boiled and she mixed the drink in the mug with the Smiley face on it which Amanda liked.

'Mince pie?' she asked.

'Mm, please,' said Amanda, who had already eaten two with her meal. 'It's lovely and warm up here tonight, Gran. What have you done?' Then her gaze fell on the new convector heater. 'Oh, you've got a new fire,' she said. 'That's good. About time.'

Alice had forgotten the need for secrecy and had not hidden the fire when she heard the car. Would Amanda mention it to her mother? Alice worried away for a minute or two, wondering whether to ask Amanda not to, then decided that she could not make the child a partner in a conspiracy against her own mother. She would have to risk it, and, if Helen made trouble, have some sort of show-down.

Thus bravely resolved, Alice settled down to hear Amanda's account of the holiday and was soon laughing at the girl's barbed description of her sister's swain.

Terry came striding through the entrance doors of the Rigby Arms into the oak-panelled restored Tudor foyer and walked up to the reception desk. Sounds of typing came from the office beyond, whose door was open, and he rang the bell on the counter.

Almost at once, Sue came through the doorway, her dark hair swept up round her small, neat head into a French pleat, making her look strangely austere. The professionally attentive expression she wore on her face was replaced by a look of surprised delight when she saw Terry.

'What are you doing here?' she asked him.

'I've come to see you, haven't I?' said Terry, grinning.

'I'm on duty. I can't really talk,' said Sue. 'Bruce will be here soon to go through the bookings.' Bruce Troughton was the manager.

'I'll take you back when you finish,' said Terry.

'Great,' said Sue. On this shift they could have more than two hours together before Jonathan came home.

'I thought I'd go over now and see the old lady,' said Terry. 'I might take her out for a spin somewhere.'

'You're not working.' It was a statement, not a question.

'Not just now,' Terry agreed. 'I'm looking around, in actual fact. Anything going here?' He gazed about him at the heavily beamed hall which had an oak settle against one wall and a log-effect electric fire in the hearth. Sporting prints hung on the walls.

'Like what?' asked Sue.

Terry shrugged.

'I can do most things,' he said. 'Bar, maybe?' There would be chances, there, to fiddle the till. 'Or maybe there's a vacancy for a waiter.' He flourished an imaginary table-napkin over his arm and said, in an affected voice, 'I can thoroughly recommend the scampi, madam.'

Sue giggled, then frowned, furrowing the smooth pale skin of her forehead.

'Not at the moment,' she said. 'We're fully staffed.'

'Pity,' said Terry. 'It'd be nice to be here with you.' He wanted to stay in the area while their plans, still not discussed, evolved, and he would have to get a regular job for a while as he needed a car for visiting Harcombe. He couldn't start taking them from Westborough; the town was too small and the police would soon notice and be on the alert. He would buy some clapped-out old heap that would last as long as he needed it.

Sue was leaning towards him over the counter, and he reached across, walking his fingers along her arm in its black cardigan, worn over a plain white blouse. She shivered. He turned her on as no one else had ever done.

'We'll have to see,' she said. 'Something might turn up.'

'See you later,' said Terry, and walked away, his head an aureole of crisp curls against the pale sky as he went through the doorway, not looking back. In that moment it seemed to Sue that if she were never to see him again she would die.

She had never felt like that in her life, never felt such acute desire. The urgency of it forced everything else to the back of her mind. Since leaving school, her one aim had been to protect and promote her own well-being, heedless of any person or object that got in her way, for no one else was likely to do it for her. Jonathan had been the exception; he cared for her, and for a while she had weakened, feeling kindly towards him, but now she was bored. His devotion was cloying; there was no spare money for discos or even the cinema; and since Christmas he had started to talk about Hilary and the children in what seemed to Sue a stupid, soppy way. They had had several rows, with Sue accusing him of wishing he had never left home, and Jonathan retorting that it was all her fault that he had. They had made it up, each time, in the usual way – in bed. But now, in the evenings, Jonathan spent more and more time sitting glumly silent and brooding.

Without thinking too much about the future, Sue knew that it would not last, though she would not leave Jonathan until she had something better lined up. Now Terry had come into her life and she saw in him someone akin to herself, someone quick to seize the moment. When he was around, she felt able to tackle things she'd never dreamed of before.

Like finding him a job at the Rigby. Bar work, he'd said.

There were two on duty in the bar at night: George, the regular barman who lived in the town and had worked at the hotel for years, acting also as cellarman in conjunction with the wine waiter. In the evenings a rota of married women worked with George, who managed alone at midday with occasional help from her or the other receptionist, or sometimes the manager, if he was pressed – say, at weekends or on market day.

Every day, certain duties had to be done in the cellar. The pipes must be cleared after switching off the night before – the stale beer in them emptied. The barrels had to be spiled, the taps cleaned. Fresh supplies had to be taken up to the bar and stacked neatly behind what was already beneath the counter – bottled beer, spirits, mineral waters. New stock had to be checked in when deliveries came. George spent a lot of time down there in the morning, before the bar opened, carrying out these regular tasks. It was his job, too, to turn the beer on every day, and to turn it off at night, and to turn on and off the CO_2 for the keg beer.

Each day he came to the office to fetch the key before going down there. He had already completed his routine work today.

Sue did not plan it consciously. She just let it happen spontaneously when the chance arose the morning after her talk with Terry.

When George came into the office to collect the key, there was no one around. No one waited by the desk for Sue's attention; the guests checking out had already gone and the telephone was silent. Bruce Troughton was conferring with the chef about a forthcoming Rotary dinner.

Sue quietly followed George, hanging back while he unlocked the cellar door and turned on the light, then began to descend the old stone steps. He never heard her behind him, though he felt the sudden hard push she gave him in the small of his back and he gave one faint, gasping cry as he fell. He struck his head on a keg near the foot of the steps and then lay silent.

Sue had not waited. She was back behind the reception desk answering the telephone before he lost consciousness. The manager, passing the open cellar door some time later, was the one who found him.

George was not dead, but he was still unconscious when removed in the ambulance and he had broken one leg and some ribs. It was possible that he had fractured his skull. X-rays would show the extent of his injuries. He was not a young man to sustain such a fall, and his condition was serious.

Sue's intention had simply been to get him out of the way but she felt no remorse when she heard how badly he had been hurt; she was glad. He wouldn't remember what had happened.

Meanwhile, the Rigby Arms urgently needed a barman.

Bruce's immediate plan was to enlist the aid of the women who worked there regularly while he sought someone, but Sue told him she knew of an experienced barman who might be free. She was not certain if he understood cellar work, but no doubt that could quickly be learned.

When Bruce saw Terry – young, but not too young, clean, conventionally dressed, he thanked his stars. He accepted Terry's explanation that he was between jobs because he had just returned from abroad, and alas, his references had temporarily got lost. He could supply addresses, if the manager wanted to check, but – and here Terry took a chance, but you had to when the stakes were high – Mrs Armitage senior, at Harcombe House, knew him well, and would vouch for him.

The old lady wouldn't be able to say a word against him. Thanks to him, she was living in far greater comfort than before, and he had proved himself honest over money when buying the heaters.

Bruce took Terry on at once, and gave him a room in the staff quarters where he and Sue made frenzied love during her lunch break before he went off to Swindon by bus to fix himself up with a car and collect his belongings.

Sue did not tell him how George's accident had occurred.

Bruce intended to ring Mrs Armitage up about Terry when he had a moment, but he kept putting it off because there was so much else to do straight away. Terry soon proved his competence, and it seemed pointless, then, to bother.

11

The staff at the Rigby Arms were shocked at George's accident. It was hard to accept that such a thing should happen after so many years of daily descents to the cellar.

'Maybe he had a heart attack,' Sue suggested while she and Bruce Troughton were having lunch at a corner table in the restaurant after most of the guests had finished. She was eating a large rare steak; she felt very hungry, more so than usual, though she always ate well and enjoyed her perk of a first-class meal elegantly served.

'You could be right,' said Bruce. 'He is getting on a bit, after all. It can happen to anyone.' It had happened before now to guests, involving their hasty removal from the public area, which was hard to combine with proper concern for the victim. 'It was lucky your friend Terry Brett happened to be free. At least it will give us time to find someone permanent, if George isn't able to come back.'

'Yes,' agreed Sue demurely, piling *pommes frites* and cauliflower on to her fork and wondering what sweet to choose; the cold trolley held a wide choice but the chef had made steamed syrup pudding today and she rather fancied that.

'I do hope poor George will be all right,' Bruce went on. He had had the sad task of telling George's wife what had happened, considering it part of his duty.

Sue thought it would be so much easier all round if he wasn't. She cut into her steak from which the blood oozed pinkly. George was old; he'd nothing left to live for, she thought, dismissing him.

Giles, postponing his return home that evening with a visit to the Rigby Arms, was surprised to find Sue still there, for her shift should have ended in the afternoon. She was behind the bar with Mavis, one of the regular barmaids, and a new young barman with a mop of crisp brown curls.

She seemed pleased to see him.

'This is Mr Armitage, one of our regulars,' she said to Terry, nudging his leg with her knee so that he paid extra attention. 'He likes a double Scotch with ice and soda. That's right, isn't it?' and she smiled at Giles in such a way that his heart turned over. She looked like a ballet dancer, he thought, so small and slight, with her pale oval face and her smooth dark hair drawn back in its pleat. What would that hair look like spread out on a pillow? It would be like fragrant silk. He dragged his mind back to the present.

'What's yours – both of you?' he invited, taking a ten-pound note from his wallet.

'Oh, thank you very much,' Sue said promptly. 'We'll have it later, if that's all right with you.' She did not have to explain to Terry how this was done, the money stacked and saved for the end of the day; he knew all about that sort of thing. 'Terry's helping out,' she explained to Giles. 'George is in hospital.'

'I'm sorry to hear that,' said Giles, gulping down most of his drink. 'Nothing serious, I hope.'

'He had a fall,' said Terry. 'He broke his leg.'

'Oh dear. That means he'll be off for some time,' said Giles.

'Could be,' said Terry, polishing a glass. He moved away to attend to another customer, not liking to think about George in pain.

'And you're lending a hand too?' Giles said to Sue.

'Just getting Terry started,' said Sue. 'It's a while since he's worked in a bar. He's got to get used to the prices and that.' He was good, though; he had just the right way with the customers. She felt proud, watching him pull beer, getting the head on the glass just right. 'He'll be all right now, with Mavis,' she said, and knew what would follow. It did.

'Like a lift home?' Giles asked.

'Please,' said Sue, with that quick curving smile which lit up her serious face. She had rung Jonathan to say she'd be late because of George's accident and that she'd telephone when she could get away. Jonathan had grumbled a bit. Although they had no money to spare, he had intended to take her out to dinner that evening. He wanted to try to recapture some of the earlier magic.

Sue had wanted to spend all the evening there in the bar with Terry – go back with him to his room, even if only for just a short time since Jonathan would wonder why she wasn't ready at closing time. But it would have been tricky: there were the barrels to close down, the CO_2 to turn off – all the late-night routine work which Bruce would be going through with Terry tonight and for some time until he could do it alone.

Now Giles had come, and that was great. Sue didn't know quite what she hoped for from him; she had never blackmailed anyone for money, and she didn't yet know that this was Terry's main occupation, but Giles was rich and knew important people. Faces familiar on television had been seen at the parties at Harcombe House. Through Giles she, and Terry too, now, might enter that glittering world. Opportunity would come, if she cultivated Giles; besides, it was always a challenge to try to make a man; to Sue it was automatic.

Driving back to Harcombe with Giles, she gave no thought to George, felt no guilt.

George died in the night.

The police came round to the Rigby Arms the next morning. There would have to be an inquest, Detective Sergeant Rivers explained to Bruce, and he must present an account to the coroner of how the accident happened.

'It's shocking,' said Bruce, collecting his jacket from the back of his chair and putting it on. He was never seen in the public part of the hotel dressed other than formally in his dark jacket and pinstriped trousers. People needed to know who was in charge and he did not want to be mistaken for a guest. 'He'd been down those steps hundreds of times – thousands, probably – in his working life, and never once, as far as I know, even stumbled. Now this.' Bruce was very distressed; he had been fond of George, a most reliable man.

He took Detective Sergeant Rivers along to the cellar and unlocked the door with the duplicate key he had in his own set.

'Has anyone been down here since the incident?' asked Rivers, noticing how Bruce turned on the light at the top of the straight stone staircase with its uneven treads.

'Oh yes,' said Bruce. 'There's work done down here every day. I've been doing the routine myself, but I've taken on a temporary barman.' He explained what had to be done. Terry and he together had moved the stock that morning and cleared the pipes. 'George had been going to do these jobs when he fell,' Bruce went on. He remembered Sue's theory. 'Perhaps he had a heart attack?'

'Maybe,' said the sergeant. 'The post-mortem will show what he died of.' That was in progress this morning. The hospital thought that the head wound had been the cause of death, but a heart attack would account for the fall.

'People must have been coming up and down here for centuries,' said Bruce. 'There was an inn here three hundred years ago.'

'Is that so?' Rivers was unimpressed. He had lived in the area all his life and was familiar with its heritage; he had visited many an old tumbledown cottage and many a renovated one, too. 'Dangerous, though,' he commented. 'No rail.' He indicated the sheer drop to the right of the steps. On the left was the painted brick wall.

'I suppose it could be – well, falling down any staircase could be dangerous,' said Bruce. The steps were so narrow that fitting a banister rail would have restricted the freedom of a man carrying boxes of bottles up the stairs. 'I don't think George thought of them as dangerous,' Bruce went on. 'You're always careful carrying bottles.' He wondered about the insurance; the hotel was well covered in case of accident to an employee and such matters were usually settled smoothly, but it would be unfortunate if there were to be any suggestion of negligence.

'He had his own key?' asked Rivers.

'No. He collected it from the office,' said Bruce.

Rivers examined the area. There was a small stain on one of the worn flagstones of the floor, and he looked at it carefully. The dead man had sustained a head wound of great severity and the skin had been broken, though it had not bled severely. Most head wounds bled freely and Rivers had expected to find evidence of this at the scene of the accident, but the keg on which George had struck his head had already been replaced with a fresh one.

The stain had best be examined, Rivers decided, circling it with a piece of chalk, but there had been so much traffic up and down the steps since the accident that any evidence of how it had happened would be covered with more recent traces.

'We have to make sure it was an accident, Mr Troughton,' Rivers explained, and when Bruce looked puzzled, he added, 'I mean, that he wasn't pushed.'

'Pushed? George!' Bruce was appalled. 'What a dreadful idea! Who would want to push poor old George down the stairs?'

'It doesn't seem likely, I agree,' said Rivers. 'But we have to be certain. Now, who would have known that he would be going down there?'

'Everyone,' declared Bruce. 'All the staff, that is. As I say, it was routine.'

'And he went at the same time each day?'

'More or less. He comes – came on at ten. He works – worked late, you see.' He had had time off every afternoon.

Rivers nodded.

'I'd like you to keep people out of here, just for a while, Mr Troughton,' he said. 'We'll want to look around. It won't take too long.'

'The wine waiter may need to come down,' Bruce warned.

'Well, I expect that can be managed,' said Rivers. Traces from him must already be present in the cellar. 'And I'd like to see the staff. Every one of them. Find out who was about that morning and may have seen him.'

'It's quite possible that no one did,' said Bruce. 'Just the duty receptionist when he collected the key. She'd be busy in the office. The domestic staff would be working upstairs – all the public rooms, except the restaurant, which is wanted for breakfast, are cleaned early.'

'Anyone with a grudge against the deceased could slip down, though,' said Rivers.

'Well – yes, I suppose so. But no one had a grudge against him,' said Bruce.

'I expect you're right, Mr Troughton,' said Rivers. 'But it's my job to make sure.'

While he was making the necessary arrangements word came through from the hospital that the post-mortem had shown no sign of a heart attack; for his age, George's heart was in good condition. A thorough enquiry must be made to establish that no foul play had occurred.

Sue was the first of the staff to be interviewed.

She said she had not seen George the morning of the accident, though usually they exchanged a few words when he fetched the key. She might have been in the washroom when he came for it; he would simply have taken it from the desk drawer, which she had unlocked earlier after opening up when she came on duty.

'Did this often happen?' asked Rivers.

'You mean, was I often in the washroom when George fetched the key?' asked Sue, bristling slightly.

'I mean, did he often fetch the key without your knowledge,' said Rivers patiently.

'Sometimes,' said Sue. 'If I was busy with a guest, for instance, I might not notice him.'

'And you didn't notice that he hadn't brought it back?' asked Rivers.

'I never thought about it,' said Sue, truthfully.

It took the police some time to question everyone. No one had specifically seen George go down to the cellar that morning but some of the kitchen staff had spoken to him when he arrived and found him in his normal cheerful frame of mind. Everyone knew his cellar visits were routine.

Detectives inspecting the cellar found nothing suspicious. There were no fingerprints that could not be accounted for and explained as belonging to someone with a reason for being in the cellar.

Sue had touched nothing: not the door, nor the light, nor the wall: only George, and he could not tell.

The inquest was opened and adjourned to allow time for tests on various organs. These would show if the deceased had taken any drugs which might have made him giddy. Bruce Troughton, having found the body, had attended the inquest. The widow was there, dressed in grey, her face pale and drawn, her married daughter beside her.

'Everything can change so suddenly,' the daughter said to Bruce. 'In minutes – just like that. No warning. That's the hard part.'

'I know. It's dreadful,' said Bruce. 'We'll miss him a lot,' he added, and went on to offer what personal help he could with the funeral arrangements.

'He'd have been retiring in two years,' said the widow, dry-eyed, still in shock. 'We'd so many plans.' She looked bleakly at Bruce.

'I'm very sorry,' said Bruce again.

'They said he wouldn't have known anything about it,' said the daughter. 'He never came round. That's a comfort. But there was no goodbye.' Her soft, pretty face crumpled as she began to weep.

Bruce drove them home and rang the undertaker. The funeral could go ahead now, and was arranged for the following Thursday, the earliest date the crematorium could offer, for January was always a busy month.

Sue learned the result of the inquest when Bruce returned to the hotel. He explained about the adjournment, saying this was usual.

'Upsetting for the family,' he said. 'Means it's all to do again.'

'Can I help at all?' asked Sue. 'We want to have a collection among the staff – for a wreath, you know. I'm arranging it.' It had been the housekeeper's idea.

'Oh, good,' said Bruce, who hadn't got that far in his thoughts. He pulled a ten-pound note from his wallet and gave it to her. 'I should order some nice flowers and give the balance to the family.'

'Some of the bar regulars might like to contribute to that,' Sue suggested. 'Shall I ask Terry to fix up a tin?'

12

Alice was surprised to learn that Terry was working at the Rigby Arms. She did not know he was free to take on a new job.

'Oh, I thought you knew I was looking for a change,' he told her airily.

'What exactly were you doing before?' Alice asked.

'I was an agent,' said Terry. 'I handled various lines. It was a bit up and down. Now I know where I am – regular hours and regular pay.'

'I thought you must be something to do with cars,' said Alice. 'You seemed to have a different one each time you came over, and you do know a lot about them.' She remembered how he had mended her Metro that day.

He hadn't thought that she'd be so observant.

'That was the firm's policy,' he improvised. 'They own a lot of cars and you just take whichever one's handy when you set out for the day.' He rushed on, before she could query this system. 'Of course, now that George has died, they'll be wanting a permanent barman at the Rigby, and I'm not sure about that, but I'm staying for the moment. I'll be able to come and see you often. I get time off in the afternoon because of all the late nights.'

Did she want that? Alice wasn't sure. Sometimes he made her uneasy, though she was grateful to him for making the flat so snug.

Terry's mind had turned towards Giles.

'I've met your son,' he told her. 'In the bar at the Rigby. He's one of the regulars.'

'Is he?' asked Alice, a slow dismay filling her.

'Didn't you know?' smiled Terry. 'Likes his drop, doesn't he? But he can hold it,' he finished, deciding that now he could end his visit. He hadn't seen the old girl for a few days because he'd been busy getting the hang of the job, and he was eager to see Sue; while she was on the early shift their hours restricted their time together.

He had brought Alice a plant in a pot, a small, rather weak cineraria he had bought in the market when the stall-holder had knocked down his prices at the end of the day. Alice sat staring at it while she pictured Giles in the bar, holding his drink.

She hadn't known about that. Oh, a drink or two, yes, like everyone else; but Terry implied that he was a heavy drinker. No wonder he gave Sue lifts so often.

She tried to put it out of her mind in the weeks that followed and went up to London three times, seeing two matinées and a film, though there was little on that appealed to her. She rang up her friend Audrey in Bournemouth several times but could get no reply. She went to supper one evening with Violet Hedges and Nancy Wilson, and then worried for days about how to invite them back, at last telling Terry, who said she must take them to dinner in a restaurant.

How easy it seemed, when he made the suggestion. He was perfectly right, yet she hadn't been able to think of the idea for herself. She'd no one to talk things over with; only Terry, when he came on his brisk visits. Gradually Alice's reservations about him were dispersed. She found herself looking forward to seeing his cheerful face and curly head. How springy those curls must be if you touched them. She supposed he had lots of girlfriends.

'Well, I have had,' he admitted, when she asked him one day, teasingly. 'But now there's just one. Someone rather special.'

'Who?' asked Alice, and then, frowning, added, 'Not Sue, is it?' She knew he saw Sue most afternoons, for the old red VW he drove now was parked outside the lodge every day. He brought her back when she was on the first shift, and took her in to the Rigby Arms when she was on the late one, for in each case he, himself, was free until just before opening time after his lunch-time stint.

'No, you silly,' said Terry. 'It's you, isn't it?' and he laughed at her in a kindly way.

It was all just his fun. He was such a joker, thought Alice. He certainly cheered her up.

A verdict of accidental death was returned at the resumed inquest on the dead barman. No trace of any drugs had been found in his body, and there was nothing to show why he had slipped. His shoes had been examined and were sound: no loose edge of sole could have caught anywhere, no slippery substance adhered to them. He might have felt suddenly giddy, though there was no trace of disease. The wound to his head was the cause of death; possibly he had toppled forward as he fell and in this way could have caught it against a keg. It was suggested that a hand rail be fitted to the cellar steps to avoid another such accident.

Sue, by this time, had almost forgotten the part she played in the incident. More important to her, now, was the deterioration in her relationship with Jonathan. Since Christmas he had become increasingly morose. He was often irritable, constantly complaining about her short-comings. When she was on the early shift, why couldn't she have a meal waiting in the evening? Didn't she want to eat too, in spite of the fancy lunch she had every day? And couldn't she at least shop for food when she was on late herself, leave something ready for him to cook? They must pull together, he said; work out a system. Couldn't she do the washing sometimes? He seemed to be always the one who went to the launderette, and no one but ~~he~~ him ever used the vacuum cleaner or dusted round.

Often, it ended in argument, with loud, angry shouts from Jonathan who then stormed out of the lodge and went off for a furious walk round the lanes, even at night. Sue sometimes wondered if he would be run over on one of these nocturnal expeditions. But there wasn't much traffic around Harcombe at night.

Jonathan was finding Sue's careless ways increasingly hard to bear. He was tired of collecting her dirty clothes from wherever she let them fall. He was tired of finding no bread in the house when he came back from work, and only cheese in the refrigerator. But he still liked to hold that thin, insatiable body in the crumpled double bed.

One day, returning the children after a weekend spent with them at his parents' home, Jonathan hovered beside the car while he watched them walk up the path to the front door of the house where they had lived for all their short lives. Hilary stood there, waiting for them. On impulse, Jonathan strode up the path to speak to her.

'Hilary,' he said. 'Don't – ' He wanted to stop her from closing the door in his face.

'What is it?' She faced him, the children, inside the house, peering round her at him. Her eyes were hostile in her pale face. She had lost a lot of weight, he noticed.

'Oh – I just wondered if you were all right. Is there anything you want done? Any little jobs in the house?' he asked.

'You've made it very clear that you don't want that sort of responsibility,' said Hilary.

'You hate me, don't you?' said Jonathan.

'Are you surprised?' asked Hilary curtly.

'Couldn't we – couldn't we be a bit more friendly?' he pleaded, and looked down at the children who stared back at him, round-eyed. 'For them?'

'You should have thought of that before,' said Hilary

mercilessly. 'Goodbye, Jonathan,' and she shut the door on him.

When he had gone, she burst into tears, quite frightening the two children.

Now, Jonathan was depressed and afraid. He saw no good long-term future with Sue, and if they parted, he would be quite alone.

Perhaps even that would be better than things as they were, he began to acknowledge, when Sue turned away from him in bed. She had never done that before.

Jonathan could not know that Sue had spent an extended session in this very bed with Terry that afternoon, and for the first time in her life was attaching emotion to the experience. Why should she bother with Jonathan, who was now so bad-tempered most of the time and had become such a nag? If she moved back to the Rigby Arms she would see much more of Terry but she would lose the opportunities to be alone in the car with Giles, which she knew Terry wanted her to take; Terry wasn't into the money, and Giles was.

'Would you want to live here, if you could? In the big house, I mean?' he'd asked her.

'Only if I could get away from it often enough,' said Sue, who did not know what she really wanted from life except an improvement on the present.

'To what? Bermuda or somewhere?' Terry quite fancied spending a few weeks lolling in the sun, though after a while he'd probably want to move on to some fresh excitement.

'Something like that,' said Sue. She had been to Spain and to Greece with various fellows. The hotels, concrete blocks, had been poorly plumbed and their food didn't compare with the Rigby, whose chef was first class. 'I'd like the best,' she declared. 'Only the best for me,' and as she said it she smiled a slow, lazy smile.

'You could get that Giles, you know,' Terry had told her, his hand on her thigh. He had seen how the men watched her at the Rigby, seen how she lapped up their admiration. She fed on it. 'Make him fall for you, I mean. He's halfway there already. Then he'd give Helen the push and you'd have the lot. Old Alice, too – she'd like that. She doesn't go much on Helen, as we know.'

'You mean marry Giles?' Sue asked.

'If you like. In time,' said Terry. He traced a circle round her nipple; funny how they jumped up like that when you turned them on: some of those poor, bored cows on the estates hadn't known about that and were they grateful when they found out! 'Of course, I'd be part of the family too. We'd both be all right then.'

It was said, put into words between them at last.

'You'd have to make him think he couldn't live without you,' said Terry 'Like in bed.' Then, later, she'd have to make him pay for it.

Sue stroked the few pale wispy hairs on Terry's chest.

'I could get him in here easily enough,' she said. 'When Jonathan's off with his kids. I could say I needed strong masculine help for some job. He is the landlord, after all.'

'He's drinking a lot. You'd have to choose a good time,' said Terry. 'When he's able.'

'And before he drinks himself to death,' said Sue. 'He could do that afterwards, couldn't he? When we've got the lot.'

Giles was spending more and more time at the Rigby Arms. Until Sue and Jonathan moved into the lodge, his habit had been to stop at different bars on his way home; now, knowing Sue might be glimpsed behind the reception desk, he forsook his other haunts and went there every evening, though when she was on the early shift he missed her. Terry, however, always greeted him warmly and would talk to him in the intervals of serving other customers before the bar became crowded. Terry was acquiring the smattering of knowledge needed to keep conversation going among lonely men postponing returning home to their wives. He would run his eye down the sporting page of the paper every morning as soon as he opened up, gleaning the latest football, golf, or racing news. There was cricket in distant climes; there were sometimes athletic feats worthy of note. He could turn on the patter with ease.

Giles seemed uninterested in any sport. The state of the pound was more his concern, and Terry, who cared only about the pound in his pocket, not its international value, found that by nodding and making encouraging noises he could coax Giles into almost a monologue, which didn't require much effort. Mrs Armitage was quite a sporty old thing, in Terry's opinion, but her son was a pain. Terry found most of the older men in the bar a boring lot; things cheered up when the younger element came in later.

When Sue was on late, more and more frequently Giles stayed on until closing time and took her home. Sometimes he had something to eat in the restaurant – in the evening the Rigby did not serve meals in the bar. But often, drinking steadily, he forgot about food. Helen never waited for him; her arrangement was that she ate at eight; if he wasn't there, too bad. His meal was put in the Aga. Often it was still there in the morning, dried out but not quite a cinder. Helen never looked; she didn't want to know. It was Mrs Wood who daily investigated and removed the evidence. She had some sympathy with Giles; she thought Helen a hard piece and in her opinion the girls were left to themselves too much in the holidays, though they seemed to keep busy, what with the pool and the ponies, and they both played tennis, though the older girl was too good for her sister and often grew bored with the uneven game. Mrs Wood saw it all, from the separate bedrooms to the empty bottles that went out with the rubbish.

There was no risk of meeting Helen when Giles came home so late to the hostile house that he called home. He knew that some would call it beautiful, though in his eyes it was too grey, too cold, too gaunt with its high gabled roofs. Inside, the elegant decor reflected Helen's taste, and the furniture was right for the setting, but pieces he liked tended to disappear as Helen sold them to clients. She had a contact who bought items at sales, restored them as required, sometimes cutting them down to make them acceptable in smaller houses than those they had been designed to grace, and then passed them to Helen who would place them among her customers. Even her own bedroom, with its oak fourposter draped in cream silk, was not safe from this pillage. Various chaises longues had already moved in and out of it, and three different dressing-tables.

When he brought Sue home, Giles would stop at the lodge to let her out of the Rover, always with a single soft kiss on her warm mouth, and then drive on to the barn to garage the car. He drove carefully at a moderate pace, aware that if he made any error on the way back to Harcombe, or was involved in any one else's driving misdemeanour, he would fail a breathalyser test. For her part, Sue was not nervous with him. The distance was not great and there was seldom much traffic about once they left the town, and, as Terry had told Alice, he could carry his drink. It was the one thing about him, apart from his life style, that she admired. Drink made Giles neither cheerful nor aggressive; it merely dulled his misery.

Walking from the barn to the house after leaving the car, Giles was freed from the need to concentrate. He would gulp great breaths of the night air, and that, combined with the alcohol, would at last make him befuddled so that he often had difficulty unlocking the front door. Sometimes he stumbled in the hall or on the stairs, but in the end he would reach his bedroom, at the opposite end of the landing from Helen's. His bathroom – not yet renovated – was stark: an old-fashioned tub with curly feet; a mahogany-seated lavatory with a wood surround. Here, he would pour himself a glass of water into which, as a nightly routine, he dropped two Alka seltzers. Then he would fall into bed, sleeping heavily, snoring. In the morning, three cups of strong black coffee and some aspirin would clear his head enough for the drive to work.

He had got much worse in recent weeks. Helen, glancing at him at breakfast in the kitchen, could see that. He had looked quite fit when they came back from their skiing holiday; now there were threads of veins on his nose and his colour was high.

She had noticed him drinking a lot on their honeymoon, which they spent in Greece. It was very hot, and they had swum and water-skiied. Giles was a good swimmer, having grown up near the sea, but his natural balance was poor and he never stayed upright long on the skis. Helen, however, soon became expert. It seemed to him that she excelled at everything she attempted, and he could not believe his luck in capturing this wonderful girl.

He was the failure. Helen lay passive in bed, her head turned away, enduring with martyred patience Giles's tentative efforts to stir her. He trembled with nerves, humble yet urgent. By the time they returned home he had begun to feel that he was gross and his touch an insult, and he had started to drink in a search for courage.

Once installed in their bright new house, Giles put all his energy into his new job, determined to succeed. It occupied his mind and took up much of his energy, so that he was able to ignore the bitter disappointment he already felt in his domestic life. Helen was still beautiful; she was his wife; and she was pregnant.

She was angry about that. She had not wanted a family yet – not until she had established herself in the best social circle available to them then. Later, because everyone had a pair of children to set them off, so would they. She had not allowed herself to dwell on the cruder aspect of the production process, but now she was made acutely aware of just how fundamental it was. She felt sick; soon her body grew ugly and heavy.

Giles, secretly exultant and proud, showed anxious concern. He hovered about, offering to fill hot bottles or make cups of tea. These were the only attentions she permitted for the whole of her pregnancy and for a long time afterwards. It was only when he had built up his nerve with several drinks that he ever dared to approach her intimately, and then his overtures were more often rebuffed than suffered. They had not been to bed together since Amanda's birth.

Giles no longer thought a great deal about this side of his life. He was not an overly sensual man, and because he had never experienced shared physical rapture he was not aware of what had been missed in his marriage. The family joined a country club; he swam, played tennis poorly and squash still worse, and enjoyed the company of his daughters who, when they were small, were very affectionate. He and Helen never quarrelled, but they communicated on an increasingly superficial level. The years went by, and the girls drew apart from him more as their outside interests grew. Sometimes Dawn looked at him, now, with an expression on her face just like her mother's, as if she despised him; but Amanda still twined herself round his neck when she came home from school and allowed him to help her with Mr Jinks. He

107

thought that his life must be little different from that of many men. Others in his place would, he knew, look for a mistress, but he lacked the drive even for that. Whenever he felt unduly depressed, alcohol helped dull his thoughts. He had expected a big improvement after the move to Harcombe, building a fantasy in which, surrounded at last by the setting she craved, Helen would fall in love with him all over again. For surely she must have loved him once, or why had she married him?

Now he knew that this was a delusion. She had never loved him. She wanted a husband because girls of her class, in her generation, expected to marry, and early. He did not know what made her accept him for the role.

Helen had recognized his manageability. The husband she had to acquire must be one whom she would have no problems controlling and guiding into the pattern she ordained.

She had met other suitable men, but all had sheered away before making any commitment. Helen did not know that the appeal of her moneyed background and personal elegance had not been enough to outweigh the apprehensions of these other suitors. She would be hard to live up to; she would expect too much from them; above all, though she was lovely and desirable, she lacked warmth. The more experienced young men sensed that she would be difficult to arouse, and none of them put this theory to the test.

Helen, tireless where she was interested, was absorbed by her work and was often late home. She would notice that the Rover was still out when she parked her Volvo, but there were always patterns to match, plans to inspect, other details to attend to in her own sitting-room. She would have a drink, then help herself to the meal prepared by Mrs Wood and left ready. Sometimes there were dishes to heat through in the Aga; often there was a casserole dish or a pie already in the slow oven and a salad in the refrigerator. Helen ate sparingly, and she never put on weight. She would spend the evening in her sitting-room, working, or watching television. Giles, if he wanted to see some programme, used the girls' set in their sitting-room.

She would get his mother out in the end. That was her long-term plan. At the moment Alice was useful. She took messages efficiently and dealt with minor matters when Helen was out. The moment she fell really ill or made any mistake, she would be condemned. She could go to some sheltered home or other, Helen thought; local councils ran places for elderly people, with wardens in charge. At some point she must put Alice's name down for somewhere appropriate that would not cost more than the old woman's pension.

The only cloud on Helen's horizon was the fact that her father's business had now been taken over and Giles would never be chairman. He had never had the ability. But he still had his job, which kept him out of the way all day and paid a large salary.

She might have to look into this drinking. She did not want him disgracing himself, making scenes, though that wasn't his style.

13

Sue was not one to waste opportunities. A chance came, and she took it. In just such a way she had, on impulse, enrolled for a short hotel training course when her husband left her with enough money to keep herself for a year. She had known about the course because a girl she was at school with had done it and had secured a job with a big hotel group. Sue saw hotel work as a way to move upwards; she had the tenacity to tackle the course because of the goal; she would meet a lot of people. You never knew who might book in at a good hotel, and what pickings there could be.

Now she turned her mind towards Giles. The idea of trapping him amused her, and she didn't think it would be difficult, but sometimes older men grew sentimental and Sue found that irksome. She thought he might be one of those.

Would she really consider marrying him? Marriage need not be permanent, but it put restraints on liberty. He was certainly rich and the idea of living in Harcombe House had its attractions. The first thing she'd do, if she moved in, was to sort out poor old Alice, give her a suite of rooms on the first floor and treat her properly. That was it, she thought: move in. There was no need to get married. But if Giles were to die, and they weren't married, she might not get the money. There was Helen to be got rid of, too. Perhaps Helen would take off when she knew about Sue. Like that Hilary, throwing Jonathan out. If Giles was thrown out, he and Sue would set up somewhere just as grand, Sue thought. And Terry would be there in the background, waiting.

In idle moments Sue's thoughts wandered along these attractive lines, and in the evenings, because she was on the late shift, Giles took her home. He had been doing this continuously, and at the weekend her shift would change.

In melancholy tones he mentioned this as they drove along.

'It won't be long till I'm on late again, you know,' Sue said lightly.

'It'll seem a long time to me,' mourned Giles. 'I'll be counting the days.' His heart beat fast at his own daring words.

Sue did not reply, but she moved a little in her seat, edging nearer to Giles although their seatbelts and the handbrake kept them apart. His heart was thundering. He peered out at the night as the black road rolled out ahead in the headlights. They turned into the lane, and the big, powerful car, a warm cocoon humming through the darkness, seemed to Giles to be heading for paradise. Tonight he did not stop at the lodge but drove straight into the barn, where he parked the Rover in its usual place and switched off the lights and the engine. Then he sat motionless, breathing heavily. He undid his seatbelt.

'What's this, then?' asked Sue, smiling in the darkness. 'Abducting me, are you?' She groped for the catch on her seatbelt.

'Here, let me,' said Giles. He fumbled about and freed it. Sue pulled it off as he clumsily seized her and began mumbling into her hair. 'How little you are, and how lovely,' she heard and then she felt schoolboy kisses landing all over her face.

She wanted to laugh. He really hadn't the least idea, she thought, turning her open mouth to him.

110

He hadn't. It was obvious, and Sue spared a moment of pity for Helen, who had been married to him for years. Even Jonathan had been in a more advanced grade than this, she thought, guiding his hand.

They couldn't do it here, in the car. It would be too uncomfortable, and he had drunk so much. In fact, she wondered if maybe he'd drunk too much altogether.

'Oh Giles,' she sighed, her fingers making sparks fly in his mind, as well as his body.

'Come into the house,' he croaked hoarsely. 'Come in with me, Sue. Helen's away.'

She was up in Yorkshire, inspecting work on a house she was decorating there.

'All right,' Sue breathed, and broke free. She got out of the car. A dim light filtered in from the lamp outside the barn, enough for her to find her way round to the driver's side and help him extract himself.

Giles's head was swimming as they went together to the house. His arm was around Sue, but she was supporting more than embracing him.

Alice had heard the car return. She had watched from her window as it turned in at the barn without dropping Sue at the lodge, so she thought Giles was alone, but he didn't come out of the barn for some time. Alice began to worry. Was he ill? She stayed there, watching, until at last she saw them both moving together across the gravel sweep to the house, their arms entwined, a large dark blur of two bodies closely linked.

'Oh no!' she whispered aloud. 'Oh no, please!'

She stayed at the window, her mind refusing to accept what she had seen, until after some time she saw Sue return alone and walk down to the lodge, whose porch light still burned. Then the light snapped off.

Alice went to bed, but not to sleep.

Various explanations for what she had seen came into her mind, and each seemed as dreadful as another. The only one she could bear to admit was that Giles had been taken ill and Sue had seen him into the house and up to his room.

She decided to believe that theory. It was the safest.

*   *   *

When Jonathan heard the Rover pass the lodge without stopping, his first feeling was irritation. Now he would have to turn out to fetch Sue. He was sure she had said she would ring if she wanted a lift. Giles had brought her back every night that week, and Jonathan had been grateful. He was increasingly tired these days and it was no fun turning out on a cold night to collect her. This evening he had ironed eight shirts and cleaned the bathroom, which was filthy. Then he'd had a bath, dressed again in his flannels and jacket and gone to the Bull in Great Minton for steak and chips at the bar. He'd stayed quite late.

He went out to the window and looked across at the barn. The doors were still open, but sometimes Giles left them overnight and Jonathan, the first to leave in the mornings, found them so when he went to fetch the Granada. He let the curtain fall back. Giles spent too much time in the bar at the Rigby, but that was none of Jonathan's business. It had not yet crossed his mind to feel jealous; he imagined Giles in the bar, and Sue at reception, simply together in the car for convenience. It was his naiveté that had made Jonathan fall prey to Sue; until now the same innocent outlook had let him ignore the perils of propinquity.

He dialled the number of the Rigby Arms.

The telephone rang for several minutes before it was answered.

'Rigby Arms,' said a male voice.

'Who's that?' asked Jonathan. It might be the manager.

'Terry Brett, the barman,' said Terry. 'Can I help you?'

'Oh – Terry – this is Jonathan Cooper. Is Sue still there? Is she expecting me to collect her?' asked Jonathan.

Terry grinned to himself as he sat at the switchboard. It was lucky the call had come through before he switched the line to the manager's flat, as happened at night. Sue hadn't wasted much time. What now, though? He couldn't say Sue was still at the hotel and let Jonathan come over in vain. That would only start a hue and cry. He glanced at his watch. She'd had long enough, he thought; long enough for starters, anyway. The main course could follow another time. He could trust her to play her hand solo.

'Mr Armitage was giving her a lift,' he said. 'Perhaps they broke down?'

'No. His car's back, but Sue hasn't come in,' said Jonathan.

'Well, perhaps they're just having a chat,' said Terry soothingly.

'At this time of night?' said Jonathan. 'What sort of chat would that be?'

'You tell me,' said Terry silkily.

'Goodnight, Terry,' Jonathan snapped, and replaced the receiver. Then he began pacing round the room as scenes from the past came into his mind. He remembered Hilary angrily asking him why he was late, and his answer that he had met a man in a pub and had stayed talking too long. Then Hilary had asked who the girl was he'd been seen lunching with, who'd also been seen in his car. He had replied that she was a business colleague. There had been lies and excuses then on his side, with Hilary the one deceived. Sue had been free to do as she liked, and in a moment of revelation Jonathan saw that she would always want that freedom. The miscarriage that had ended her marriage – she had told him her husband had left her after that – had been the key that opened the door. There had been other men besides him; she had not denied it when he asked her.

'It's only fun, isn't it?' she had said.

Was it happening again, with Giles, who was ten years older than Jonathan, flabby and red-faced, already going to seed?

Was she out there in the car with him, smooching like some adolescent? She'd done it with him, after all.

Jonathan opened the front door, on the point of going to see; then drew back. What would he do if she was? And what if she wasn't – what if neither was there? The implication of that possibility was much more serious.

By the time Sue came back to the house, Jonathan had worked himself into a fit of jealous rage.

'Well, where have you been?' he demanded. 'In bed with Giles Armitage?'

She mustn't break with him yet. It was too soon for Jonathan to flounce out of the lodge. Tonight nothing had happened. Excitement and alcohol had proved too much for

Giles and he had passed out as soon as they reached his room. Sue had left him sprawled on the bed. She had removed his shoes and tie, and covered him up, as she would for anyone over the top, and left him to sleep it off.

There would soon be another chance. Jonathan would be off visiting his kids again before long.

'He wasn't feeling well,' she said smoothly. 'I helped him into the house. Helen's away, so I made sure he was all right before leaving him. I gave him some aspirins.'

'Oh yes? And what else?' sneered Jonathan. 'Held his hand, I suppose, and bit more too?'

'What on earth's bugging you?' Sue demanded. 'I told you, he felt ill. He drinks too much,' she added.

'And whose fault is that? Your friend Terry's, I suppose,' said Jonathan, the blood pounding in his head.

'Terry just does his job,' said Sue.

'And what's that?' asked Jonathan. 'Next thing, you'll be fucking him too.' He hadn't meant to say it: the words seemed to rise up from some awful pit of suspicion deep in his brain. He stood glaring at her, his mind seething, and saw her slow smile. Suddenly, crystal clear, he realized what had been happening in the weeks since Christmas. There had been all those times when Terry had come over here, ostensibly visiting Mrs Armitage, the lifts that Terry had given her. 'By Christ, that's it!' he cried. 'It's been Terry in the morning and Giles at night, and I'm the poor sucker in the middle. You bitch!'

He raised his hand and struck her across the face.

It was a determined blow, and though tears of pain filled Sue's eyes, she didn't pause for thought. She had seen her father go for her mother and pull fistfuls of hair from her mother's head; she had seen her mother's eye blacked. No man would ever do that to her. In one quick action, Sue looked round and saw the heavy iron poker in the hearth. She grabbed it and brought the handle down hard against Jonathan's temple.

He stared at her for one instant before his knees sagged and he toppled over.

Sue stood gazing down at him, panting, the poker still in her hand. He lay still.

114

'You bastard,' she said. 'That'll teach you to try that sort of thing on me.'

Jonathan did not move. Sue replaced the poker. She looked at him. Faking hurt, she thought, wanting her to fall on her knees and say she was sorry. Well, she wasn't. She'd do it again.

She went upstairs and got ready for bed. He'd soon give up his silly trick. But he didn't, and she fell asleep.

Some time later she woke, feeling hungry. She got up and went into the kitchen to find something to eat. There were some chocolate biscuits in a tin and she crunched up six with her sharp white teeth. Then she went into the sitting-room.

Jonathan still lay where he had fallen. He was dead.

Sue would not believe it at first.

'Get up, Jonathan,' she ordered, prodding him with her naked toe. His head was turned to one side, and she went down on her knees beside him, patting his cheek hard. Nothing happened, and she moved his head to face her. It was heavy, and flopped to the other side, the jaw open, the eyes staring. Sue shook him, and one arm that had lain across his body fell back with a thud to lie limply, the hand turned palm upwards, the fingers half curled.

Sue was terrified. She moved backwards, gazing down at him in horror and disgust. She'd only meant to stop him from hitting her again. What did he mean by going and dying? It wasn't fair.

What was she to do? She looked around the room as if something there would give her the answer, and saw the poker. She took it out to the kitchen and washed it thoroughly, wiping it dry before replacing it in the hearth.

The police, she thought: she ought to ring up the police. But they would want to know why she had not telephoned straight away. Leaving Jonathan lying on the floor for hours wouldn't look good. What about saying they'd thought they'd heard someone in the house and Jonathan had gone down to investigate? She could make it look as if someone had broken in. Yes, that was the thing to do. Then she remembered the bruise on her cheek. She could cover it with

115

make-up but there was a mark and a tiny graze where his signet ring had broken the skin. They might notice and be curious. Sue felt a great reluctance to let the police come nosing around here. Suppose they grew interested again in George's accident and began asking about that? She felt concern for neither victim, but a lot for herself.

She sat down on the sofa to think. The room was cold now, and shock hit her; she began to shiver. That wouldn't help; she must keep her head.

Sue got up and crossed to the sideboard, where she poured herself a good tot of whisky from a half-empty bottle, their last. Then she went over to look at the body again. Why had he died? She had struck one single blow, and she could see no blood. Gingerly, she lifted a lock of his dark hair and saw bruising on his temple. There was a tiny abrasion; it had scarcely bled. His eyes stared up. She knew you should close a dead person's eyes, but she had never seen a corpse before and was aware only of revulsion. She went into the kitchen and fetched a white polythene bin liner which she put over Jonathan's head, biting her lip while she did it, concentrating on the task, heaving his heavy head up and rolling the bag over it.

That was better. Now he could not stare at her with those brown unblinking eyes. Next, she rolled him away to the side of the room where he would be out of the way. It was an effort; he was very heavy and his limbs flopped as she edged his torso over, using her knee and leg muscles. She tucked him neatly against the wall beside the storage heater. Then she fetched a spare blanket from upstairs and covered him up.

Terry would know what to do. She came to this decision as she tidied Jonathan away with the same concentration she showed in her work but lacked in domestic matters.

After that she went back to bed. She couldn't get hold of Terry until the morning.

The shuddering began again as she lay there in the darkness. Sue turned on the bedside lamp and sat up hugging her knees, telling herself not to be frightened. She had been afraid as a child and had overcome her fears; she had learned not to let her feelings control her head.

No one had suspected that George's death was not an

accident. She had got away with that, and she would do the same now. Terry would know how to deal with things; he would be able to spirit Jonathan away.

She sat up in bed until the sky grew light.

No one saw the glow from the bedside lamp.

14

With the morning, confidence began seeping back. It was no good dithering and wondering what to do: that had never been Sue's way and now she could act.

The body lay where she had left it, a long mound under its blanket.

Sue made herself some strong black coffee and sat drinking it while she waited for the duty receptionist to start the early turn at the Rigby Arms. She wanted to by-pass the manager over this.

At last it was time. Sue asked Anthea to get Terry to ring her back as soon as he could.

'Jonathan's not well,' she added. 'But I'll be in as usual. It's lucky I'm on the late shift.' And after today, she had forty-eight hours free. Terry would think of something, somewhere to take Jonathan and get rid of him. Soon it would all be over.

As she ended the call, the milkman's float stopped in the drive and she heard his brisk step on the path. Sue remained motionless. Often, if she was up when he came, she would open the door and exchange some backchat with him; he was a cheerful middle-aged man who had been doing the village round for years. She heard the bottle clank down on the stone floor of the porch and his retreating tread.

She left the sitting-room curtains drawn, in case anyone looked in, though if they did, they wouldn't be able to see Jonathan who lay close up to the wall to one side. Luckily almost no one called at the lodge apart from Terry. Sue sat in the kitchen drinking more coffee until Terry rang.

'Come over, will you?' she asked. 'Right away. It's serious.'

'Well, I've got to do the cellar,' said Terry. 'It'll have to be quick. Can't you tell me what it's all about?'

'No,' said Sue. 'You must come, Terry.'

He had never heard her speak like that before. Her voice was steady – too steady, the words all uttered in a monotone.

'Jonathan isn't well, I hear,' he said.

'No.' She didn't elaborate.

'I'll be right over,' said Terry.

She was waiting for him, dressed, now, in black slacks and tight sweater, her long hair in a pony tail, no make-up on, and she opened the door as he came up the path.

He saw the mark on her face at once, even before she cast herself against him.

'What is all this?' he asked, holding her away from him and laying a finger against her cheek. 'What's happened, Sue? Where's Jonathan? Is he in bed?'

Sue shook her head.

'He's over there,' she said, and began to tremble as she pointed to the bundle against the wall. 'He's dead.'

Terry stared at her.

'No!' he gasped. 'No!'

'He is,' said Sue.

'Why? How? What happened?' There had been some sort of accident, obviously. Terry let go of Sue and went over to the long blanket-covered heap, drawing back one end of the blanket. He saw the white polythene bag. 'Suicide?' he said, but he knew it wasn't, not with the body tidily placed like this beside the storage heater.

'No. He hit me,' said Sue. 'I didn't think, Terry. I picked up the poker.'

Terry covered the dead man's head again and stood up. He came over to Sue and looked again at her face, inspecting the bruise and the tiny scrape.

'Oh dear,' he said. 'Better tell me what happened.'

'Let's go into the kitchen,' said Sue. 'I don't like him being there.' It was as if Jonathan could hear himself being discussed.

Terry didn't care for it either. They went into the kitchen

118

and sat at the table. Sue told him the story exactly as it had happened.

'Jealous bugger,' said Terry. 'He shouldn't have hit you.'

'No,' said Sue. 'I was scared.' But that wasn't true. She hadn't been scared until later; she had been ragingly angry.

'If you'd called the police, you could have said it was self-defence,' Terry pointed out. 'You could still do that, Sue. You could say you panicked and that's why you didn't do it at once. Did he die straight away?'

'I don't know. I didn't look,' said Sue. 'I thought he was putting it on, for sympathy. I went up to bed.'

Terry gulped.

'You mean you left him there – you didn't –?' But he knew she had not tried to find out how badly hurt Jonathan was. He swallowed, horrified. How could she just leave him?

'He'd hurt me, Terry,' said Sue. 'He hit me.'

'You'd better ring the police, Sue,' Terry said.

'I can't,' said Sue. 'They'll think I meant to do it.'

'Well, you can prove he hit you. You've got a bruise to show for it,' Terry said.

'It's not just that,' said Sue. 'I can't risk the police, Terry.'

'Why not?' Terry could see it would be tough for her, especially if the police realized she hadn't tried to help Jonathan. Perhaps she could say he had died straight away, or she thought he had, and had panicked. That made sense.

Wasn't he going to get rid of the body for her? Sue had been so sure that he would.

'You've got to get rid of him, Terry,' she said, on a rising note.

'But – but –' How could he? Where to? Terry didn't like this sort of thing at all.

She had to persuade him. How far dared she go?

'If we tell the police, they might think I'd had something to do with George's accident,' said Sue.

'Oh no! They wouldn't do that,' said Terry. 'Why should they?'

'They might,' Sue insisted. 'Just because I was around at the time.'

'But you – how?' Terry stared at her, unable to follow her reasoning.

'They might think I'd pushed him,' said Sue, keeping her voice level. 'After all, you got his job because I'd recommended you. They might say I'd done it deliberately to get you in at the Rigby.'

'Oh, but that was just a coincidence,' Terry began, and stopped, for he realized that the police could look at it differently if they took it into their heads to consider the matter again. Sue would have no defence if they set out to build up a case against her; she'd been at work as usual that morning with no witness to say that she had never left the reception area. He saw the danger there could be for both of them if this happened. The police might even accuse him of having conspired with her to remove George, so devious were they, in Terry's opinion. At best, they would investigate what he had been doing recently, and Terry couldn't risk that happening. Some of his deals would not stand up to inspection.

On the whole, the wisest course would be to get rid of all trace of the accident and its victim.

'Let's see,' he said, beginning to plan, and Sue saw that she had won. 'You told Anthea he wasn't well,' Terry went on. 'What about his office? What were his plans for today?'

Sue didn't know. She had never been interested in how Jonathan earned his living.

'His diary,' said Terry, almost irritably for him, to Sue's surprise. He was never cross. 'Where does he keep it?'

'In his pocket, I suppose,' she said.

'Would he have been making calls or going to the office?'

'I don't know,' said Sue.

'We'd better find out,' said Terry grimly. 'We don't want his boss ringing up wanting to talk to him, do we?'

He was going to help her. He would deal with it. Sue relaxed a little. She followed as Terry returned to the sitting-room and began unfolding the blanket. The body had not yet begun to stiffen, for Jonathan had not been dead so very long. The inter-cranial haemorrhage that had killed him had not taken fatal effect at once.

Terry held his breath as he felt in the dead man's jacket and found Jonathan's slim black leather diary in his inside pocket. His wallet was there, too. Terry left it. He turned the diary pages until he came to today's date. Several names and times were entered, and his office number was listed on the page provided for personal notes.

He gave the diary to Sue.

'Ring up his office. Say he's ill and give them these names. Say you don't know what's wrong exactly but that he's been very depressed lately. That's the thing, depression.' It would make suicide, if somehow this death could be arranged to look like that, understandable.

Terry covered the body again while Sue went to the telephone. Her voice was calm as she made the call.

'Depressed, yes,' she said. 'For some time, really. Since Christmas. Yes, yes. Thank you. I'll tell him.' She hung up and turned to Terry. 'They said he'd better see a doctor if he isn't all right by Monday,' she told him.

'I'll have to go now,' Terry said. 'I'll come back as soon as the bar closes.'

'But we can't leave him here all that time!' Sue exclaimed. 'Suppose someone calls?'

'Who's likely to? Only Alice, and you can tell her Jonathan's ill and you can't let her in. You'll have to sweat it out this morning, Sue. I'll be thinking of something to do, meanwhile.'

'What if Helen comes?'

'Does she ever?'

'She might, to see what we're up to.'

'Do the same to her – say Jonathan's ill and sleeping. Ask her to come back another time,' said Terry. 'You can handle that, Sue.'

She could, of course.

'You will come back?' she asked, clinging to him.

'Of course I will,' he said, unwrapping her arms and moving towards the door.

He thought about it, driving away. He could clear out, be gone, leave Sue to cope. Seeing that large, log-like bundle tucked against the wall, feeling in the jacket pocket, had really choked him.

But they would be able to get rid of it – he and Sue: careful planning would be needed, and he thrived on that. It would be safer for his own skin than lighting out.

* * *

Sue went back to bed after Terry left. She could not stay in the sitting-room with that shape beneath its blanket lying there by the wall. She drank some coffee laced with whisky and swallowed four aspirins – she had no sleeping pills; Sue never went near a doctor – and slept for over two hours.

There was still a long time to fill in until Terry came. She dared not go out, not even to see Alice, in case someone came to the house. She had a bath and got dressed, then leafed through some magazines with the radio on. She could not watch television because the set was in the room with the body.

Terry arrived just before three. He always came then, when she was on late shift. They would go to bed and then he would drive her in to work. Alice would not think it odd if she noticed his car outside.

'Have you got a plan?' she asked. 'What are you going to do?'

'Put him in the boot of his own car, to start with,' said Terry. 'Then, when there's more time, fake an accident.' He hadn't worked out the details yet, but they'd come to him. He was rather surprised that a splendid plan had not yet sprung into his mind, for usually his ideas rapidly grew from the needs of the occasion. The trouble was that this wasn't his kind of thing at all; he'd never been mixed up with anything violent. But Jonathan had hit Sue. Terry told himself that without this trigger it wouldn't have happened. 'Who's about the place today?' he asked. 'It's Thursday. There's the cleaning woman, isn't there?' He had seen Mrs Wood on her cycle several times, a doughty soul with head-scarf and boots, steadily pedalling.

'She's gone.' Sue had seen her ride past the windows earlier. 'She has her lunch and then goes.'

'What about that gardener fellow?'

'I don't know if he's there. He comes when he feels like it,' said Sue. 'There's Alice.'

'Yes. Well, it won't take very long to wheel – er – him over to the garage in the wheelbarrow,' said Terry. He had developed an aversion to uttering Jonathan's name.

'What if the gardener is using it?'

'Oh!' Terry had not thought of that.

'There's that truck Giles uses for moving the logs,' said

Sue. 'It's kept in the barn. It's bigger than a wheelbarrow. A sort of handcart.'

'Ah! Well, I'll use that, then,' said Terry. 'Now, you go and see what the gardener's doing. Check that he'll be busy for about twenty minutes. It won't take longer than that. See if he's digging a big patch – ask him.'

'But I never go and talk to the gardener,' Sue said.

'There's always a first time. Tell him that – er – Jonathan's at home ill and beg a cabbage or something off him. Say you want to cook something special. If he's leaving and packing up we'll have to wait till he's gone.' Terry didn't fancy that. He didn't want to be forced to take Sue in to work and then return and extemporize alone: not over this.

'Why not bring the car out – park outside?' Sue said.

'And have someone see us piling him into it? No. Besides, if he really was ill, he wouldn't be using it. It must stay where it is,' said Terry. 'Things must go on as normally as we can manage. Off you go – chat up the gardener. Be as quick as you can but make a good job of it.'

Sue put on her coat and boots and went off round the side of the house. She was gone nearly ten minutes but it seemed much longer to Terry as he waited alone with the corpse.

Sue came back with a tight green savoy cabbage.

'He's digging a patch for sowing beans,' she said. 'He'll be busy for a bit yet.'

'How do you know?'

'He'd been drinking his tea – he had a flask – when I got out there. It's to last him till he finishes that strip of ground,' said Sue. 'He said so.'

'Right,' said Terry. 'Now you go and visit Alice. Get her to make you some coffee. Keep her there talking. Do a sob-stuff act – tell her – ' he made an effort. 'Tell her that Jonathan's been acting strangely lately. Say he hit you. You can say he's sorry – that he was drunk. That won't be anything new to her, seeing what Giles gets up to. The main thing is to keep her away from the window.'

Sue nodded.

'How will I know when you've finished?' she asked.

'You won't. Stay as long as you can, leaving time for us to get you to the Rigby on the dot. Leave this end to me.'

'You're wonderful, Terry,' said Sue, meaning it. He was so firm and decisive. She moved against him, but he pushed her away.

'No time for that now, Sue,' he said. 'Get going.'

He watched from the window as she walked up to the back door and pressed the bell. Soon the door opened and she went inside. Terry gave them three minutes to get settled. Then he went over to the barn, looked around for the cart and finally saw it at one end, beside the pile of neatly stacked logs. He wheeled it round to the back door of the lodge.

The task of moving Jonathan was almost too much for Terry. He couldn't lift the body but had to drag it by the heels across the floor, bumping into furniture and the door-posts, hauling it into the kitchen. The blanket came unwrapped and he had to bundle it up again, rolling it up like a carpet. The head and shoulders were stiffening. Terry knew nothing about rigor mortis and did not realize that the warmth of the storage heater had delayed the process some-what as he managed to heave the heavy torso into the cart and roll the legs in after it. Then he went round to the front of the lodge and glanced up and down the drive.

There was no one in sight.

He pushed the cart briskly into the barn, elated until he realized that he had forgotten to get the keys of the Granada from Sue and he had not brought his own set of keys with him. He ran back to the lodge and was searching for them when the doorbell rang. Looking out of the window, Terry saw a white van outside. For a wild moment he imagined that a policeman stood on the step. He thought about leaving the bell unanswered, but he had not closed the front door when he came in to search for the keys.

A small man with ginger hair and a large book stood on the doorstep: the representative of the electricity board come to read the meter.

Terry didn't know where it was, but the man did; it was in a cupboard under the stairs, reached through the sitting-room. A short time earlier, a dead body had lain, wrapped in a rug, not ten feet from the cupboard door.

Terry smiled pleasantly at the meter man, standing beside him while he noted the figures, showing him out, watching him drive on in his van to the main house. Sue would have a turn when she saw him, he thought.

Those few moments when he had to be calm had steadied Terry. He remembered seeing keys on a hook on the kitchen dresser. They were there.

He'd forgotten his gloves. Terry found a pair of Jonathan's on a shelf in the small lobby and went back again to the barn, chiding himself for being so careless.

He opened the boot and steeled himself to lift the body in.

He was sweating when he went back to the house to wait for Sue.

'Oh, my dear!' exclaimed Alice when she saw Sue's face with its pale bruise under the delicate skin, and the small abrasion. 'Oh, how dreadful!'

Sue found it easy to cry in the aftermath of tension. She allowed Alice to pat her arm soothingly and lapped up the expressions of concern which Alice was uttering.

'What shall I do?' wailed Sue. 'Oh, what shall I do?'

'He can't have meant to hurt you,' said Alice.

'He was jealous,' said Sue. 'Jealous because I come home from work so often with Giles. But he should be glad. It saves him from turning out to come for me.'

Alice remembered what she had seen, the intertwined figures crossing from the barn to the house, and Sue's return alone. She hadn't been in the house long. How long was long enough, wondered Alice.

'Perhaps it isn't very discreet,' she said.

'Well, he's lonely, isn't he?' said Sue. 'Giles, I mean. Helen's out such a lot, and so busy.'

'That's true.' Alice sighed. 'It wasn't a good idea, my coming here. I thought if Helen had the sort of house she'd always wanted – ' her voice trailed away.

'You should think of yourself, not them,' Sue said, and meant it. 'You aren't at all happy here.'

'Well, it's been better since I got to know you and Jonathan,' Alice said. 'Are you planning to marry?'

'Not really. His wife won't agree to a divorce. You can easily get one in two years if you agree. If not, it takes much

125

longer. And I'm not sure about anything permanent. He's been acting so strangely lately. We've had several rows, but he's never hit me before.' Sue found it surprisingly easy to give this truthful reply.

'Perhaps you should give up taking lifts from Giles,' Alice suggested. 'If it upsets Jonathan?'

'You don't think – ?' Sue began, and Alice broke in.

'No, of course not.' But however innocent Sue's presence in the house last night, the temptation was there. What had they been doing? She found that she did not want to know the answer.

'You must make it up with Jonathan,' she advised. 'When he comes home tonight.'

'He hasn't gone in to work,' Sue said. 'He's in bed. He won't talk to me. Terry's with him now. I thought if I left them together – ' she wrung her hands and looked at Alice in a genuinely anxious way. How was Terry getting on? Had he done it?

There was Terry, too. She had got them all in her thrall, thought Alice and was astonished at the direction of her thoughts. *La Belle Dame Sans Merci*, that was; Walter had quoted it sometimes when he was doing the crossword. In her own young days, one's reputation was precious; girls guarded it by avoiding conduct that might be misinterpreted. Nowadays, nobody seemed to care about that sort of thing. Alice remembered feeling doubtful about Terry and Sue being alone in the lodge together that very first day.

Sue said she must go. It was nearly time to leave for the Rigby and she had to change and do her hair.

Perhaps she would leave the lodge, Alice thought when she had gone. Perhaps this quarrel would prove to be final. It would be much better for Giles if Sue were to leave.

15

During the night in which Jonathan died alone in the sitting-room at the lodge, Giles had woken to find himself lying on his bed fully dressed, with the eiderdown over him. His shoes lay untidily on the floor a yard apart; his tie was on a chair.

He woke just in time before vomiting.

In the bathroom, he splashed cold water on his face and tried to remember what had happened the previous evening. He'd been in the bar at the Rigby Arms where by now he had friends among the regulars. Two were keen punters and told him of their betting successes, not referring to their failures; Giles took a courteous interest in their fortunes.

He had brought Sue home. Slowly, painfully, Giles dredged up the memory of the night. He had driven straight into the barn and, in the kindly darkness, begun to make love to her.

Love. Even in his fuddled state, Giles knew that what he felt for Sue was not love. But she had been responsive. He'd experienced delicious sensations.

Memory blanked out after they'd got out of the car. He'd passed out, obviously. And just as obviously, he hadn't been sober enough to get far with Sue.

No doubt he'd made a crass fool of himself.

Giles took off his clothes and crawled into bed, where he tossed and turned for a while before he slept again. In the morning he had a foul taste in his mouth, and his head throbbed. Luckily Helen was away, so he did not have to listen to any breakfast-time comments on his pallor. Before leaving for the office he looked at the engagement pad by the telephone. They were going out to dinner on Saturday and on Sunday there were guests for lunch. It wasn't a weekend when the girls came home so there was nothing to look forward to at all.

He had a meeting that morning, and in the afternoon had to go through some complex figures. He liked that; he was good with figures; you knew where you were with them. In between, there were letters to answer and routine matters to handle. At lunch-time he sent out for sandwiches, surprising his secretary, for usually he took himself off to a nearby pub. He worked on hard through the day, intending to be home in good time that evening, wearing a welcoming expression when Helen came in, if he should be first, or greeting her with a display of pleasure if she were already home from

Yorkshire. Should he buy flowers? He thought about it. He never did, except for form's sake on her birthday.

At three o'clock he sent his astonished secretary out to buy three dozen carnations. He gave her the key of his car and asked her to put them in it. At five o'clock he left for home, and soon after six walked into the house. He knew she was back. Her car was in the barn.

Helen was in her sitting-room writing up some notes about the house in Yorkshire. Giles's footsteps in the passage were muted by the Persian runner that covered the stone flags. He paused. Of course I don't have to knock, he told himself. This wasn't her bedroom. He took a deep breath, opened the door and walked in.

'Ah – Helen – you're back,' he said. 'Did you have a good trip?'

'Very.' Helen pushed her glasses up on to the top of her head and tilted her chair back, drumming impatiently with her fingers on the paper before her. Now what?

'And a good run back? It's nice that you're home early,' he tried, and swallowed. Then he proffered the flowers, which he had been carrying head downwards by his side. 'I thought you'd like these,' he said.

Helen turned to look at him. She saw a flabby man who had once been slim and handsome. His face, now, was florid, but not with the glow of health; there were pouches beneath his eyes and he had a small paunch. At the moment he was looking at her with the apprehensive, eager expression of a small boy who has committed a misdemeanour as yet undetected for which, in advance, he wants to make amends.

Helen interpreted all this perfectly.

'Well!' she said. 'Flowers! And it isn't my birthday! What have you been doing, Giles, while my back was turned?'

'Just going to the office as usual. What else?' asked Giles.

'I don't know. You tell me,' said Helen. She waited, watching him, a cat alert for prey.

'I – er – I've missed you.' Sweat broke out on Giles's forehead, and the flowers, still thrust forward, wavered in his grasp.

'I doubt it,' said Helen. 'Since we seldom meet.' She turned back to her work and settled her glasses back on her nose. 'If you're having an affair, Giles, I don't want to know.

Just be discreet. And you needn't think I'll ever divorce you, for I won't. You keep your goings-on away from here – I won't put up with gossip. You can give your flowers to your girlfriend. I don't want them. And grow up, for God's sake. Just look at you – you're drinking so much you're falling apart.' She gave him a last scornful glance. 'I'm surprised that anyone will look at you,' she told him. 'You're a walking disaster.'

Giles turned on his heel and walked out of the room without another word, still holding the flowers, and Helen returned to her work, putting him out of her mind.

Giles went straight out to the car and drove to the Rigby Arms. He'd tried and Helen had snubbed him. She had only herself to blame for what happened next. He'd give the flowers to Sue, and he'd be sober when they parked in the barn.

But that night she asked to be dropped at the lodge. Jonathan wasn't well, she said, and they were going away the next day for the weekend.

'Some other time, Giles,' she promised, opening her mouth to him, making him gasp.

'He's forgotten to put the outside light on for you,' said Giles.

'Yes. Never mind,' said Sue. 'I can see all right.'

He waited while she went up the path. He saw her use her key to open the door. There were no lights on in the house. Jonathan must have gone to bed, Giles supposed, driving on, putting the car away.

Because of her make-up and the surrounding darkness, he hadn't noticed the bruise on Sue's face.

She'd forgotten the flowers. They were still in the car. Giles took them into the house and flung them into the kitchen waste bin, where Mrs Wood found them next day. She revived them with plenty of water and took them home, where they bloomed for some days giving her a great deal of pleasure. Her guess as to how they had come to be thrown away was not very far from the truth.

That afternoon, as they drove to Westborough leaving Jonathan's body stowed in the boot of the Granada, Terry had told Sue that he wouldn't take her back after closing time, as she had proposed.

'But you could stay,' she said.

He was shocked.

'I couldn't,' he said. 'He's supposed to be upstairs in bed, remember.'

'But you'll be dumping him somewhere,' said Sue. 'You can take the car out and drive it into a river or something. Make it look as if he's had an accident.'

'Not just like that, I can't,' said Terry. 'There's got to be a proper plan. He wouldn't just drive off.'

'He might,' said Sue. 'He's been going for walks at night.'

'No,' said Terry. 'It's got to be thought about.' And he needed time to get over the revulsion he felt about the whole business to which now, it seemed, he was committed. 'Tomorrow,' he said. 'We'll do it tomorrow. You're off then, aren't you, for the weekend?'

'Yes.'

'I've got it!' Terry felt the sudden lift that came with a good idea. 'You and him – ' he still avoided using the dead man's name. 'You book in at a hotel for a weekend. You've had a row and you're making it up, see?'

'But – '

'No, wait!' Terry liked his plan more as it began to take shape. It was vital to get the dead man away from the district so that any hunt for him, when he was missed, would not be local. The problem would be to fit it in with his own shifts at the bar; he had to keep his routine going. 'Pick somewhere about thirty or forty miles away – not too far. Near the motorway. I'll have to do a lot of travelling around.'

'You will?'

'Well, you can't drive, can you? And someone's got to be at the hotel with you, taking his place.'

'But you don't look like him,' objected Sue.

'No one's going to see me – or only in the distance. You'll check in, saying I'm not well. Or rather, he's not well. It will have to be a motel or somewhere like that, where the rooms are away from the main block and reception area. A place where guests can get out at night without a hall porter.'

'Money,' said Sue promptly. 'It's going to cost.'

'I'll find some,' said Terry. He'd get Sue like this, he saw, bind her for ever, and she in turn would get Giles; it would be an investment. He hardened his heart as he turned his mind towards what had to be done. 'During the night, while you're in the hotel, I'll get rid of him,' he said. 'Somewhere where he'll never be found. Or at least, so that no one will ever find out what happened.' What had? Why had a single blow been fatal? He'd heard of paper-thin skulls; was that the explanation?

'Like setting the car on fire, do you mean?' Sue asked.

'That's a good idea,' said Terry. 'Yes, something like that. It's better if you don't know too much about it. Leave that to me.' He'd work it out as he went along.

'How will you get back to Westborough?' Sue asked. 'By train?'

He'd lift another car, but he couldn't tell Sue that. There were some things it was better for her not to know about him; at the moment he was the one with the upper hand.

'Yes,' he said. 'Or I'll hitch a ride.'

'Had we better go to a hotel in a town, then?' said Sue.

Terry didn't like that idea. There were always people about in a town, busybodies minding other people's business. A car driving off in the night might be noticed, and the fact that the driver had not emerged from the hotel be seen and remembered.

'Somewhere quiet would be better,' he said. 'And you'd go somewhere in the country, wouldn't you, to make it up? Somewhere romantic.'

'There's that place at Twistleton,' said Sue. 'The Court Grange Hotel. It's got an annexe block. We've often booked touring Americans in there and we've just had a couple who'd been there. They liked it a lot.'

'Twistleton?' Terry was trying to place it.

'It's not far from Swindon,' said Sue. 'There'll be something about it in the office.'

She checked when they reached the Rigby. Terry was still off duty and looked Twistleton up on the map. It was only a mile and a half from the motorway.

'Book yourselves in tomorrow for the weekend,' said Terry. 'Two nights. We'll plan later.'

'Two nights?' asked Sue.

'Two nights,' confirmed Terry. 'A weekend, remember. In the annexe.'

How had he got himself into this? It was way outside his normal scene. Terry wished Sue could drive, it would make things so much easier. She could have done it herself, once it was in the car. It was easier to think of Jonathan as it than as him, a person once warm and breathing.

The thing was, if Sue had done the obvious, rung the police when it happened, they would have given her a hard time and she might have found herself going down for manslaughter, and it was an accident, after all. But it would work out all right. All Sue need do was act sad for a while when she came back from that place, the Court Grange Hotel, saying Jonathan had gone off and left her there alone.

Terry had told her that he would hitch a ride back, but he wouldn't. Before he nicked a car, however, he'd have to get clear of the Court Grange. It wouldn't do to lift a car out of their yard. Pity about that: there'd be some good ones there, for sure. What a waste!

Terry told Mavis, the barmaid who was on duty with him on Thursday evening, that his car needed a repair and he knew this bloke who was going to do it cheap over the weekend, but he'd be stuck for getting about. Would she lend him her bike?

Mavis's bike was a small folding one, and she wouldn't be on duty over the weekend.

As she hesitated, Terry smiled at her winningly and explained that there was this bird he wanted to visit who'd be ever so upset if he couldn't get over.

Mavis said she could spare the bike if he'd run her home tonight after work. She sometimes went out cycling on Sundays with her children, but as it happened, this weekend her mother was coming to stay and there wouldn't be time.

'Thanks, Mavis. You're a true pal,' said Terry, and kissed her cheek.

Mavis, a plump forty-year-old with blonde-rinsed hair who worked to earn money for holidays and for music lessons for her daughter, blushed and pulled his ear.

'You'd charm the hide off a monkey, Terry,' she told him.

Had he thought of everything? Terry lay in bed that night going over his plan, only a fragment of which he'd so far told Sue. The timing would be so tight, but he dare not risk asking for any time off in case, later, it was remembered and thought an odd coincidence. He mustn't be seen with Sue so he must leave his own car outside Harcombe where it would not attract attention and where it would be safe until he could go and collect it on Mavis's bike. There was Alice to think of, too. What if she looked out of the window and saw him? In a coat of Jonathan's, at a distance, she might be deceived, but what about Helen? She'd be back from York-shire and might take it into her head to go past the lodge just as they set off. Terry lay in bed mulling it over. Should he go to Harcombe now and move the car, in the dark? No. In the morning Giles would see that it had gone and could question their story later.

He thought of a plan, lying there, that would take care of Helen. For Alice he was going to need inspiration.

The next afternoon, Terry left his car in Great Minton, where twenty houses were being built in what had once been a patch of allotments. He drove down the unmade road past the shells of houses to where the foundations of the last few were laid. Here, a bulldozer and a cement mixer stood on waste ground at the side of the site. There was no sign of activity. At the end of the new estate two cars were parked under a chestnut tree whose buds were sticky, ready to sprout when the warm weather came. Terry turned the car round so that it faced outwards for a quick getaway and took the bike from the back. It unfolded easily and he screwed it into its working position. Then he pedalled quickly back to the main village street. One of the new houses had a sign saying SOLD pasted across its windows. Another was nearly complete, and more were ranged in varying stages of construction. Someone must be there, to account for the cars, but he could see no exterior work in progress. Perhaps there were painters and plasterers working inside, Terry thought; or perhaps the developers had run out of money. No one would pay any attention to his old car; they would think it belonged to some worker on the site. It was safer here than in the village itself, where it might be the subject of curiosity.

It was a hard ride to Harcombe on the small bike, taking up precious time. Terry's legs ached as he pedalled the last stretch. He left the bike under a hedge just before he reached the gateway to Harcombe House, and approached the lodge on foot from the back, coming in from the neighbouring field over the garden fence.

He gave Sue a fright. She was expecting him to arrive in the normal way up the drive and she knew that Helen was in, which was worrying her, although it was unlikely that she would be looking out of a north-facing window since all the main rooms faced the garden side.

Terry came in by the back door and went softly through into the sitting-room where Sue was watching by the window. He whistled and she turned, her eyes large in her pale face. The bruise on her cheek stood out now.

'Oh, you scared me!' she gasped, clasping him.

'I came the back way so as not to be seen,' said Terry. 'Mrs Wood's gone by now, hasn't she?' He held her away from him.

'Yes – and the gardener. I watched for them both,' said Sue. 'What took you so long?' She had expected him soon after the bar closed.

Terry explained about the bike.

'I'll tell you the rest as we go,' he said. He was pleased with his plan. 'What about Helen and Alice? Are they in?'

She told him that Helen was, but there had been some luck about Alice. Sue had gone over, as instructed by Terry, to tell her that she and Jonathan were going away for a honeymoon-type weekend.

'What a good idea!' Alice had said, and the next minute she had decided to go away too. She had telephoned a hotel in Bournemouth not far from where she used to live and booked herself in. She had left before lunch.

'I've packed two cases,' Sue said. 'What he'd need for a couple of nights, and my own.' She indicated the bags by the door.

'Good. And I'll need one of his coats and a hat. I suppose he's got some sort of hat?'

134

Jonathan sometimes wore a tweed cap in cold weather. Sue had teased him about what she called his 'toff's hat'. It hung in the lobby together with an anorak and raincoat. Terry put on the bulky anorak and the cap, pushing his curls up under the cap, and laid the raincoat over the suitcases.

'How's that?' he said, posturing before her.

'Someone might take you for him on a dark night, at a distance,' said Sue doubtfully. 'But not up close. You're thinner. Oh Terry, someone else might come, like the meter reader yesterday.'

'Even if someone does, it probably wouldn't be anyone who knows him,' said Terry. 'People see what they expect to see. Don't lose your nerve, Sue. I'm going out to get the car now. I'll park by the gate while we put the cases in. You dial Helen's number on the telephone while I'm getting it, and then hang up when she answers. Now, where are the keys?'

He'd left them on the sideboard the day before; they were still there, beside Jonathan's diary. He picked them up and went to the door.

'Now dial,' he told her.

The Granada started first go. Terry backed it out of the barn and drove up to the lodge gate, where he left the engine running. He put the two cases and Jonathan's raincoat on the back seat of the car. When he went into the house again Sue was standing beside the telephone, the handset in place on the rest.

'Dial again, and leave the phone off,' he instructed. 'As soon as it's ringing, leave it and run.'

'The back door!' Sue said. 'It's not locked.'

Terry went quickly through and locked it, then came back. Thank God she'd remembered, but he should have thought of it. He forced himself to concentrate and to ignore the reason for what they were doing, that long silent form in the boot of the car.

'Dial now,' he said.

Helen's voice was clacking into the receiver as they hurried off down the path and into the car. They left the village by the Great Minton road, stopping to pick up the bike from where Terry had left it and covering it up, in the back of the car, with Jonathan's raincoat.

Helen gave up on the telephone when nobody spoke, as she had the first time it rang. In the lodge, the receiver lay on the sideboard beside Jonathan's diary, emitting the whirr of a line that has not been cleared.

16

Terry would not think about what lay in the boot of the Granada as he drove fast towards Twistleton. Every minute was precious if he was to get back to the Rigby Arms by opening time. He outlined his plan as he went along, and Sue became more confident as she saw that unless something went wrong with the journeys he had to make, it would work. He seemed to have thought of everything, even the fact that if the Granada was in the hotel car park on Saturday morning because of some hitch, there was still another night in which it could be disposed of; and he told her how, if that happened, she must get through the day, ordering meals in the room to make it seem as if Jonathan was there with her, feeling unwell.

The hotel stood at the foot of a hill beyond the village of Twistleton. A river wound towards woods in the distance. Picturesque cottages, most of them thatched, bordered the village street which was deserted on this Friday afternoon.

Terry drove through the gates and up to the main entrance. At the side was a row of cottages made from what had been the stable block of the mansion which was now the hotel. There was parking space beyond. There might be a second gate, a tradesmen's entrance, at the further end.

'It looks expensive,' said Terry.

'It is,' said Sue.

'We'll drive on and have a look round,' he said, sliding the car into gear and going on past the cottages. Sure enough, at the far end a gate led into the lane. Terry drove back up the hill and turned off along a narrow road which went to the church. He had noticed the spire from below.

'I forgot the bike,' he told Sue. 'I can't risk taking it out of the car down at the hotel. I'll leave it in the churchyard. That should be safe enough, for Christ's sake.'

Sue waited in the car while he wheeled the bike through the gates leading into the churchyard. He vanished between the graves. In a few minutes he returned, grinning. He had left it by a fence under a yew beyond the church. Then they drove back down the hill to the Court Grange Hotel. Its mellow brick was soft in the last of the day's slanting sunshine. Ancient trees studded the lawn. A gate led into a walled garden where there was now a swimming-pool complete with changing pavilion. What a place, thought Terry, peering from beneath Jonathan's cap as Sue went in to register and collect the key. An elderly couple, arm in arm, walked past as he waited. They took no notice of him.

Sue soon returned with the key, relieved at accomplishing the first task. She had registered herself and Jonathan in their correct names – she didn't want trouble over that later if there were any enquiries – and had remembered to glance at the registration number of the car before approaching the desk, aware from her own job that it would have to appear on the form.

'It's number five,' she said, getting back into the car, nodding towards the annexe.

'Good.' Terry had noticed as they drove past that the lowest numbers were nearest the main building; the further away they were, the better.

He parked outside number five and carried in their cases, hesitating over the raincoat, then took that in too. Afterwards, he parked the car at the furthest end of the parking area, close to the rear gate. He need only slip in through that and drive away. Then he walked quickly back to the annexe where Sue was waiting. He shouldn't be doing this, he thought: he should have gone at once, but he had to seem to be Jonathan, in anorak and cap, in case anyone noticed.

Sue sprang at him as he entered the room, eager and ardent, turned on by the excitement.

'Isn't this great?' she exclaimed, twining her arms round him, effectively blocking his view of the pretty room with its yellow sprigged curtains, pale carpet, and bleached furniture picked out with gold. 'Makes the Rigby seem a dump.'

Terry firmly detached her, holding her away, not letting her press herself against him.

'I've got to be back at that dump, as you call it, by six, remember,' he said. 'And I need all my strength for that bloody bike.'

Sue's expression hardened.

'What am I going to do all the evening?' she said. 'I'll be bored out of my mind.'

'You've got the telly,' said Terry. 'You can look at that. Or read a good book. They're bound to have some here.'

But Sue never read more than magazine gossip about the jet set and the showbiz world, and the fashion news.

'You can go over to the bar later,' said Terry. 'Bring a drink back for – ' he swallowed – 'Jonathan. That will be a natural thing to do. You can order dinner while you're there. Make a bit of a thing about it, apologizing for causing trouble and that. Charm them.'

'All right,' said Sue. She caught him again, fiercely, and pecked little kisses all over his face but once again Terry held her away from him; he felt no desire at all.

'Have a look out of the window,' he instructed. 'See if there's anyone about.'

Sue obeyed.

'There's an old woman with a dog,' she reported. 'She's going down towards the river. I can't see anyone else.'

Terry had kept Jonathan's gloves on all this time. Now he removed them while he took off the anorak and cap. He laid them on the bed and put on the dead man's raincoat. His curls sprang up in their usual manner as he ran his fingers quickly through them. He took the car keys from the anorak pocket and then replaced the gloves.

'I won't see you now until it's all over,' he told Sue.

'What – not tonight? You'll come in then, when you get back, won't you?'

'No. Someone might see me. I'm off now,' he said, and was gone, closing the door quietly behind him.

Sue watched from the window as he left the building and walked quickly away through the rear entrance. He did not glance back. His head was held at a jaunty angle and he looked quite unlike the apparently thickset man in the anorak and cap who had entered earlier.

Sue patted the wad of money he had given her to pay the bill. There was plenty. She had decided not to ask him where he had got it. They were both playing for high stakes now, and this was his investment in the future.

Terry, carrying crates of beer and mineral waters up to the bar from the cellar, had taken more exercise lately than for a long time, but his leg muscles ached with protest as he pedalled towards the motorway. Once out of the village the road looked level, but the small bike found and fought every rise.

Terry had passed a few people as he walked to the church to collect the bicycle, and as he pushed it out through the churchyard gate a woman had approached carrying a basket containing brass-cleaning equipment.

Terry held the gate open for her.

'Thank you,' she said, adding, 'Hasn't it been a lovely day?'

Terry agreed. He was hoping it would stay dry until the night was over.

'It won't be long now until spring,' said the woman. She looked curiously at Terry.

'That's right,' agreed Terry. An explanation of why he was there occurred to him, and he gave it. 'I've just been looking for my granny's grave,' he told her.

'Oh – did you find it?' asked the woman.

'Yes, yes,' said Terry, sure that if he said no the woman would offer to help him.

'That's good,' said the woman. 'It's among the old ones, then?'

What could she mean?

'Right,' said Terry. 'I must be off now. Goodbye,' and he mounted the bike to speed away before she could ask more questions.

He put her out of his mind as he pedalled on. Close to the slip road leading to the motorway, he left the bike in a field under a hedge, noting the place carefully as it would be dark when he returned. Once on the motorway, a lorry soon stopped to pick him up. His luck was in for it was going to

Swindon. Terry got the driver to drop him close to the town centre. Now he was on familiar ground.

It was weeks since he had lifted a car. He walked into the nearest pay-and-display parking lot and looked around for an unlocked car. He'd brought his sets of keys with him and soon found a Honda Accord whose passenger door had not been locked. He got in, started up, and drove away whistling. The first part of the plan had gone better than he had hoped, and there was enough petrol in the stolen car to last for the trip to Westborough now and the return late that night.

He left the car in a side road near the Rigby Arms and was in time for a bath before going on duty. If he'd been even five minutes late, Bruce might remember and connect it with the weekend of Jonathan's disappearance, once that was known, and though certain that nothing could ever be proved against him, Terry wanted to run no avoidable risks. He thought that he wouldn't stay at the Rigby much longer; he and Bruce had agreed a three month trial on both sides before deciding on anything permanent, but perhaps he would leave before then. The regular hours were beginning to pall and with Jonathan out of the way there would be no problem about visiting Sue. He would still need money, but he'd find some other project while she worked on Giles. Terry thought about that quite calmly. His attitude to Sue had hardened; he'd got her, now; she could never escape, once this weekend's work was done.

He soaked his aching muscles in hot sudsy water, dreaming of future opulence, and shaved and put on a clean shirt before going on duty.

Terry always liked to be clean and neat.

That afternoon, at Harcombe House, Helen crossly replaced the telephone receiver after finding no one there for the second time. The call that had not come through could have been from an important customer who might be discouraged by failed attempts at dialling. She waited for it to ring again, but in vain, and as she did not need to make a call herself that day, she did not discover that the line had not been cleared.

Giles returned from the office in a subdued frame of mind.

140

He sat in his study drinking until sounds from the kitchen indicated that Helen was dishing up the fish *au gratin* which Mrs Wood had prepared earlier.

'Oh, so you're here tonight, are you?' she said, when he appeared in the doorway.

He did not reply and they ate in silence. When the meal was over they shared the tasks of clearing away and stacking the dishwasher, still not speaking, until Helen reminded him that they were dining out the next night.

'We're alone here all weekend,' she said. 'Sue and Jonathan are away and your mother's gone down to Bournemouth. She left me a note.'

'Oh,' said Giles. 'I didn't know she was going anywhere. Did you?' He meant his mother, but he thought also of Sue.

'No, but neither you nor your mother tell me what you're doing,' said Helen.

Giles stood at the sink drying a cut glass sherry glass which Helen had used and which was too good to go into the machine.

'Do we have to go on like this, Helen?' he asked. 'Can't we at least be civil to one another?'

'Am I being uncivil?' asked Helen. 'Oh, I do beg your pardon, Giles.'

'We should be so grateful to mother,' he said. 'Without her, we wouldn't be living here in this house you wanted so badly.'

'I don't see it like that at all,' said Helen. 'She should be grateful to us for taking her in. Many families wouldn't. But for us, she might be living alone in some nasty little seaside villa or flat.'

Giles did not say that his mother might be much happier doing just that. What was the point? He hung the tea towel carefully in front of the Aga and walked back to his study where he poured himself another tot of whisky. He had tried.

The stolen Honda was still parked where Terry had left it when he went to collect it late that night. After the bar closed and he had turned off the beer and locked up, he had gone to his room and changed from collar and tie into a dark roll-neck sweater. He put on his own car coat and a pair of soft shoes and pocketed his key collections. Tonight there would be no tough cycling; he'd use the bike only to coast down into Twistleton village. It had lights, but if he could see without them, he'd leave them off.

He did not go through Swindon, where the car, by now, had no doubt been reported missing and local police would be watching for it. Terry joined the M4 at the next junction and headed west at a steady seventy miles an hour. There were more cars about than he had expected so late; weekenders, he realized, delaying their departure from London until the main rush was over. He made the journey without any problems and collected the cycle from where he had left it. He would need it again after dumping the Granada. Terry thought in terms of disposing of the car, not what was inside it; he had never found it hard to suppress uncomfortable thoughts.

He abandoned the stolen car on a grass verge above Twistleton village and freewheeled quietly down the hill towards the Court Grange Hotel. He had to use the lamp, for the few street lights in the village were out and there was no moon. Even the hotel was in darkness. Terry folded the cycle and left it a short distance from the gateway. Then he walked quickly back and got into the Granada.

What if it wouldn't start?

But again it fired at the first touch and in minutes Terry had loaded the bike into it and set off up the hill to safety.

Sue heard him go. She had watched television until it closed down, then lain waiting on her bed in the dark. When all the exterior lights at the hotel went out, she had been very relieved, for at the Rigby one burned all night in the car park as some of their guests kept very late hours.

She ran to the window in time to see the Granada's brake lights flash and then disappear.

That was that. That was the end. It was over. Now there was nothing to think of until the next day.

Sue had had her drink in the bar, as Terry had recommended – vodka and lime – and ordered the meal, confiding that her companion had been unwell for a while and that this was why they had come away for a break, but that now he didn't feel up to dining in the restaurant. She had chosen their dinner carefully – a fish dish for Jonathan who, she said, wasn't very hungry, and steak for herself. Sue liked a good piece of rare steak and often chose it at the Rigby. When the two waiters who brought the dinner over to the annexe came into the room they could hear the sound of water running out of the bath. Sue had watched for them with the bath filled and as they knocked on the bedroom door she had pulled the waste plug and closed the bathroom door.

They had brought the whole meal at once; Sue had particularly chosen cold starters and a cold sweet for herself, and cheese and biscuits for Jonathan, to make this possible.

'That will be easier for you and less disturbing for us,' she had said, smiling at the Spanish head waiter.

'I hope the gentleman will be better tomorrow, madam,' the head waiter had said.

As they set out the folding table and arranged the dishes, the main course keeping warm balanced over a flame, the waiters heard Sue call out to Jonathan.

'Dinner's here, darling. Don't be long.'

She gave the waiters a pound each for their trouble. It went against the grain with her, but she knew it was wise insurance.

Sue was very hungry. She had eaten nothing since her sandwich lunch, and she demolished one avocado with prawns, Jonathan's fish dish and her own steak, her cherry *torte* and his cheese and biscuits. She flushed most of the extra vegetables down the lavatory leaving a new potato and some spinach on Jonathan's plate for effect, and she spread his toast with his *pâté de maison* and set it aside for herself later. She poured what was left of the wine into a toothmug. Then she put the table and all the dishes on the landing outside the room and hung the *Please do not disturb* sign on the door.

When the waiter came to remove the table and dishes, he could hear the television on in the room. It drowned any possible sound of voices.

Sue finished the toast and *pâté* and the tumbler of wine when Terry had gone with the car. Then she went straight to sleep and did not wake up until eight o'clock the next morning.

She remembered to muss up Jonathan's bed and crumple his pyjamas as if they had been worn before getting dressed and going over to the main hotel for breakfast.

In the dining-room she expressed surprise at not seeing Jonathan. He had already dressed and gone when she woke, she explained, and she thought he must have decided to go ahead without her. Perhaps he had gone for a walk. She ordered coffee and toast, and ate the whole rackful that was brought, and two warm, crisp rolls.

Then it was time to discover that the Granada was gone, and to ask at the desk if Jonathan had left her a message.

Needless to say, he had not.

17

Terry knew about the old gravel pits from visits there with various ladies afraid of entertaining him in their own houses too often. In summer, it was pleasant among the leafy undergrowth bordering the pits which had been filled in with water and now formed deep dark lakes. He had only to get Jonathan into the driving seat of the car, turn on the ignition so that if the car was found the key was in the right position, and push the car over the side. The fact that it was out of gear would not matter; the impact might have jolted it free.

It was better to do this than set the car alight. Someone would see the blaze and there would be an investigation. This way, Jonathan's disappearance would, in time, be noticed and even looked into, but unless he was found there could be no full enquiry. Water would do its work on the body. Terry did not like to think about all that, but the longer it lay undiscovered, the better.

It took him less than an hour to reach the place, making speed on the motorway though keeping within the limit. He was not in a stolen car now, but he did not want to be stopped by some nosy copper with nothing better to do than harass the innocent. When he turned into the side roads he went on steadily, the headlight beams piercing the darkness. He met no oncoming lights when he reached the lanes.

What a shame to ditch this good car, he thought, enjoying its power. There were years of life in it, and it was worth a tidy bit.

The old pits lay up a track leading away from a lane a mile from the nearest village. It would be all right if the lights were seen; Jonathan, if it were he who was coming here to commit suicide, would need a light to find his way, but the place was so isolated that the chance of witness was remote. He left the track and drove along the rough ground at the edge of the artificial lake, looking for a place where the bushes thinned out and it would be easy to tip the car into the water. In summer people came here with canoes, but it was too small for a marina, as had been suggested by some people. Children had drowned here, stumbling to their deaths down the steep sheer sides. By night it was eerie, too silent: no creatures squeaked or moved in the darkness and all Terry could hear was the sound of his own breathing and the noise of his movements as he got out of the car and went round to the boot. Now came the hardest part, the part he had not practised in his imagination: the fitting of Jonathan in behind the wheel.

As soon as he opened the boot, the sweet sick smell of putrefaction met him; the smell of death. Terry hadn't thought of that, nor had he any experience of it. He held his breath as he took a grip on the blanket and dragged out the body. Rigor mortis had come and gone and the body sagged as he heaved it out of the boot and on to the ground. Terry pulled the blanket off and the dead man's head lolled over. The bag that covered it must be removed, and Terry pulled it away, casting it from him. Bile rose in his throat as he dragged the body towards the door of the car. The sickness seemed likely to overcome him, so he laid the corpse down and moved away to gulp down cold fresh air. This was terrible. Jonathan had been a decent enough fellow who didn't deserve to die so soon. Still, he had struck Sue, Terry reminded himself; he had hurt her and frightened her. That was why he was here now, a dead man to be disposed of. Terry inhaled new resolution with the pure air and returned to his task, putting his hands under the armpits, lifting Jonathan up, heaving him towards the car.

Why do it this way? Why not just tip Jonathan over the edge of the pit and into the water? Then he could go off with the car. It would be so much easier than putting the body behind the wheel, and without the car it might be lost for ever. There was always the risk of part of the car remaining above the surface or being reflected upwards into someone's vision. And getting away with the car would be a piece of cake; he could simply drive off, and in two hours' time or less be in London, where he knew someone who would pay a good price for a Granada. It would soon be a different colour and have a new number plate, no questions asked and money in Terry's pocket that would keep him for two or three months without needing to work.

The decision was easily made.

Soon Terry was on the road to London, driving hard again but watching the limit. Jonathan's body lay beneath the dark still waters of the gravel pit, the surface restored to the glassy calm that had been broken by one loud, single splash.

Early traffic was entering London as Terry reached Hammersmith. He blended with it, driving down the side streets that led to the innocent-seeming workshop which fronted a thriving unofficial used car business. This was a place where someone was on duty all round the clock and Terry soon concluded his deal. He pedalled away on Mavis's bike and reached Paddington station with time for a really good breakfast before catching the train back to Westborough.

The blanket that had covered the body was in the boot of the car.

Sue sat in the hotel lounge after breakfast looking at *Country Life*, which she found dull. It was full of advertisements for houses like Harcombe and bigger. At intervals she rose and went to the door to look out. Twice she walked up to the car park and looked around her as if seeking the Granada.

Major Smythe, the hotel proprietor, noticed the restlessness of his pretty guest as he moved to and fro himself on hotel business. Sue judged her moment and told him that either during the night or early that morning Jonathan had got up, dressed, and driven away without waking her and without leaving a message. The major looked at her warily, hoping there would be no trouble. A conventional man himself, he had opened the hotel with his wife's money on his retirement and he did not like unmarried couples who openly signed the register; a decent concealment of adultery was only good manners, in his opinion. This time, if the fellow didn't turn up, there might be an unpaid bill to chase as well as a missing guest.

He saw the bruise on Sue's cheek, and noticing his gaze Sue touched the place with her own long fingers, their nails newly varnished blood red.

'Odd that he left no note,' the major suggested.

'Yes.' Sue sighed the answer, turning her head so that the light fell more directly on to her face. 'He's been very depressed,' she explained. 'His wife won't divorce him, you see, and we had a quarrel.' She touched her cheek again and the major felt chilled. 'This was to be a sort of honeymoon weekend, to forget.'

'You're not thinking of telling the police?'

'Oh no!' Sue looked directly at the major. She had large, dark, tragic eyes. How could the fellow go off and leave her? 'He'll come back,' she said. 'Won't he?'

'Of course he will,' the major assured her, relieved that she didn't seem panicky, simply sad. 'Perhaps he's just thinking things out,' he suggested. He wanted no scandal at the hotel. It would help no one to have the police here when all that had happened was a domestic dispute. Major Smythe was on good terms with the Chief Constable and had been grateful for police discretion before now when dealing with pilfering staff. So far, no guests had reported problems more serious than the loss of a few trinkets. A notice warned them to place valuables in the hotel safe and absolved the management from responsibility. You couldn't watch everyone all the time.

With luck the fellow would reappear in time to pay his account and go.

Somehow, Sue got through the day. There was nothing at all to do. She strolled in the grounds and round the village. At twelve she had a drink in the bar and started talking to a middle-aged man who was waiting for his wife. The wife looked daggers at Sue when she found the pair of them in lively conversation. Sue smiled inwardly as she recognized the look. It was so easy. You just had to make them think themselves important, flatter their stupid male egos; then they ate out of your hand, as Giles was doing.

Giles. Her thoughts hardened. She wouldn't wait long: just a decent amount of time while people accepted that Jonathan had left her. Once Giles knew that Jonathan had hit her, he would be Sir Galahad himself, Sue thought.

Lunch was not included in the weekend terms, so she had cold ham and chicken in the bar. The other couple ate there too, but did not ask her to join them. The husband made a small, sad *moue*, shrugging silently as he caught Sue's eye. She sat demurely with a second vodka and lime – the first had been bought by her new friend – and her meal, exchanging glances with him while his wife's attention was fixed on her own plate.

It passed the time.

She had a bath and repainted her nails before dinner, using a different varnish: bright coral. The maid had tidied the room. Jonathan's anorak and cap were both in the wardrobe. Sue lay on the bed watching television before going over to the restaurant.

Major Smythe was in the hall greeting his various guests. He asked Sue if she had had any news, but there was nothing to report.

'Have you tried ringing your home?' asked the major. 'He may be there.' He assumed they lived together.

Sue thought quickly. It was a reasonable suggestion.

'I've tried,' she said. 'There was no reply.'

'You mentioned his wife,' said the major, with some embarrassment. What messy lives people led! 'Might she know where he is? Do you know her address?' This was more tactful than suggesting that Jonathan had returned to her.

'I do, but I couldn't ring her,' said Sue. 'She hates me. She won't let her children meet me.'

'Tch, tch.' The major pondered. 'Should I ring her?' he wondered aloud. 'Just ask for him? If he's there, she'll say so. If he comes to the telephone you can speak to him and ask him his plans.' And I, perhaps, can refer to the account, the major reflected. 'Perhaps a male voice – ?' he added.

Sue turned the idea over in her mind. It could do no harm.

'I'm not sure – ' she began, but the major broke in.

'Surely it's reasonable?' he insisted.

Sue understood the major's problem about the bill, though she would not allude to it; what would Bruce do at the Rigby in such a case? And what would be wisest for herself? Terry had not foreseen this complication.

Sue did not want to offend the major. She gave in and went with him to his office while he looked up Hilary's number in the complete set of directories which he kept there. While he dialled and the number rang, Sue sat in a deep leather armchair trying to wear an expression combining the right amount of concern and apprehension; it was not difficult.

'Oh – ' she heard the major say. 'May I speak to Mr Jonathan Cooper, please?'

There was a curt reply. The major glanced across at Sue, shaking his head.

'Not there? I see. Where can I find him, do you know?'

There was a further short squawk from the telephone.

'Yes, I have that address,' said the major suavely.

Sue could hear the interrogative note in the next remark from the telephone.

'My name is Smythe,' she heard the major answer. 'I am the owner of the Court Grange Hotel, Twistleton. Mr Cooper has been our guest and we want to get in touch with him.'

Hilary said something else.

'I quite understand,' said the major calmly. 'I'm sorry to have troubled you. Goodbye,' and he replaced the receiver. 'She hasn't seen him for two weeks, since he last visited the children,' he told Sue. 'I'm sorry.'

Sue turned a tearful face towards him.

'Thank you,' she whispered.

The major himself escorted her to a quiet corner of the restaurant and ordered her a half bottle of the best burgundy with the compliments of the house. He murmured to the head waiter. Sue received assiduous attention throughout the meal, some of it from the two waiters who had served dinner in the room the previous night.

She knew she should peck at her food, but she couldn't hold back.

'Worry always makes me hungry,' she told the waiter, with truth. So did anger and sex.

Everyone disappeared from the residents' lounge as soon as their coffee was finished. Off to fuck, Sue thought. She would not stay there alone, and she did not want to talk to the major again. She went to her room where she took off her black dress, loosened her hair from the tight knot in which she had worn it for dinner, and lay on the bed watching television.

After a while she began to day-dream about the future when Giles would be eating out of her hand, granting her every whim. They would go to Barbados or Nice in the winter, she planned, and with them would be Terry. Perhaps he could become Giles's valet or chauffeur, or maybe his secretary. Giles would age rapidly and they would have plenty of chances to be together. The fact that Giles would need to earn his living was ignored in this scenario.

She wished she could ring Terry, to see how things had gone, but the call would be billed and might be traced. She blessed the day Alice Armitage had crashed her car into Terry's. They would be kind to Alice; she was resolved about that; they would take her about with them when they travelled, and find her some nice flat. They wouldn't want her around all the time.

The one flaw in this bright future was Helen. Would she make trouble? She might use some of the money. She could have an accident, Sue mused, lying there in the warm, comfortable room alone, while in other apartments in the hotel guests soothed old hurts with caresses or tried to recapture youthful illusions. Terry knew a lot about cars; he could fix Helen's in some way. They must be ready to snatch any chance that came for although they were both young, now was the time for the good things in life before you were too old to enjoy them. Look at Giles. What was the good of having all that money and being too miserable to enjoy it?

Restless, she got up from the bed, put on slacks, sweater and jacket and went out of the building into the grounds. Lamps were placed here and there on the paths and walks so that guests could safely ramble after dark. The night was full of sounds. A dog fox barked in the distance, although Sue did not know that that was what it was. Some silent creature brushed past her face as she wandered along – a bat? Horrified, Sue put her hands to her head, holding her long hair tight against invasion. There were small squeaking sounds in the grass, and a faint singing came from the river. Sue reached a small bridge that spanned it and looked down at the dark water sliding by.

She shivered, standing there, and turned back towards the brightly lit block of the main hotel, an urban product hurrying back to known comfort.

Sue slept badly that night and dreamed of Jonathan wringing his hands and weeping, with blood pouring down his face from a wound above his eye.

18

Sue dropped off into a heavy slumber with the dawn, and did not wake until nine.

She rang for breakfast in her room, thinking to hell with toast and coffee and ordering eggs and bacon. She ate every scrap of food that was brought.

It was nearly eleven o'clock by the time she was ready for the day and went over to the main building. Major Smythe saw her enter the hall and could tell from her expression that she had had no news.

He suggested that she should telephone Harcombe again. By now the wanderer might have returned. Sue saw that he would think it unreasonable if she refused and allowed him to put through the call.

The line was engaged, he told her, coming out of his office all smiles.

'Engaged?' How could it be engaged when no one was there?

'If you ring again soon, you'll be able to speak to him,' said the major.

Sue's heart was thudding. Then she remembered the call she had made to Helen before she and Terry left Harcombe on Friday afternoon. The phone had been left off the hook.

'Yes,' she said, and then, 'No, I don't think I'll do that – I think I'll just get back.' She opened her eyes wide at the major. 'Not to make a fuss, you know.'

The major didn't. He thought the whole thing most regrettable. Sue asked for her bill and the major himself made it up.

'There's no phone call on it,' he said, frowning. 'You said you had telephoned your home.'

'Yes – yes, I did,' said Sue. Drat him! He was out for every penny he could get.

'Our mistake – never mind,' said the major, determined to check the arrangements for billing telephone calls, as if one was missed, others would be and that must be stopped. The major presented Sue with the totalled account, less telephone call.

Sue paid it in cash with some of the money Terry had given her. That would finish the matter as far as the major was concerned. She asked about trains, and the major looked them up. There was one in just over an hour.

Sue doubted if she would be ready in time to catch it as she hadn't yet packed, but the major, although he thought her a taking little thing, wanted this ended. He assured her that there would be plenty of time and ordered a taxi. He had been relieved to see that her wallet was comfortingly full of banknotes.

She was eager to leave, but when the taxi dropped her at the small country station, she saw a blackboard notice on the platform announcing that the train she had come to catch had been cancelled. British Rail regretted any inconvenience.

'You can say that again,' muttered Sue. She left her cases in the ticket office and went into a pub near the station, where she had two vodkas and lime and a ploughman's. It was after four when she reached Westborough and she took a taxi straight to the Rigby.

'Terry about?' Sue asked Anthea, on duty at reception.

'He was. He's gone off,' said Anthea.

He would have, of course, since the bar was closed. Their plan had ended with her taking a taxi back to Harcombe but now she had altered the script. She went down the yard and up to his room.

Terry, exhausted after his night without sleep on Friday

and all his physical exertions, had arrears of sleep still to make up and was lost to the world when she tried his door. It was locked, but she rattled it, calling his name, and he woke with a jerk, hurrying over to open it, finger to lip, his expression furious.

'What are you doing here?' He hissed the words at her.

Sue came into the room.

'What do I do now?' she asked.

Terry put a hand over her mouth. One of the waiters slept in the next room and was probably in there now.

'Don't say anything,' he whispered, nodding at the thin dividing wall, and then, more loudly, 'Oh – Sue – did you have a nice weekend?'

Sue stared at him. Then she got the message.

'Well – er – no. Jonathan went off,' she said.

Terry nodded encouragingly.

'Went off? What do you mean?' he said.

'He disappeared on Friday night,' said Sue. 'Took the car and vanished. I don't know where he is. I waited until today, but he hasn't come back.'

'Oh, I expect he'll turn up,' said Terry easily. 'Maybe he'll be at home when you get there.'

'Do you think so?' said Sue.

'Yes, I'm sure of it,' said Terry. 'Better get back, hadn't you, and see?'

She stared at him. Surely he would take her?

'Get a taxi,' Terry said, impatiently. Then, as she still stared at him blankly, he whispered, 'I haven't got the car yet. My car.'

'Oh!' Sue was briefly at a loss, but then she said softly, 'Come with me.'

Terry pondered. He must collect his car as soon as he could. If they went in a taxi to Great Minton, he could fetch it and drop her off at the lodge. It would save him a bus ride or a trip on the small bike – he hadn't decided yet how to go. He grinned.

'All right,' he said.

He would leave Sue at the gates to Harcombe House. She would have to manage the next bit alone; he had done his part for the present.

*   *   *

Alice's weekend visit to Bournemouth had not been a great success. She had felt adventurous setting off on the spur of the moment and making such a long trip, for all her recent journeys had been short ones in the Westborough area. The hotel she had chosen was in a side road not far from the sea and only a mile from Windlea. It was small and quiet; there was a bathroom just along the corridor from her bedroom. Alice unpacked her case and set out her bedroom slippers, pink fluffy mules, ready for use. You soon grew accustomed to having everything near at hand, she thought, feeling strange for a moment. Then she pulled herself together and went down to the hall where there was a pay-phone.

Alice dialled her friend Audrey's number. Perhaps, when Audrey heard how near she was, she would invite Alice round for dinner. Alice waited patiently for an answer as the telephone rang in Audrey's house, but there was no reply. There was nothing for it but to make the best of the evening on her own.

The drive had tired her. She went in to dinner promptly at half-past seven, finding three other elderly ladies ahead of her at the door as two strokes on a gong rang out. A friendly middle-aged waitress showed her to a distant table, smiling pleasantly. Dinner was served at a good speed. Alice enjoyed a glass of the house burgundy with her meal, and took coffee later in the lounge. The other three ladies and a couple all finished eating at much the same time. The couple, after conferring together in low voices, left the room, and the three ladies asked Alice if she played bridge. When she said that she didn't, they looked disappointed.

'We can often make up a four with a weekend visitor,' said one of them.

Alice discovered that they lived in the hotel. In the winter they had excellent rooms, but in the summer they had to move to lesser apartments, leaving the best rooms free for holiday guests. Their weekly payments helped to keep the hotel solvent through the winter. The three began complaining about the meal, which Alice had thought was good. Wearied, she soon said goodnight and went up to her room where she whiled away the rest of the evening watching television, just as she did at home.

154

In the morning she telephoned Audrey and again there was no reply. Alice put on her coat with the fur collar and went for a walk past Windlea. She stood in the road looking up at the house. The room with the bow window on the first floor had been hers and Walter's; there they had lain together in unexciting contentment through most of their long marriage, their roles at home calmly dove-tailed. The years of Walter's retirement had been, in some ways, the best. He had spent happy hours at the bowls club; Alice had joined a flower arranging group. Never great walkers, they often went out for the day in the car to look at country houses and Walter became interested in paintings because they saw so many. At home, he gardened while Alice cooked or read novels from the library. They did not talk a great deal because most of the time they knew each other's wishes and views. Each, now, accepted the other's limitations and strengths. We trusted one another, Alice thought, noticing how the window frames had been painted blue. As she walked on she could see a swing in the garden. It was good to know that other children would enjoy the garden where Giles had bowled to Walter and where they could climb the old apple tree and build a camp fire in the spinney.

Giles should have married some local girl who would have been content with the unambitious security he could offer. He was orbiting around in a world he wasn't equipped to deal with. Amanda and Dawn were growing up; soon they would be leaving home and what would be left for him then? Alice had made a dreadful mistake in letting herself be persuaded to join them, but how could she pull out now? She could never get her capital back – or not without a terrible row involving the sale of the house, and that, she saw, would break up the marriage. She switched off her mind at this thought. Alice belonged to a generation who took its marriage vows seriously.

She came to Audrey's house. It had the blank look of one that was empty. She turned away and went to the end of the road where she caught the bus into town, an easier thing to do than taking the car on a busy Saturday. She spent the rest of the morning strolling round the shops and bought a new pair of bronze patent shoes with ankle straps and slim heels and a <u>fawn</u> fluffy sweater. Then she had lunch in a salad bar which was new since she left, and after that went to the cinema.

She left Bournemouth straight after breakfast on Sunday without making contact with any of her former acquaintances, and as she drove home the painful tears came into her eyes. She belonged nowhere now.

She put the car in the barn. The Granada was missing; Jonathan and Sue would not be back until later from their weekend away, she supposed. Alice hoped it had been more successful than hers. There were two strange cars parked outside the main house; Helen's guests for lunch, presumably.

Letting herself in, creeping upstairs, afraid of meeting her son's awesome wife, Alice wondered how she could go on living like this for what might be another ten years – maybe more. What would happen then, when she could no longer manage the stairs? Would she be packed off to some home for the ancient, to spend her days propped up in a row amid other old people with no teeth and few wits, waiting for death? It would be better to get there first, to beat the fiend. Helen would not mind at all, she thought bleakly; indeed, she would be relieved. Dawn would scarcely notice, though Amanda, for a while, might miss their Scrabble and Horlicks and her grandmother's interest in Mr Jinks. What about Giles? Would he grieve? Would it lift her from his conscience?

She knew that it wouldn't; she would remain on it for ever if he found her one day with a plastic bag over her face.

Perhaps she could build up some sort of life, if she really tried. Mrs Duncan, for instance, was pleasant and friendly, though forceful and always busy. She was not in the least pretentious. Could Alice ask her round for a glass of sherry, or even supper, here in the flat? Or Mrs Hedges, who was perhaps less alarming? But then she must invite Miss Wilson too, and there wouldn't be space.

Alice thought she would try Mrs Duncan. She spun a brief fantasy in which, instead of accepting Alice's invitation, Mrs Duncan asked her down to the Old Vicarage.

But the telephone was out of order. Alice jiggled and pushed at the receiver rest but could get no dialling tone. At first she thought someone was there, connected and listening silently to her own tense breathing as she held the receiver to her ear. But no one spoke. The line was dead.

Later that afternoon, Alice was asleep with the television set on when Giles came in.

'Oh mother, you're here,' he exclaimed in surprise. 'I didn't think you'd be back yet.'

Alice abruptly woke from a dream in which Helen had turned into an octopus and was slowly strangling Giles with one tentacle after another. Now, she focused on her unstrangled son who stood before her, a middle-aged man with a high complexion and fleshy nose, thinning hair and a harassed expression. How had that pretty little boy, to whom she had read about Winnie the Pooh and Toad, turned into this defeated figure? Where was the long, lean lad who had played cricket on the lawn at Windlea with his father and keenly followed the Test matches?

'Oh – yes, dear,' Alice said, blinking. 'I'm back.'

Giles, in his turn, was for the first time seeing his mother as really old. She was always so elegant and had kept her neat figure, and though her face was lined, he never saw her without her extensive make-up. Now, surprised in sleep, she sat up in the armchair with her hair disordered and her face blotchy. She couldn't have been crying, surely? He peered at her more closely.

'Are you all right?' he asked. 'Didn't you enjoy your weekend?'

'I'm quite all right, thank you, Giles,' said Alice. 'It made a nice break.' There was no point in telling him otherwise. She looked at him questioningly. There must be a reason for this visit – and at a time when he expected her to be out. She was guiltily aware of her illicit heater burning its head off a few feet away.

He was explaining.

'I came to see if your phone was working,' he said, anxious that she should not think either he or Helen might pry round in her absence. Old people's privacy was important. Old people: he reminded himself that his mother was old. 'Ours is on the blink,' he went on. 'I thought perhaps it was just us and that yours was all right.'

In fact, Helen had suggested that Alice might have left hers off the hook, though Giles had pointed out that if she had – and such carelessness was right out of character – the instrument would be buzzing. Now he could see that the receiver was in place. Before Alice could say that she had already discovered her telephone was out of order he had lifted the receiver and pressed the rest. Nothing happened.

'No,' he said. 'It's dead too.'

'Oh dear,' said Alice. 'Do you want to make a call?'

'Helen does,' said Giles. 'No one's called us for a couple of days but we haven't wanted to ring out so we didn't realize something was wrong. Helen wants to speak to a client. It's important. I'll have to report it.'

'They won't mend it today, will they?' asked Alice. 'Not on a Sunday.'

'No, I suppose not,' said Giles. 'Well, I'm glad you're back, mother.' Then he lost his head. 'Come down and have supper with us, will you? I'm sure there's plenty.'

Alice's heart glowed and she smiled at her son, whom she loved. She knew he would regret the words as soon as he realized he would have to tell Helen what he had done, so she saved him in advance.

'Thank you, dear, but I won't, if you don't mind,' she said. 'I'll probably eat early and go to bed. I'm a little tired after the drive.'

Giles's slow-moving mind had caught up with her thoughts in just the manner she had anticipated and he heard her with relief.

'Another time, then,' he said. 'When Helen's out. She's out a lot these days. Just the two of us, eh?'

Alice nodded, eyes bright.

Giles glanced round the room. He had noticed how cosy it was when he entered, and was pleased; she must be quite snug up here. Now he saw the convector warmly glowing. Funny: he hadn't seen it before, but then he so seldom came up here. He thought she had just the fire and the fan he had bought.

Alice followed his glance and again forestalled him.

'I see you've noticed my new heater,' she said briskly. 'I don't leave it on when I'm out, and it was rather cold.'

'No – well – ' Giles hoped Helen wouldn't discover what Alice had done. 'It'll be better next year, when the new heating system's in,' he said lamely.

Alice wept a little more when he had gone. He was trapped. And so was she.

'What an age you've been, Giles,' said Helen when he returned. 'Well?'

'Well, what?'

'What about the telephone, of course? Had she left it off?'

'No. It's dead,' said Giles shortly.

'Well, I must ring my client,' said Helen. 'I'll use the telephone in the lodge and report this out of order at the same time.'

'Jonathan and Sue are away,' said Giles.

'I know that,' said Helen. 'But I've got a key, haven't I? I can go in and use the telephone, for God's sake.'

'Couldn't you go down to the call-box in the village?' said Giles. 'They may not like you wandering round the house while they're out.'

'I shan't be wandering round, as you put it,' said Helen. 'I'll simply be using their telephone, and I'll do it through the operator, ADC, and refund them the cost. Will that satisfy you?'

Giles saw that it was useless to argue. He went off to his study with the *Sunday Times* while Helen, in her tight black pants and padded Indian jacket, took the spare keys of the lodge from her desk and walked off down the drive.

Some ten minutes later the telephone rang. There were three instruments in Harcombe House apart from the one in Alice's attic, and one was in the kitchen. Giles crossed through and lifted the receiver.

'Hullo?' he said.

'Oh – so it is working now,' said Helen's voice. 'How strange. I thought I'd just try it, after I'd made my call. The receiver here was off the hook. How very odd. Ring back, will you, when I've hung up, to make sure it's all right.' She cut the line.

Giles hung up, waited a short time and then dialled the lodge. Helen answered at once.

He worked it out while she was on her way back to the house. Jonathan or Sue must have called on Friday, been somehow distracted and failed to clear the line before going away. Sue had been ringing him, he thought fatuously, forgetting that this must have happened during the afternoon, while he was at work.

'How extraordinary to go away leaving the telephone off the hook,' Helen said, so puzzled that she actually spoke to Giles about it. 'I had two false calls on Friday afternoon – I answered but no one was there. I suppose that was just coincidence.'

She hadn't understood, Giles thought, almost tittering in delight that here was something she wasn't so wonderfully clever about. He didn't tell her. Let her work it out for herself.

It was strange that Sue had rung twice, without speaking either time. Perhaps the first call had been some other misdial, and Sue, hearing Helen, had realized that he would be out and had lost her cool, leaving the receiver off.

The flattering nature of this deduction blinded Giles to its oddness; by the time that dawned, he had learned that Jonathan was missing.

19

Alice was restless when Giles had gone. She fidgeted about, tidying the already tidy sitting-room. Then she washed through stockings and underwear worn in Bournemouth. After that she looked out of the window wondering if Sue and Jonathan were back.

She could see a thread of light between the drawn curtains at the lodge window, and outside, in the rays cast from the exterior light, she recognized Terry's car.

What was he doing there?

Spending the evening with Jonathan and Sue was the obvious, straightforward explanation, but Alice was not certain just how straightforward a person Terry was. Things happened when he was about, and not always for the best.

As she stood at her window, watching and wondering, the lodge door opened and Terry emerged. He walked quickly down the path, got into his car, started the engine, turned on the lights and drove off. A moment later the door opened again and Sue came out. She walked up to the front door of the main house, just out of Alice's line of vision. There was an instant when a panel of light fell on the ground as the front door was opened and then all was dark once more.

Sue had gone for advice.

She and Terry had discussed what to do, what would be natural had things been as they seemed

'Was it all right? No one saw you?' she had asked him, and he'd reassured her, not giving any details.

'It's not nice, manhandling a dead man,' he told her. 'I don't want to go into it.'

'Well, what now?' Sue had said. 'I can't just go on as if nothing's happened, can I? There's the rent, for a start. It's paid to the end of the month, but I can't manage after that on my own. And there's his work – Jonathan's. Do I get in touch with his boss?'

Terry pondered. What would be best? She was right, she couldn't just do nothing; but if anyone reported Jonathan missing, the police would start nosing around looking for him. They would not find him, of course – nor the car. It would be an unsolved mystery. He did not want Sue to find out what he had done with the car but he was very glad that he'd changed the plan. That money under his mattress was a nice little piece of insurance. Though it went against the grain to do it, he had paid back what he had borrowed from the till. That alone justified selling the car, for if the money had been missed, he would have been the obvious suspect. He would have had to find some cash – and fast – otherwise, and had not looked ahead to that beyond thinking that Mrs Armitage would come up trumps if he pressed her.

Funny that he didn't fancy Sue any more. She hadn't changed. She was still lively and pretty, and Christ, did she want it! But he didn't, now. She was the only girl he'd ever truly fancied for herself, but he'd suddenly gone right off her.

'You're on good terms with Giles,' he said. 'I think you should tell him. Go up to the house and ask their advice – both of them. That would be normal.'

'And then?' asked Sue.

'Do as they say,' said Terry. 'If they think you should ring his boss, do it.'

'What if they think I should tell the police?'

'Oh – stall. Say you'll give it a bit longer in case he just comes walking in, as then you'd feel silly. Besides, he might be angry.'

Sue nodded. She had wanted to go to bed then, but he wouldn't, so when he had gone she went straight up to the house.

Giles opened the door.

'Why, Sue, oh!' His delight at seeing her was plain. All the sagging folds on his face lifted, his mouth curved into a smile of joy, his eyes crinkled. Sue thought he looked quite nice when he was happy. 'Come in, come in,' he said.

Sue stepped over the threshold. She wore a red suede jacket over her slacks, and her long dark hair was loose. She smelled of the scent she always wore, plus that indefinable other essence that was always about her and which Giles did not recognize as sheer femininity.

'I don't know what to do, Giles,' she said, standing close to him, looking up at him. The bruise on her face was fading now. He would be furious if he knew that Jonathan had hit her.

'Why, what's wrong?' he asked. He led her into the big drawing-room where they had held Alice's party and where a log fire burned. The air was smoky from the cigars and cigarettes of the lunch-time guests. Though she never smoked herself, Sue liked the smell of tobacco. 'Come and sit down,' said Giles, leading her to a seat by the fire. 'Shall I take your coat?'

She let him, allowing the weight of her hair to brush

against his hand. Now was her chance to make a bid for sympathy. She sat at one end of the long sofa, hoping that Giles would think of sitting beside her. He might not; he was so dumb.

But he did, timidly placing himself not at the further end, yet not too close to her. To see her clearly he must either put on his glasses or keep a distance between them.

'Now, what's wrong?' he said.

'Jonathan's gone,' said Sue.

'Gone? What do you mean?' cried Giles. 'You don't mean he's left you?' That couldn't be true.

'I don't know. He just vanished while we were at Twistleton,' said Sue. 'Took off in the car during the night while I was asleep, and never came back.' She told him what had happened at the hotel – how Major Smythe had telephoned Hilary and how in the end she had come home alone.

'You should have rung me,' said Giles. 'I'd have come for you.' He forgot that their telephone had been out of order.

'How could you? You had guests,' said Sue in a gently reproving tone. 'But what shall I do, Giles? If he doesn't come back – ' she did not end the sentence.

'Oh, he will – he'll get in touch, anyway,' said Giles. What a scoundrel the mild-seeming Jonathan must be! 'He'll want his things – his clothes and so on, if he's really left. I'm sure he'll come back, Sue.' How could he not return to this delicious girl? 'Perhaps he's ill. You said he was depressed. It's the only explanation, isn't it? Maybe he had a blackout. Have you rung the hospitals?'

She had not thought of doing that, she told him.

'I'll do it,' said Giles, becoming masterful.

It took him quite a long time, and while he was telephoning, Helen came to speak to Sue.

'Giles told me what's happened. I'm sorry,' she said. 'Beastly for you. Embarrassing.'

'Yes,' said Sue.

'You paid the hotel?'

'Oh yes,' said Sue, surprised that this should be Helen's first question. Giles hadn't thought of that. Money wasn't important to him, but it mattered to his wife, just as it did to her.

'I'll get you a drink,' said Helen. 'I'm sure you need one. How did you get back?'

Sue told her about the train and added that she had gone to the Rigby Arms and Terry had brought her home.

'Oh, of course – he's an old friend of yours, isn't he?' said Helen, who had seen him about the place. 'I suppose you'll move back to Westborough, if Jonathan's gone for good.' I'll need new tenants, she thought. She'd put up the rent.

'I don't know,' said Sue. What if Terry shared the lodge with her? That would be great. He would keep out of the way while she worked on Giles.

'Oh well – time enough to decide when you know what's happened,' said Helen.

She fetched Sue a vodka and lime and a gin and tonic for herself, and began to tell Sue about a house she had been asked to do up near Slough, for a pop star. She had never done that sort of place before and was finding it hard to adapt her ideas to his wish for psychedelic effects. Sue found the conversation fascinating.

'Not your scene, really, is it?' she said.

'No. I thought of turning it down at first,' said Helen. 'But one should seize every opportunity that comes along. You never know where it may lead.'

'That's right,' agreed Sue, who also never passed up a chance.

She had almost forgotten why she had come by the time Giles returned, having drawn blank at all the hospitals he had called.

'The next thing to do is to tell the police,' he said.

'Oh no!' exclaimed Sue. 'Nothing can have happened to him. If he'd had an accident, the hospitals would know.'

What if he'd been killed, wondered Giles.

'You'd hear, if he'd been in a road accident,' said Helen. 'The police would get in touch with you.'

'Would they?' asked Giles. 'Wouldn't they tell his wife?'

'What address would he have on him?' asked Helen.

Sue didn't know. She said the car belonged to the firm but she did not know if it was registered in their name or his.

'Shall I ring his wife?' Giles suggested. 'It's some time

since the hotel rang her, after all, and maybe she's heard from him by now. He's fond of his children, isn't he?'

'If he's lost his memory or something, he'll have forgotten about them,' Sue said, rather wildly. She didn't want anyone ringing Hilary again.

But Helen thought it could do no harm. She poured Sue another drink while Giles made the call. He came back shaking his head.

'Would you like to stay here for the night, Sue?' he offered, and went blithely on, ignoring Helen's frown. 'Perhaps you'd better not be on your own?'

'He might come back in the night,' said Helen bluntly. 'You'd better be there.'

Giles escorted her back to the lodge door. He kissed her chastely on the brow.

'Poor little Sue,' he said. 'Let me know if there's any news – anything I can do.'

'You can take me to work in the morning,' said Sue promptly, and he beamed.

'Of course.' He squeezed her hand. Now he had something to look forward to.

'I'm so glad I've got you to turn to, Giles,' said Sue as a sweetener, and went into the house.

The storage heaters kept the chill off, but the fire was not lit and she had nothing for supper except what might be in the fridge. Sue looked round in distaste. Terry hadn't even taken the cases upstairs: there they were, in the middle of the sitting-room.

Sue left Jonathan's where it was and took her own up to the bedroom where the bed was unmade and her discarded clothes were strewn about. It was all very different from the luxurious room at the Court Grange where she had spent the last two nights. A maid – someone to clear up after her – that's what she needed, Sue thought, opening her case and flinging a few garments about. That pop star Helen was working for had one for sure. Sue couldn't think why Helen had only Mrs Wood from the village. Of course, in a place that size you didn't get into such a mess, she thought; there was space for things to lie about. Sue forgot that things were never left lying about in Helen's tidy house.

How could she get through the evening?

Sue went down to the kitchen. Half a loaf of bread, mouldy now, sat on the kitchen table where she had left it on Friday. There was no fresh milk.

Alice would have some. Alice would offer her something to eat, even if it was only scrambled egg. Sue was starving. She had had only a scratch lunch in the pub near the station and now two vodkas and lime.

She had better ring the old girl.

Sue went to the telephone to dial Alice's number. As she waited for the old woman to answer, she was aware of something not quite as she expected it to be, but it was not until late that night, when she was in bed among the grubby, tumbled sheets, that she remembered she had left the telephone off the hook when she went off with Terry on Friday. Who had replaced it? Terry?

At the big house, Helen, too, forgot about it until after Sue had gone.

'We never asked her what she or Jonathan rang up about on Friday,' she said. 'And why they didn't hang up.'

'It must have been Jonathan,' said Giles. 'Perhaps he put the phone down while he fetched something and then forgot about it. He seems pretty mixed up just now.'

'It's all very unsatisfactory,' said Helen.

Giles thought that Jonathan might be having a breakdown. Things might simply have become too much for him, a state with which Giles himself had some sympathy.

Sue had forgotten that when Giles and Helen were in, telephone calls to Alice had to be put through from the main house and she was disconcerted to hear Giles's voice on the line. He switched her through without comment.

'Can I pop up and see you?' Sue asked, when Alice answered.

'Yes, of course, Sue,' said Alice. 'That will be lovely. I'm all alone.'

Giles was listening, and he felt fresh guilt. The main house was so large. Why couldn't his mother be downstairs now, in the warm drawing-room beside the log fire? Their guests had gone and Helen would be spending the evening in her sitting-room. He sighed. He saw no way out of this toil, but if Jonathan didn't come back, he resolved to offer his mother the lodge, no matter what Helen said. He could see that Sue would not stay there alone; she couldn't afford it, and without a car she would be marooned.

But of course Jonathan would return, though surely his future with Sue must be uncertain now. Had he known of their quarrel, Giles's thoughts might have pursued this line in relation to himself further than he let them tonight.

When Sue told Alice what had happened at the Court Grange, the old woman was appalled. There was so much sorrow about; she hated to think of it. She suggested that Jonathan might have felt remorse about having struck Sue and had gone off to think things over, but it was thoughtless to have left no explanatory note. And leaving her in the hotel without paying the bill and with no means of getting home was irresponsible, to say the least.

'I'd have fetched you, my dear,' she said, just as Giles had done.

'You were away,' said Sue, and asked Alice about her weekend. She laughed at Alice's description of the permanent guests at the hotel and their complaints. She had worked in a hotel like that before coming to the Rigby.

'Have you had supper, Sue?' Aliced asked, and when the girl said no, at once began fussing round looking for something to feed her on. She had intended to have a boiled egg herself.

Sue felt slightly ashamed at having forced Alice's hand over providing the meal, but reminded herself that she was cheering the poor old thing up in her solitude. They had baked beans and poached eggs, with toast, and Alice opened a tin of peaches. They ate with their plates balanced on magazines on their knees watching television, and it was really quite cosy. Sue left when she saw that Alice was having trouble concealing her yawns. She promised to let the old lady know at once if there was news.

'Do you think I should ring his boss in the morning?' asked Sue.

'Oh yes,' Alice said, and Giles agreed when she consulted him on her way in to work the next day.

She telephoned from the Rigby. She'd forgotten to bring Jonathan's diary, so she had to look his firm's number up in the directory and she couldn't tell his employer what calls he had arranged for that day. Mr Prentiss sounded rather annoyed, but it wasn't her fault, Sue told him. She explained what had happened.

Mr Prentiss sat fuming in his office after the call. Jonathan Cooper was not the world's most wonderful salesman but he was conscientious, his figures were reliable and he was popular with their customers. He could be replaced without any trouble if he was developing a temperament, but it was to be hoped that this was some brief folly which would soon be over.

At eleven-fifteen a customer whom Jonathan was to have met earlier that day telephoned to enquire where he was. Mr Prentiss soothed him. Then he rang Hilary. She was the man's wife, after all, and if she would not report the man missing, Mr Prentiss most certainly would.

Hilary was on the defensive at once, as soon as she knew who was calling, and why.

'How should I know where he is?' she asked. 'You'd better ask that woman – Mrs whatever-her-name-is.'

Mr Prentiss was not so hard-hearted that he did not recognize the anguish in Hilary's voice, nor was he deceived by her pretence of forgetting the name of her supplanter.

'She doesn't know,' he told her. 'He walked out on her during a weekend break they were having at Twistleton. 'And she rang last Friday to say that he wasn't well. I'm so sorry to distress you, Mrs Cooper, but I need to know what's happening.'

So did Hilary. This was the third call she had received about Jonathan, and her livelihood and the children's depended on him.

'What do you want me to do?' she asked.

'Report him missing to the police,' said Mr Prentiss. 'I understand that his landlord telephoned the hospitals last night, with no result, but the police will make a more thorough job of doing that. He may not have rung them all.'

'Oh!' There was a shock in Hilary's voice.

'Or I will, if you prefer,' said Mr Prentiss. 'But in any case I'm sure they will want to ask you about him.' He was thinking that Jonathan was unlikely to have been involved in a motor accident, for in that case his car would have been checked out by the police and his identity discovered.

Hilary was still Jonathan's wife.

'I'll do it,' she said. 'If you really think it's necessary.'

'He may need help,' said Mr Prentiss. The man had such a nice, if rather earnest wife, and the children were sweet. What got into people, wondered Mr Prentiss wearily; what made them fly off in their middle years? The fear of missing something? 'The sooner we know where he is, the better,' he said and added that unless she called him first, he would telephone later to see what the police had said.

Hilary sent the children next door to her neighbour while she made the call. It would not do for them to overhear this sort of conversation. She explained the trouble briefly, in whispers. Her neighbour was kind and helpful and had been a great support in the early days of Jonathan's fall from grace; it was she, when she heard of it from someone else, who had felt bound to tell Hilary about his affair.

Hilary kept her voice steady on the telephone. She explained to the female voice which answered that she wanted to report her husband missing. She was asked to hold on and then connected with a different voice, male and slow-speaking, which asked for her name and address. Hilary's control wavered then, and her words came out jerkily as she related what she knew about Jonathan's disappearance.

She was told that an officer would be with her shortly to take down the details.

Very soon, an area car drew up outside and a woman police officer in uniform came to the door. Hilary showed her into the sitting-room. WPC Grace Ferris took a quick look round to gain an impression of where she was. She saw a beige carpet, sand-coloured curtains at the long windows, books in a recess. There were prints on the wall, a Canaletto over the fireplace and Redouté roses on the other walls. It was a relief to see two toy cars parked on the hearthstone and knitting bundled up on the sofa, for the room looked clinically clean and bare.

'It may all be a fuss about nothing,' said Hilary nervously.

'It's not about nothing, if you're worried,' said the policewoman. 'Tell me why you're anxious.' She smiled encouragingly at the pale young woman much her own age who wore a beige shetland sweater over a brown shirt, and a baggy beige tweed skirt. 'Let's sit down, shall we?'

'Oh yes – sorry,' Hilary put her hand to her mouth. She was very near tears. 'We haven't been living together for some time,' she said.

'I see.' Patiently, Grace Ferris extracted the facts: how the man from the hotel had telephoned first – Hilary understood, now, the reason for that call, and went off at a tangent to wonder how Jonathan could afford to stay at a place like that with 'that woman'. Eventually Grace Ferris learned when Hilary had last seen her husband, and obtained a description of him as well as details about his work. He had parents living; they were in Tenerife just now.

'He might be at their house, though?' suggested WPC Ferris.

Hilary had not thought of that. They dealt with that possibility at once by telephoning his parents' number. There was no reply. Grace Ferris did not tell Hilary that this was not proof of his absence. He might be there, perhaps dead: the local police would soon find out.

'How did he seem when you last saw him?' the police officer asked.

'Oh – I don't know. As usual,' Hilary said. But he had wanted to talk to her, and she had not let him.

'I see. Well, we'll get busy and be in touch,' said Grace Ferris. 'Have you got a photograph of him?'

Hilary took one from a drawer. It was a holiday snapshot showing the four of them – the two children, herself and Jonathan – on holiday in Cornwall.

'That's two years old,' said Hilary.

'I don't suppose he's changed much,' said Grace Ferris. She admired the children and asked their names and ages, and where they were now. Then she explained that if Jonathan was traced and found safe, the police were not obliged to tell Hilary more than just that. If he did not want his whereabouts known, his confidence would be respected.

'You might tell him to get in touch with his boss,' said Hilary bitterly. 'Or he'll lose his job.'

Grace Ferris said that he would be told.

'Most people turn up quite safely, you know,' she said.

When she had gone, Hilary went back to the sitting-room and indulged in the luxury of tears for a full ten minutes.

How could he behave like this? How could he?

20

While Jonathan's body lay in the ice-cold water of the old quarry, police all over the country went about their routine work. They patrolled the roads; strove to control the unruly; attended accidents; investigated robberies, muggings and cases of arson; enquired into fraud; pursued murderers.

An officer in an area car on normal patrol in the Twistleton area saw a Honda Accord parked on the grass verge above the village. There was no sign of a driver and the car was not locked. He checked it out, and in minutes established through the computer that it had been stolen from a car park in Swindon on Friday. It was soon taken away, to be returned to its owner.

Other officers began the task of trying to find Jonathan Cooper, aged thirty-six, five foot eleven inches tall, dark hair, brown eyes, pale complexion. Police at Westborough were asked to send an officer to the missing man's address in Harcombe to interview Mrs Sue Norris, with whom he had been living.

When PC Graves rang the bell at the lodge there was no reply so he went up to the main house, where Mrs Wood opened the door and in response to his question said that Mrs Norris was probably at work. Annoyed at being interrupted as she turned out the kitchen, a fortnightly task, Mrs Wood said, 'Why don't you ask the old lady?'

'Old lady?'

'Mrs Armitage senior. She lives upstairs. Very friendly

she is, with them two,' said Mrs Wood, and then, showing some interest, 'Not in trouble, are they?'

Graves ignored the remark.

'Tell me, Mrs – er – ' he began in his most benign tone.

'Mrs Wood,' supplied that lady.

'Mrs Wood, do you know Mr Jonathan Cooper?'

'By sight, yes,' said Mrs Wood. 'Not to talk to. He's normally out at work when I'm here, but I have seen him when he's had days off, like. It's different with her – that Sue. She's often about – works shifts.'

'Where does she work?' asked Graves.

'At the Rigby Arms in Westborough,' said Mrs Wood.

'Mrs Armitage senior?' Graves pursued.

'It's her son owns this place,' said Mrs Wood, unbending, and added graciously, 'I'll take you up.'

So it was that Alice opened her door to the middle-aged constable with greying hair and a spreading waistline, one who had never sought promotion because he liked the job on the ground. As soon as Mrs Wood – reluctantly, now – had departed, he asked when she had last seen Jonathan.

Alice was glad to know that proper enquiries were under way. She told Graves about Jonathan's alleged depression, the bruise on Sue's face and the weekend away to mend relations between the pair. She hadn't seen Jonathan for some time, herself; he'd been in bed on Friday when she left for Bournemouth. She told Graves what Sue had said about Jonathan disappearing during the night from the Court Grange Hotel.

'Do you think he's had an accident?' she asked.

Graves said that he was not the victim of any accident so far reported, although the possibility could not be ruled out. It was more likely to be a domestic matter; perhaps he wanted to get away and think things over on his own.

Alice thought this was very possible. She said that Sue would be back from the hotel around five, if she came on the bus; sooner if she got a lift. In either case it wouldn't be long for Graves to wait.

When Sue's shift ended that afternoon she went over to Terry's room at the Rigby, but he wasn't there. He was returning the bike to Mavis, though Sue had no way of knowing that.

Sue felt totally abandoned. She did not want to go back to the empty lodge. There would be no one around except Alice. She thought of hanging about in Westborough until opening time, then going into the bar to see if Giles would come in; he'd take her home. He'd be sorry for her. It would be easy to get him to go into the lodge with her.

It was too soon. She knew it. She'd have to wait – not because of any scruples of her own but because of Giles's. He would want to be sure that Jonathan had really left her; then his pity would drive him to comfort her. Sue smiled, imagining it. Perhaps he'd fix her up with a nice flat somewhere, she mused. Why not? She'd rather that than marry him; she thought Terry's idea of that was going too far, although she supposed from the money point of view it would be best. But she didn't like the idea of any restraint on her freedom. She needed to talk to Terry, work it all out.

At the idea of shifting responsibility for some of her actions on to him, she felt easier. He was so inventive. He'd think of a way of getting her somewhere nice to live quite soon, she was sure. She couldn't stand that place on her own, not for long, but she saw that there was nothing for it now except to return there. She caught the bus which dropped her at the end of the lane and trudged the last mile to the village.

A white police Ford Escort was parked outside the lodge as Sue walked through the gates. She felt a moment of panic. What did it mean? Had they found Jonathan's burnt-out car and discovered who it belonged to? They'd be able to trace it if the number plate hadn't burned.

She was ready to receive this news in an appropriate manner as PC Graves got out of his car and came towards her.

'Mrs Norris? Mrs Sue Norris?' he asked.

Sue nodded. It wasn't hard to look solemn.

'I'd like a word, please, Mrs Norris,' said Graves. He remembered seeing her before, when there had been that unfortunate accident at the Rigby not long after Christmas and the barman had fallen down the cellar steps.

Sue remembered Graves, too, but he had not interviewed her; a sergeant had taken her short statement.

'We've met before, Mrs Norris,' said Graves as Sue took out her key and opened the door.

'Yes,' agreed Sue. 'Why are you here now?'

'I'm making some enquiries about Mr Jonathan Cooper,' said Graves. 'He lives here, I believe?'

'Yes, that's right,' said Sue. 'You'd better come in.' She led Graves into the house, took off her coat and settled herself down on the sofa, indicating that Graves should face her in the armchair.

'He's been reported missing, Mrs Norris,' said Graves. 'When did you last see him?'

Sue switched her line of thinking. Mr Prentiss must have rung the police: it had to be him. She must tell her story calmly. It wasn't the first recital, and her other hearers had accepted it easily.

'On Friday,' she said. 'We went away for the weekend.' She clenched her fists on each side of her thighs and spoke steadily. 'We were staying at the Court Grange Hotel at Twistleton for the weekend.' She swallowed.

'Yes?' prompted Graves.

'He went away in the night,' said Sue. 'Or early on Saturday morning while I was asleep. I woke up and he'd gone.'

'I see.' Graves wrote it down in his pocket book. 'Did he take his things? Pack his case?'

'No.'

'So what would he have been wearing, Mrs Norris?'

They couldn't have found the car. That was obvious. If they had, the man wouldn't be asking all these questions.

'Well, I don't know – what he wore for the trip down, I suppose.' What had Jonathan been wearing that other evening when it happened? Terry hadn't thought of this, in his planning – how she might be questioned in such a way. She frowned, trying to remember. 'Dark flannels –' She was going to say he'd been wearing a sweater when she remembered Terry feeling inside Jonathan's jacket pocket for his diary. 'A tweed jacket,' she went on with more confidence. 'At least, I didn't pack it to bring it back, and he wore it for the trip.' But Terry, posing as Jonathan, had worn the anorak – well, Jonathan might have put it on over the jacket. Anyway, the anorak was here, in the hall. She'd hung it up

174

herself. Luckily she'd taken Jonathan's case upstairs this morning, though she hadn't unpacked it.

'What colour?' asked Graves.

'Brown tweed,' said Sue. 'And a shirt – brown checks, maybe – I'm not sure. I could look through his things and see what's missing. But even then, I might not be right,' she warned. 'He did his own packing.'

'Shoes?' tried Graves.

She could see his feet in brown lace-up shoes sticking out as she tucked the blanket round them. She described them.

'What do you think has happened?' she asked.

'What's your opinion, Mrs Norris?' countered Graves. 'Weren't you worried?'

'Well, in a way, but you see we'd had a quarrel,' said Sue. 'Just a few days earlier. He'd been very depressed.'

'Why was that?'

'It was after seeing his children,' said Sue. 'He often got low, then.'

'You've no idea where he might have gone?'

'No. We had dinner in our room – he didn't feel like going to the restaurant – watched television for a bit, and then went to sleep. Or anyway, I did,' said Sue, regarding Graves with a steady gaze.

'Had he any friends he might have gone to see?'

'Not that I know of. He'd rather lost touch with the people he saw before we joined up,' said Sue.

'I see.'

'You'll let me know if you find him?' she asked. 'No matter what – ' she did not end the sentence.

'Have you any reason to think he might have wished to take his own life, Mrs Norris?' asked Graves. 'Had he ever threatened to?'

'No – no! It was just that he was so depressed, and then going off without a word,' said Sue.

'I expect he'll turn up, safe and sound,' said Graves. 'You'll be at the Rigby Arms during working hours,' he established.

'Yes.' Sue explained about her shifts.

Graves got up to go. He glanced round the room. A fine film of dust covered most of the hard surfaces. He saw a slim black diary beside the telephone.

'Is that Mr Cooper's?' he asked.

'Yes,' said Sue.

'I'd like to take it, Mrs Norris,' said Graves. 'It might help us to trace him – addresses and such.'

Sue couldn't object. What harm could it do?

'What if he comes back and wants it?' she asked.

'Then he can collect it straight away from the station,' said Graves, and added, 'We'd like to know if – when – he does return, Mrs Norris. Save us going on with our enquiries, you see.'

'Of course,' said Sue.

Graves faithfully noted their conversation in his report.

It was strange that the car hadn't been found. You'd think it would make a lot of smoke and someone would have seen it. Still, if Terry had found a really remote spot, anyone noticing it from some distance away might think it was just a bonfire.

Sue said as much to Terry when she saw him the next day.

'Yeah – well, I did find a place miles from anywhere, didn't I?' he said. 'I told you I would.' Sue had waylaid him when he came up from the cellar carrying a crate of ginger ale bottles. 'Who sent them poking around, did they say?' He hadn't been pleased to hear of the visit from the police.

'Must have been his boss, I suppose,' said Sue. She didn't tell Terry about Giles ringing Hilary and the hospitals. 'I suppose it might stay lost for months – years, even. The car, I mean. Like those planes from the war. They've found some, haven't they, lost in woods?' She'd heard someone talking about it in the hotel, some old guy with a lame leg who'd been in the war. Creepy, it must be, with the bodies still there in their uniform.

'Of course it might,' said Terry. 'I shouldn't think we'll hear another word about it. He'll be one of those missing persons who never turn up.' He glanced round. It was risky to talk like this; someone might hear them. 'Didn't bother about the house, did he? The copper, I mean?' he asked, needing that reassurance.

'No. Just wanted to know what he'd been wearing,' said Sue, and decided not to mention the diary.

Terry thought warmly of the wad of notes under his mattress. He'd fade away while the search went on. In the end the police would give up and by then the body in the water would be unrecognizable. He'd return and present his account to Sue when she'd got things set up nicely with Giles. She wouldn't take long over that; she'd need some sort of anchor man; she couldn't operate on her own, as he could.

Terry was paid weekly. He didn't want to provoke any ill-feeling with Bruce so he thought he would tell some tale about his mother being ill and needing him at home, something to counteract any resentment at not working out the full trial period he and Bruce had agreed at the start. It might be useful to be able to quote Bruce as a referee. Terry knew he had given satisfaction; he always did. He wouldn't need to think about work for some time; he might even go off to Barbados or somewhere like that: there'd be pickings, for sure, in those sort of places.

It was weird how he hadn't been able to get enough of Sue at first, and yet now she didn't turn him on at all. Pity, really; it had been great for a while. He'd always be able to find her, for she wouldn't be moving far from Giles – not unless someone else turned up, some better chance, but he'd take care that she wouldn't know how to find him.

Polishing glasses, pouring out doubles, pulling pints, smiling and jesting with the customers, Terry planned for the future.

Morgues and accident reports were checked. There was no sign of either Jonathan Cooper or his car, but the police did not regard the search for him as urgent. He was no small child that might have been abducted; he was a man in a domestic mess who had probably gone somewhere to think things over.

Graves handed the diary in and made his report. In time, someone would ring round the possible contacts but meanwhile other business had to be dealt with too.

Jonathan's parents' home was visited by the local force. There were no signs that it had been entered while they were away on holiday, and a neighbour produced a key so that the police could make sure Jonathan was not there, either dead or alive.

Hilary Cooper lay sleepless at night, wondering where Jonathan had gone. Why was there no news? Her resentment was greater than any anxiety; how dared he do this on top of everything else?

By day, she presented her usual impassive face to the children, occupying them with Plasticine or paints until she was ready to take them out. At half-term she always planned expeditions of varying kinds, mainly for edification. She wondered about telephoning her parents to tell them what had happened. They lived in Suffolk, where her father, a schoolmaster, was nearing retirement, and she always took the children to visit them in the school holidays. If she rang, what could they do? They wouldn't be able to find Jonathan and it would only add to their already great worry about her and the children. Time enough when he turned up and she knew what was behind his disappearance. Had he had some sort of breakdown? She thought again of his attempt to talk to her. What had he wanted to say? What if she'd let him? Would it have made any difference? The mess they were in was entirely of his creation; she had always done her part – cooking, cleaning the house, caring for him and the children. There were always ironed shirts in the cupboard and a meal ready each evening; she had nothing to reproach herself for in that way. Naturally, with two small, demanding children, she was tired and had lost some of her youthful looks, not that she'd ever been much of a one to bother about her appearance beyond being clean and neat. Life wasn't about that; it was about providing a secure home for your family; teaching your children to develop their skills and the right degree of independence appropriate to their age; ensuring they got the best possible education to take, in their turn, a responsible place in the world. Jonathan had seemed to share these views until that little slut got hold of him.

People did have breakdowns. You'd think, though, that she would be the one to do that, not Jonathan. But Hilary had always kept herself under control.

On Tuesday evening when the children were in bed and asleep, she telephoned the police to ask if there was any news. WPC Ferris was not available but Hilary learned that so far no trace of Jonathan had been discovered.

Most of the schools in the country had their half-term holiday that week. Though cold, the weather was dry and children ranged far and wide during their days of leisure. Some went on trips to museums or cinemas; some went shopping; some visited grandparents. Many tore about on cycles or roller skates.

Some went canoeing.

On Wednesday afternoon, two boys who had spent most of the day paddling about on the dark waters of the old gravel pit to which Terry had driven on Friday night, pulled in to the side to refresh themselves with Mars Bars and crisps. That morning they had set out on their day's voyaging armed with enough picnic food to last the day and with instructions as to taking care ringing in their ears. They'd been Indians travelling along the Mississippi, they'd shot rapids and hunted for elk. Wrapped in warm clothes, with wool caps on their heads and bright orange life jackets as protection, they had had a blissful day.

Soon the light would be gone. They must set off to base camp for the night before the snows came – they were now at the North Pole. Once they reached land, there would be quite a trudge, carrying their canoe, down the main track to their village, where the friendly Eskimos, in the shape of their families, would be cooking whale meat stew for their nourishment.

They made landfall at a slightly different spot from where they had put their canoe into the water that morning, which explained why they had missed it then.

They saw the pale white hand of a dead man, partially screened by a bush that overhung the black water of the artificial lake, breaking the surface.

21

It seemed straightforward at first: a drowned man, a possible suicide. But in sudden death the possibility of foul play as the cause must always be explored.

The doctor certified life extinct and the body was taken away to the mortuary. Papers on him – his notecase, sodden, containing eighteen pounds in notes, his driving licence and Access card, gave a probable identity. The collator soon married up the sad corpse with the missing Jonathan Cooper.

There was no sign of his car, which was odd. Perhaps it was hidden in the scrub area surrounding the quarry. Darkness had fallen by now; a search for it could begin in the morning.

Hilary was just packing up her knitting ready to go to bed when her doorbell rang. A rather young constable stood on the step, dreading breaking the news.

'You've found him,' said Hilary, one hand at her throat.

'Yes, Mrs Cooper.'

Before he went on to say that it was bad news, Hilary guessed from his sombre tone. She remained totally calm while he told her the little they knew, refusing to let him call a neighbour. She would be all right, she said. She'd been alone for months; this was nothing new.

There was the question of identifying the body, the officer said. Was there someone else who could do it? His parents? A friend?

His parents were still on holiday. She would do it. She was his wife. Must she come now?

It would do in the morning, said the officer. Someone would come and collect her. Could she arrange to leave her children with a neighbour?

Hilary was sure that she could. She saw the officer to the door and then collapsed on the sofa in a storm of exhausted tears, pounding the cushions, her face ugly and distorted.

'How could you?' she sobbed. 'How could you?'

For it must be suicide. And would Jonathan's insurance company pay up if that was the case? She'd heard that they didn't in cases of suicide.

She went to bed at last and drifted into sleep.

When she looked at the white face the next day, it was hard to believe that the dead man was Jonathan, but she saw that it was. There would have to be an inquest, she learned, and a post-mortem.

'But why?'

'To establish the cause of death.'

'But he drowned. He jumped into the water,' Hilary said.

'He could swim?'

'Yes. But even so – '

'The water was cold. The weight of his clothes would drag him down. Yes, I know. But it's routine,' said WPC Ferris, who had taken her to the mortuary.

'He might have had a heart attack,' said Hilary. 'Been looking at the water – thinking about it, maybe – then fallen?'

'Maybe,' agreed WPC Ferris.

In that case it would be an accident, Hilary thought. The insurance money would be safe. She steeled herself against any other sense of grief or loss, and decided not to get in touch with his parents. They were due back at the weekend in any case. She would not say a word to the children, either. In time they would stop asking about him. It would all pass.

The pathologist had expected a routine case of drowning which would lead to a verdict of misadventure if suicide could not be proved, but there were puzzling anomalies before he began his examination. The dead man's car had so far not been found. There had been no trace of frothing round his mouth.

Whilst he worked, police were at the old gravel pit inspecting the area around where the body was discovered, looking for signs of how it had got into the water. Now it became clear that things were not straightforward. The lungs were not in the water-logged state normal in persons who have met their death by drowning: there were no traces of ingested weed nor signs of water having been swallowed in the struggle to breathe. Decomposition was well under way, but, carefully, the alert pathologist now sought further evidence that the man had been dead before he entered the water. Inconclusive in itself, because the body had been immersed for several days, was the fact that there were no fragments of grass or weed in the hands; in cadaveric spasm a drowning man would clutch, literally, at a straw and any substance would be retained in the grasp. There was nothing under the fingernails, no soil collected while scrabbling for a handhold at the side of the pit.

The doctor had noted a depressed wound on the left temple, and an abrasion which might have been sustained in the fall from the top of the pit, but now he looked into the possibility of injury to the head that could cause death, signs of which might show in the meninges. There were other things to look for: if the body had lain elsewhere before immersion, even after days in the water, hypostasis, the typical collection of blood in what had been the lower part of the body, might be found.

He began the slow, careful search to discover the truth.

Several police divisions were concerned with the disappearance of Jonathan Cooper and the subsequent discovery of his body. Even when he had been officially identified, there was no urgency about telling Sue Norris; she was not his widow and it was not she who had reported him missing. It was simply a matter of courtesy for the investigating officers to give their colleagues in Westborough the news before it arrived automatically as the collator updated details of missing persons, and when they told Sue was their affair. She did not hear at once.

Journalists making their routine calls to police headquarters soon learned of the body's discovery, but did not hear about its identification until too late for Wednesday's papers. When the cautious pathologist had pronounced that the cause of death was a depressed fracture of the skull, and that the man had been dead for several days before immersion, the newspapers were able to state that the police were treating the case as murder.

Laboratory tests would attempt to discover how long the body had been dead before being put in the water, and to pinpoint the time of death. The pathologist had reported that the deceased had probably eaten a meal of steak and chips some hours before he died, and Detective Superintendent Howard asked for an analysis of the stomach and intestinal contents. However urgently required, results would take several days to come through.

PC Graves came to the Rigby Arms to see Sue on Thursday.

It was market day in the town and the police were busy; there were always extra cases of theft, and more parking offences and traffic problems than during the rest of the week. The Rigby Arms had a brisk bar trade and the dining-room was full.

The hotel manager could have done without the visit from Graves. Before seeing Sue, the constable told Bruce why he had come and explained that as next-of-kin Jonathan's widow was the one who counted now, but that it was only right for Sue to be told that the search was over.

'What happened?' asked Bruce. 'Suicide?' He was shocked at the news.

'We don't think so,' said Graves, and added, thankful for the cliché, 'Enquiries are proceeding.'

There was no doubt about Sue's horror. She turned white, gasped, cried, 'Oh no, it can't be true!' but she did not break down. She kept asking about Jonathan's car and Graves had to tell her that so far it had not been found.

Bruce, despite the rush of work, asked her if she would like to go home and was relieved when she said no. She was given a brandy and sent to sit down for a while. It was some time before she had any chance of a word with Terry who, in the bar, was surrounded by farmers and farmers' wives and folk from the surrounding district who had come in to the market. Terry had heard the news, though, from Bruce, and was ready when, later, she seized her chance. By then, too, his own first dismay had been replaced by his customary optimism.

'You didn't set fire to the car,' she accused him.

'I couldn't,' said Terry. 'It would have been such a waste. But don't worry. It'll never be found. It'll all die down. You'll see. They'll never find out the truth.'

'You couldn't resist the chance of making some quick money, could you?' said Sue, and he shook his head, grinning at her. 'You know me, Sue,' he said.

'You were a fool,' she said, but some of his optimism brushed off on her when he said there was no way the police could find out what had really happened. He meant that there was no way they could connect him with it.

He drove her back to the lodge when her shift ended. Bruce had asked him to do it, and although Terry did not want to be alone with Sue, facing her recriminations, he could not refuse.

She raised the subject again.

'If only you'd burned the car, as we planned,' she said.

'It wasn't necessary,' said Terry. He could not bring himself to admit that he had been unable to carry out the part of the plan that involved putting the dead man in the driver's seat.

'It might be traced,' she insisted.

'It won't,' said Terry. 'I've sold cars before, Sue. To people who are doing that sort of thing all the time.'

'You mean, changing their numbers?'

'That, yes. Painting them, too.' Terry did not want to go into it. 'Relax. The car will never be found,' he repeated. And it wasn't.

'Won't the police find out that he died before Friday?' said Sue. 'Won't they know he wasn't drowned?'

'No way,' said Terry. 'The water, you see.' He swallowed, not liking to think of it, even now. 'The water will have changed things – him.'

That was true. Sue felt better.

'Let's go to bed,' she said. She could forget like that: put it out of her mind, be reassured.

But he couldn't. Terry, who had made a career of keeping women quiet and who knew how to perform automatically, was repelled, now, at the mere idea.

'Sorry. Got to rush,' he said. 'Things to do.' He did not even get out of the car.

*　　*　　*

The news of Jonathan's death was soon all round the town of Westborough, spreading from the hotel staff to the clients and so to the streets and shops. People who had never even heard of the dead man felt briefly involved because he was local. Murder did not happen on your doorstep every day, and murder it was, according to rumour.

The facts reached Harcombe through a number of people who had gone in to the market, among them Barbara Duncan who had met a friend for lunch at the Rigby. They had bought their drinks and their bar meal from Terry, and had heard the story from gossip around them. Barbara, horrified herself at what must have been, the bar pundits theorized, a random attack by some sort of mugger, thought that Alice Armitage would be deeply shocked and upset when she heard. The old woman was on her conscience; Barbara had intended to invite her round to a meal, but one way and the other she hadn't got round to it, putting it off for small reasons which did not stand up to examination.

She telephoned Alice as soon as she returned from Westborough and suggested that, if Alice was doing nothing that afternoon, she should come round to tea.

Alice was surprised and delighted; she accepted at once and was soon sitting in Barbara's drawing-room admiring the bulbs in bowls and the burgeoning forsythia in a jug on the window-sill.

She had not heard about Jonathan. Barbara told her as gently as she could, emphasizing that while she knew he had been found in the waters of an old gravel pit, she did not know how he had got there. Time enough, Barbara thought, for Alice to hear about murder when the police gave more information.

'Oh dear, oh dear,' Alice lamented. 'He was a kind young man. Oh dear! Poor Sue!'

'And his widow and children,' said Barbara, whose sympathy lay more with them than with Sue, though how could an outsider ever judge about marriage? It was like an iceberg, only a fraction revealed on the surface. 'I hadn't met him until that party you had after Christmas. The young man from the bar at the Rigby was there, too, wasn't he? He seems to be a great friend of theirs – of Jonathan's, that is, and Sue.'

'Yes,' agreed Alice, doubtfully.

'He's popular in the bar at the Rigby,' said Barbara. 'Has quite a way with him. Rather a charmer.'

It was true. Terry had beguiled his way into the lodge, just as he had into her flat.

The two ladies talked about the tragedy for a time. Alice revealed that Jonathan had been very depressed recently but did not mention his quarrel with Sue, for, however tenuously, her own son was concerned with that. She drove home thinking uneasily about how she and Terry had first met and how he had turned the truth of that encounter on its head. It distracted her from thinking too much about Jonathan, whose unhappiness had been so great that it had sent him to his death.

And so it had, although not in the way that Alice imagined.

22

In order to discover how Jonathan Cooper had died, the police needed to trace his last movements.

He had stayed at the Court Grange Hotel for the last night of his life, leaving it some time during the hours of darkness in his car, which had now disappeared. Had he been alone? Someone at the hotel might have seen him go.

A detective sergeant and a detective constable went to the hotel to take statements from the staff, and when these were studied in the Incident Room a curious fact emerged.

No one could be found who had actually seen Jonathan Cooper. Detective Sergeant Johnson returned to the hotel to find out more. He learned that Sue Norris had made the registration. The card was produced and the clerk on duty at the time was asked about her. The girl remembered that she had said her companion was unwell but had declined help with the luggage. Dinner on Friday night had been served in the room, and one of the waiters who had taken it over, now in the restaurant laying tables for lunch, was questioned.

The young lady was very nice, he said, remembering Sue's tip. The gentleman was taking a bath and she had called out to him that the meal had arrived.

Had the gentleman answered?

The waiter couldn't remember. In any case, an answer might have been drowned by the sound of the bathwater running out, which he had heard.

His assistant, who was off-duty, was called from his quarters where he had been lying on his bed smoking and reading a girlie magazine. He remembered Sue calling out 'Darling' and had noticed an anorak jacket lying on the bed. The room had been untidy, with ladies' clothes flung here and there and madam herself wearing only a negligée but you often saw more than that when giving room service. The waiter had enjoyed his brief view of Sue's charms.

Detective Sergeant Johnson wondered if there was any record of what the late Mr Cooper had eaten for dinner that night, and the waiter recalled that steak had been ordered.

That fitted with what the pathologist said had been ingested. Johnson asked if the full menu chosen that night could be traced. After only a short delay, Major Smythe was able to tell him just what dishes had been taken across to the hotel annexe that night. These could be compared with the analysis of the dead man's stomach contents, when the lab. report came through.

Johnson pursued his efforts to find someone who had met, face to face, the deceased, but there was no one at the hotel who recognized the man in the photograph he displayed.

Major Smythe was anxious that the good name of the place should not be besmirched by this sorry affair, yet the truth must be uncovered. He supplied the names and addresses of other guests resident during Friday night; they would all be interviewed, now, by officers from their local stations. One of them might have heard the Granada drive away. House-to-house enquiries in Twistleton would begin at once. Someone could have seen or heard something unusual during the night.

If the car was found, that would help.

* * *

Officially, now, Westborough police station's collator had learned that Jonathan Cooper had died as the result of a blow to the head causing internal haemorrhaging rather in the manner of a fatal stroke.

As routine, Graves' report of his interview with Sue Norris was studied. Addresses contained in the dead man's diary had already been forwarded to the police area covering Twistleton, from which the search for the missing man had been conducted. Now, across two counties, the murder team was told that the victim's diary was in the possession of the Westborough force.

How very distressed Sue must be, Alice thought as she turned into the drive of Harcombe House after tea with Barbara. The lights were on at the lodge, and when she had parked the car in the barn, Alice went there.

Sue opened the door wearing a quilted dressing-gown which had toothpaste stains down the front. She had changed from her working clothes after Terry left, and woven a plan for the evening which would include a visit from a concerned and anxious Giles. Its course could be played by ear, she decided, but her earlier resolve that delay would be proper had been superseded by sexual hunger. Terry had gone without administering the only comfort Sue understood; she would have to seek it elsewhere and use maximum temptation to overcome Giles's scruples.

The girl's long dark hair was loose, hanging down over her shoulders. She showed no sign of tears.

'Oh Sue – I've disturbed you – were you resting?' said Alice. 'I came to say how dreadfully sorry I am to hear about Jonathan.'

Sue did a swift calculation. Giles might go into the Rigby on his way home; if he did, he would certainly hear the news there and come on at once. She could get rid of the old girl if she dealt with her briskly.

'Come in,' she said, opening the door wide to admit Alice.

'What can I say?' Alice followed Sue into the house. 'You must be heartbroken,' she said. Though the girl didn't look it. Perhaps she hadn't taken it in. 'Don't blame yourself,' she urged. 'He must have been more depressed than you thought.'

Sue couldn't think what she meant.

'It must have been suicide,' Alice went on.

So she knew very little. It was just as well, Sue reflected, reluctant to sit swapping theories about murder with the old woman.

She shrugged, standing close to Alice in the sitting-room where now the fire burned brightly. Various odours came from her: scent, and others. Alice looked at her curiously. It was almost as if she were not properly washed.

'You were going to have a bath, Sue, I expect,' she said. 'And perhaps an early night – have you something to eat?' Somehow, now, she did not want to invite the girl up to supper though that had been at the back of her mind earlier.

Sue knew that Alice would be shocked if she said she was hungry.

'I don't feel like eating,' she said. 'I'm all right, really I am. I just feel like being alone.'

'I understand. But come over if you want to,' Alice said. She hesitated. Perhaps Sue was still in a state of shock.

'Would you like a sleeping pill?' she offered, though doubtfully – still, one tablet disbursed from her own bottle could surely do no harm.

'No, thank you. I'm quite all right,' said Sue.

Alice left her, and went over to the main house feeling very confused. What was it about the girl? The word *sensual* came into her mind as she went up the stairs. That's what Sue was: even in her working garb and with her hair drawn back into a severe knot at the back of her head, she exuded some physical quality which Alice found embarrassing to think of; that was why she had been anxious about Giles spending time alone with her, Alice realized. A different sort of girl would simply have been accepting a lift and no more: but Sue seemed to be inviting attention. After all, she had lured Jonathan away from his wife.

Walking upstairs, drawing the curtains, Alice thought about Sue and slowly her mind turned also to Terry. What was the connection between them? She had felt uneasy about it right from the start. Alice remembered the day the two young people had met, straight after her own original encounter with Terry. All three had gone to the lodge and she had seen herself in the old-fashioned role of chaperon. Since then, Sue and he had met almost daily; he was always giving her lifts either in or out of Westborough.

Alice was old. Though protected by Walter, she had seen marriages broken by unscrupulous acts. Because of the love she had known before meeting Walter, she understood, though she had long since ceased experiencing it, passion. Could Jonathan have found out that Sue was having an affair with Terry?

She liked this idea. It was better than thinking that jealousy over Giles had driven him to take his life.

Alice was just in time for the early television news. Afterwards, the local station put out its own bulletin and so she learned that the police were treating the death of Jonathan Cooper as a possible case of murder. Detective Chief Superintendent Howard appealed to anyone who had seen his beige Granada on or after Friday night to get in touch with their local police or the Incident Room from which he was handling the investigation.

Murder!

No!

For minutes Alice's mind refused to accept the idea. Then she remembered that Jonathan had disappeared from the Court Grange Hotel. Some stranger – some thief or vandal – must have attacked him as he wandered about on Friday night. Perhaps someone had seen him standing by the edge of the quarry and tipped him in for the sake of the car.

The idea made sense, but Alice could not stop thinking about Terry. She cast her mind right back to the first meeting when he had turned his own careless act round and made the collision appear to be her fault. He had successfully put over that version of events at the body repairer's and in spite of that he had charmed her. He had shown thoughtful consideration, getting the heaters for her and helping Sue with the party.

More and more, as she remembered, Alice warmed to the idea that Sue and Jonathan had quarrelled about him and not about Giles, but even so, Terry couldn't have killed him.

He couldn't have followed them to that hotel and arranged to meet Jonathan, without Sue's knowledge, for some sort of showdown. Or had she known? Was Sue covering up for him?

Alice poured herself out a large glass of sherry and drank it quite fast. She was letting her imagination run away with her. Terry might be untrustworthy, a lying charmer, but that didn't make him a murderer. Sue might be amoral, even a whore – Alice's mind accepted the word and sped on – but that did not mean she was an accessory. Such things didn't happen.

But they did. Alice thought of Crippen and Christie, of wives poisoning their husbands with weedkiller. Harmless-seeming, apparently normal people could carry out appalling acts of horror and violence; the papers were full of them.

Not Terry, though. He was just a flanneller – a smooth talker. Wasn't he?

To Sue's disappointment, Giles did not call at the lodge that evening. He had not yet heard the news, and was maintaining a tactful remoteness.

Unaware of this, Sue mooched about in her dressing-gown, watching television and eating a large meal. She had shopped on the way to the bus, buying sausages and baked beans and the sort of chips you cook in the oven. After eating she felt better, more able to forget her fears about the car. It made sense that Terry would have got rid of it in some safe way, even though it was for cash: he didn't want anyone to trace it back to him.

She did not look at the news on television, so she did not see the brief interview with Detective Superintendent Howard, in charge of the investigation into Jonathan's death.

Giles stopped for her in the morning. He wore a smile which he hoped combined joy at seeing her with sympathy for her plight, and she understood his defection, as it had seemed, of the previous evening. He didn't know.

'Any news?' he asked, as she got into the Rover, and she turned her large eyes towards him.

'You haven't heard,' she said. 'I thought everyone knew.'

191

'Knew what?' asked Giles, feeling even more stupid than usual. 'Tell me.'

'He's dead. Jonathan's dead,' said Sue tragically.

Giles was truly shocked. He felt as if he had been struck hard in the solar plexus.

'Oh, how dreadful!' he exclaimed. 'What an appalling thing. How did it happen?' He reached out and laid a hand lightly on her thigh, for comfort. 'Oh, poor little Sue.'

Time enough for him to find out later what the police were saying, Sue decided.

'He drowned,' she said. 'He was so depressed. He hadn't been himself for some time.' She played with her black skirt, her finger twisting the fabric where it showed in the gap of her coat.

'You shouldn't be going to work,' said Giles. He wanted to pick her up and carry her off to some eyrie where he could protect her and keep her safe from the cruel world.

'It will take my mind off things,' said Sue, who could not have endured a day at the lodge alone.

'I'll come round this evening to see how things are,' Giles promised. 'You must let me know if there's anything at all I can do to help.'

She smiled, thinking about his offer, as they drove down the lane.

'I will,' she said.

Out of her window, Alice saw Giles collect Sue that morning. With Jonathan no longer there to take her to work on her early days, it was the neighbourly thing to do, but he was playing with fire. The girl was free now, for Jonathan was dead.

She must leave the lodge before Giles lost his head. Alice saw the need for this very clearly, although now she was convinced that it was Terry in whom Sue was interested, not Giles, who was old enough to be her father. But Sue had a warm and friendly nature; she had been kind to Alice and she might extend this kindness to Giles, unthinkingly. There shouldn't be any problem about removing this source of possible temptation: Sue would not want to stay at the lodge alone. Alice determined to move there herself. Then she would make a big effort to make her mark in the village before she became too old and frail. Violet Hedges and Nancy Wilson were not all that much younger than she was, and Barbara Duncan must be well into her sixties. They seemed to lead full, satisfying lives. She would humbly find out how they did it, learn from them. She had let things drift too long. If Giles and Helen really needed the rent, they could let her flat to a schoolteacher. What she had done in coming here had been a kindness to no one, least of all Giles, who was being destroyed before her eyes.

Alice tried not to let her mind turn to Jonathan and the tragedy of his death; it was too terrible to contemplate. His wife, with those two little children, must feel such bitter grief. The waste of a life was so wicked.

She switched on the radio news but there was no mention of the murder enquiry. The newspaper – brought to this remote village by van and delivered by a schoolboy before the school bus bore him off to Westborough Comprehensive – told her no more than she already knew.

As Alice read about Mrs Hilary Cooper, aged thirty-four, and the children, an image of Terry's round, ingenuous face with its frame of curly hair swam into her mind.

He couldn't possibly be involved, could he? And if he were, then Sue would know about it, wouldn't she?

She might not. He was very devious and had this knack of twisting things round to confuse the truth. If he had followed Sue and Jonathan to the Court Grange Hotel, he must somehow have whisked Jonathan away without Sue's knowledge. He might be jealous, but surely he couldn't have set out to kill Jonathan! Such a notion was preposterous.

Eating her toast and marmalade, Alice found that the idea would not go away. Perhaps Terry had simply intended to have a talk with Jonathan and it had got out of hand – they'd fought, perhaps; you read of such quarrels, when people were killed by accident. Things had started to go wrong, really wrong, ever since Terry had entered their lives, and now, because of his own good nature – Alice preferred not to think of Giles as weak – and the presence of a physically provocative unattached young woman with a lax moral code, her own son was at risk. In a way it was her fault: she was the one who had introduced Terry into the household, been there when he met Sue, even though he had arrived without an invitation.

The more she thought about it, the more Alice felt certain that Terry might be connected with Jonathan's death. That being so, she had a duty. The police would soon find out, one way or the other, if she was right, and the sooner they got on with it the better, before Giles was exposed to further risks.

The police had made a number of discoveries in the area around the old gravel pit where Jonathan's body had been discovered. The weather when he disappeared had been dry and very cold. There had been no rain between then and the time he had been found, and tyre marks leading to the edge of the pit had been preserved. They were not very clear; the ground was too hard for that; but in one spot soil, near a spring, was damp, and clear tread marks showed. Casts were made.

The Home Office Laboratory would be able to tell what sort of tyre had made the prints, and the garage where Jonathan's car was serviced would be able to say if they tallied.

There were small scraping marks on the ground, too; twin tracks that could have been caused by a man's heels as he was dragged to the brink. A white plastic bin liner had been found on a nearby bush and had proved to be not the relic of some picnic, but to contain several strands of human hair. It was being tested for other traces, such as saliva, and the hair would be compared with Jonathan's. Hypostasis had shown that the body had lain on its side for some time after death.

It was a puzzling case, and because no one had been found who had actually seen Jonathan Cooper at the hotel, it was developing a sinister aspect. Detective Superintendent Howard was heading away from his first idea that this was a car theft and mugging carried out by a stranger.

Enquiries went on, methodically, seeking any lead from Twistleton. And as routine, the dead man's widow was asked to account for her movements on Friday night.

Hilary's mind would not accept the fact that the police thought Jonathan had been murdered. Still less could she take in the direction of the questions which WPC Ferris was gently uttering.

She had been at home alone with the children on Friday night, as usual. That morning she had gone to the nursery school where she worked, and where Johnny was a pupil. In the afternoon, she had taken the children to the park. She had no car, and she had not known that Jonathan was staying only thirty miles away at that expensive hotel.

She couldn't have done it; Grace Ferris knew that; but she had to be officially eliminated.

The dead man's diary had arrived at the Incident Room. Well-handled by PC Graves, it held a blurred mass of prints, but it must be tested so that Sue Norris's, Jonathan's own, and those of PC Graves might be eliminated, although since it was not on the body at the time of death, the murderer's were unlikely to be there.

By such random but thorough checking are criminals caught.

When Grace Ferris had gone, Hilary sat stunned, at last taking in the full truth. It was some time before she realized that this meant her insurance money was safe. Later still, when the children had gone to bed, she began to think of her husband as the victim of a brutal attack; then, painfully, agonizingly, she started to weep and to wish she had let Jonathan talk when he had wanted to do so the last time she saw him.

A clean breast of things: that's what you had to make when you'd done wrong. Alice remembered the principles by which she had been reared and which she had tried to instil into her son. The consequences for her would be serious when Helen found out, as now was most likely, that Alice had used her car, but the worst that could happen would be that Helen would turn her out of the house, and that might be a blessing. There might be some legal way in which she could retrieve her capital.

Resolute, Alice set off for Westborough. She knew where

195

the police station was: not far from the body shop that had repaired the Volvo so efficiently. She parked in the forecourt between a van and an area car.

When she told the officer at the desk that she wanted to speak to someone about the death of Jonathan Cooper, he looked at her in surprise. This smart, elderly lady a witness? It seemed unlikely.

'Your name, madam?' he asked, and when she gave her address as Harcombe House, in whose lodge the dead man had lived, he looked at her again. She was the sort of woman whom it had sometimes been his unfortunate lot to question in shoplifting cases. He invited her to sit down and went off to find someone to see her.

'She may be a nut, but she does live at Harcombe, or so she says,' he told Detective Sergeant Rivers, who replied that anyone was welcome, nut or otherwise, who might throw light on the mystery. He came out to greet Alice and took her away to an interview room.

Alice told him the whole story, beginning with apologies if she was wasting his time, saying she could not see how there could be any connection with what she wanted to say and Jonathan's death, but she couldn't get it out of her mind and the police could be the judges. Her tale took a long time to relate. She described how she had borrowed Helen's car and been struck by Terry Brett, driving a Vauxhall – pale green. He had turned the whole thing round to make it seem her fault and had then become friendly with the young pair at the lodge, calling there most days. Rivers learned how kind he had been, buying the convector heaters and not going off with the money, as Alice had feared he might. He heard about the party arranged by Sue and Terry. Alice told Rivers how Terry had taken the job at the Rigby after the barman's accident; how he had visited Sue daily, it seemed – either bringing her back from work or taking her in, according to her shifts and his bar hours.

'He was working in Swindon when I first met him,' Alice said. 'Or so he told me. He knows a lot about cars,' she added. 'He mended my Metro.'

Rivers thought it was a hare – an old lady, worried and shocked by the violent death of someone she knew, seeking an answer, but the details must be passed on to the murder team. It would be for them to decide whether to follow this tenuous lead.

He got Alice to go through it again as he wrote it all down. They brought her a cup of tea and two biscuits while the statement was typed, and were very kind.

'I hope there won't be trouble about the accident,' she said wistfully. 'With the Volvo, I mean.'

She hadn't broken the law, Rivers assured her. No one was hurt, and both drivers had exchanged names and addresses.

Terry hadn't exactly supplied his address, Alice recalled, but thought she need not mention that fact.

They asked her to stay, even after she had signed her statement.

23

While the police were waiting for the results of the laboratory tests, they continued the painstaking elimination of irrelevance and the gleaning of facts which would clear the route to the truth.

Door-to-door enquiries in Twistleton had produced a sleepless woman who had heard a car going up the hill out of the village during Friday night – or rather, early the next morning. She was not sure of the exact time: perhaps half-past one? A man with bronchitis, also wakeful, had seen a car's headlights against the bedroom curtains. Confined to his room with his illness, he had noticed that the lights of cars turning out of the yard at the Court Grange Hotel shone on his window. Such traffic was rare in the small hours. He had put the time at one-fifteen a.m.

Another woman had noticed something odd that Friday afternoon. She had been going to the church to polish the brasses when she met a young man wheeling a bicycle out of the churchyard. She had never seen him before, and it was unusual to meet a stranger there at that time of year, although later there were tourists and visitors from the hotel. The young man had said he had been to see his grandmother's grave, and this had puzzled the woman, for the tiny churchyard was full. For the last fourteen years burials had taken place in a plot of consecrated ground across the road. She had asked if he had found his grandmother, and he said that he had. Of course, the grandmother might have died when he was a small boy, in which case his interest was touching. She gave a full description of the young man, who had a mop of bright brown curls that, had he been a girl, must have been permed. Perhaps they were. He was about five foot eight or nine inches tall, and was wearing a <u>fawn</u> raincoat. The bicycle was a small one.

With no more than these strands to catch at, the murder team was impatient for fresh news from the laboratory. When the call from Westborough police station informed them that an elderly woman, Mrs Alice Armitage, whose son was the dead man's landlord, had come in with a long story about a young man who had inveigled his way into becoming part of the scenery at Harcombe and whom she suspected of having designs on Jonathan Cooper's mistress, Detective Superintendent Howard came to the telephone himself.

'Ask her to describe this young fellow,' he requested.

Back came the answer promptly: about twenty-two, crisp brown curls, blue eyes, five foot nine or so. His name was Terence Brett.

'Keep your Mrs Armitage till we can get over,' said Howard. 'And find out where this Brett lives.'

'We know that,' said Sergeant Rivers smugly. 'He's the barman at the Rigby Arms Hotel.'

Howard ran a check on the computer on Terry before going over, himself, to Westborough. It showed a conviction for car theft two years before. So his prints would be on file. But at the moment no murder weapon, no object remotely of use as a clue, had appeared in the case.

Except the diary, and that had not been found on the body.

Alice was told that Detective ~~Sergeant~~ Super Howard, in charge of the murder enquiry, was coming over to see her.

So they were taking what she said seriously! What had she set in motion? Alice began to tremble. They would arrest Terry, question him.

Well, what if they did? If he was blameless, he had nothing to fear. The police were so clever. They would match things up – fingerprints – bloodstains – that sort of thing: Alice was vague about forensic science.

They brought her some lunch. A young woman officer stayed with her while she ate it and told her about her schoolboy sons and her husband who was also in the force but in a different division. The policewoman was small and slight: Alice thought her brave to take on such a job, and said so. The woman smiled and said it was very rewarding. Even today, the presence of a woman officer at a public house brawl, for instance, sometimes helped to cool it.

Detective Superintendent Howard was a tall, thin man with pepper-and-salt hair and piercing blue eyes. He went through Alice's statement before meeting her, then asked her to tell him her story.

She did so, sprinkling it with apologies and saying it may have been her imagination.

'How you met Terry Brett wasn't imagination,' said Howard. 'You said he took the whole thing over – blamed you and did all the talking at the car repair shop.' That part of the tale could soon be checked.

'You believe me? I might be making it up,' said Alice.

Howard looked at her gravely.

'I don't think so,' he said. 'You don't want to get into trouble with your daughter-in-law, yet you may, now, though I hope not.'

'There are worse things than that,' said Alice.

'Like murder,' said Howard.

'But Terry couldn't have –' Alice looked pleadingly at the detective. 'Surely not?' she whispered.

'We'll find out, Mrs Armitage,' said Howard.

'If he was having an affair with Sue, I suppose he might have followed them to that hotel and perhaps quarrelled with Jonathan. Something like that. An accident, though.' Alice offered her theory.

'Maybe,' said Howard.

'I'm not sure they were having an affair,' Alice said. 'Young people are so casual these days.'

'Did you enjoy driving your daughter-in-law's car, Mrs Armitage?' Howard asked.

'Yes, I did. It's a very nice car,' Alice said.

'You like driving?'

'I used to, but now there's so much heavy traffic about, and people have no road manners,' said Alice. 'I drove a canteen van during the war – only part-time, I had my small son – but Walter and I had to do what we could. He was in a reserved occupation, but he became an auxiliary fireman.'

Howard agreed with Detective Sergeant Rivers that this elegant old lady was in no sense deranged. Her story, retold to him, was consistent in every detail with her statement. It was possible that Terry Brett was involved with the case though the how and the why would have to be sought. At least, now, while the scientists probed further into what the corpse could tell them, he and his men had a name, an individual, who could, for a start, give an account of his movements during the relevant time.

'Well, thank you, Mrs Armitage,' he said. 'You'll be at home, will you, if we need you again? You're not just off to the West Indies, for instance?' She looked the sort of prosperous widow who might well take herself off in search of the sun.

'No, nothing like that. I can carry on, though, can I, as usual? Shopping? Seeing my friends?' What friends?

'Of course. Just don't leave the area without letting the station here know where you'll be,' said Howard.

'I can go now?'

'Certainly. I'll get someone to run you back.'

'I've got my car. It's parked outside. I suppose it's still there,' said Alice, with the ghost of a grin.

Howard saw her out to it, and stood watching while she belted herself in and drove off. She took extra care. It wouldn't do to crash the gears or make some careless slip while right under the noses of the police. As she drove down the High Street she felt a bit swimmy, so she decided to stop for a cup of tea. She could do with spending a penny, too.

Alice found a parking space and went into the Coffee Pot,

where she and Terry had had their coffee the day it all began. The same waitress served her. She wouldn't remember her, thought Alice, but she might remember Terry. He had talked to her – chatted her up, even.

She felt calmer after drinking her tea and visiting the cloakroom. She even called in at the library to see if any of the books she had asked for were in, and collected a fat saga about the Civil War which would be nice for the weekend.

She caught up with Sue in the lane leading from the bus stop to the village and stopped to pick her up. The girl was silent, sitting there, but Alice, guilty about how she had spent the day, chattered on, praising the fine weather and looking forward to spring.

The girl could have no knowledge of it, if Terry were involved, Alice was sure. Perhaps Jonathan had arranged to meet Terry near the quarry, slipping off without telling Sue where he was going.

If not, she was sitting here beside someone who had connived at the killing, and that was unthinkable.

Sue was silent because she was worried.

Before she left the office, she had noticed a man in the lounge reading the paper. It wasn't usual for male guests to be about the place during the day, especially not well-set-up young fellows of about thirty who looked very fit.

She had asked him if there was anything he wanted. This sort of remark often evoked a crude response but he simply shook his head and said 'No, thanks,' returning to his paper.

Sue was sure he was a policeman.

She had intended to go to Terry's room to ask him to take her home, but now she changed her mind. The safest plan was to do as Terry had said and keep away from one another; she should scuttle back to the lodge and lie low. He had been so sure that the car had been safely disposed of, but suppose he was wrong: suppose it had been found?

Even so, she told herself firmly, nothing could be proved. They had only to deny all knowledge of what had happened on Friday night and they would be safe. Terry must be right about the effect of the water making it impossible for the police to find out that Jonathan had died before then. You got washerwoman hands after only a short immersion and he had been submerged for days.

The whole thing was so unfair. All this trouble and worry. It was all Jonathan's fault for being so jealous.

Alice dropped her at the lodge without inviting her up to the flat, as Sue had expected she might. Never mind. Giles would call in that evening. She went into the lodge feeling restless, wondering how to pass the time until then.

Alice, too, felt restless. The days were beginning to draw out now, and it was not yet dark. There were great drifts of snowdrops blooming under the trees in the orchard. She decided to enjoy the last of the fine day by strolling round the garden looking for signs of spring.

She found primroses out on a sheltered bank exposed to the sun and picked some to take to the flat. Then, strolling back across the lawn, she paused beside the swimming-pool. Its waters, now, were muddied, but it had sparkled clear and blue in the summer while Helen and her friends sunbathed round it. Sue and Jonathan had come sometimes. In her mind's eye, Alice pictured Helen swimming up and down in a graceful crawl. Giles, also, swam strongly. Alice couldn't remember seeing Sue in the water, though she could recollect the slight figure in a minuscule bikini, long hair loose across her back, face down on a sun bed.

She looked round the large, lovely garden. What a perfect place it was, yet no one who lived there was happy. Well, perhaps that wasn't quite true: Amanda and Mr Jinks seemed content.

Now this dreadful thing had happened to Jonathan. It didn't bear thinking of.

Alice glanced towards the house and saw Sue approaching across the lawn. The girl had changed from her working clothes into black slacks, and she wore a black leather jacket into whose pockets her hands were thrust. Her normal bouncy stride was absent; she looked grim.

Had Terry been arrested already? Was that why she had been so silent in the car?

Alice watched her approach and saw that the girl was too deeply engrossed in her own thoughts to notice her. How black she looked, Alice thought inconsequentially: black clothes, black hair, and, as she came close, black expression.

'Why Sue, what's wrong? You do look low,' Alice said, and then, because she was going to be a coward no longer and the moment must come. 'Is it Terry?'

'Terry? Why? What about him?' asked Sue, stopping abruptly. Her brows drew together and she glared at Alice, looking suddenly – Alice sought for the word in her mind, and with a shock, found it – she looked savage.

'Well, they're bound to question him, aren't they?' said Alice. 'I had to tell them, you see.'

'Tell them what? What could you know?' Sue demanded, and, advancing, seized Alice by her upper arms.

'Let me go, Sue, you're hurting me,' said Alice, moving backwards.

Sue followed her, still grasping her arms.

'What have you been saying, you silly old woman?' she yelled at Alice, her face flushed now with rage.

Alice was suddenly terrified. The girl was like a virago. She tried to speak calmly, ignoring her thudding heart.

'I had to tell the police about Terry, Sue,' she said. 'You must see that. It was my duty.'

Sue's grip on her arms tightened.

'What have you told them?' she screamed.

'How he got to know us under false pretences. How he's so fond of you,' Alice said, trying to free herself.

Sue, who knew only Terry's version of the original meeting, ignored the first part of what Alice had said, latching on to the last sentence. She started to shake Alice, whose head was whipped back and forth, making her giddy.

'You told them what?' Sue demanded. 'What have you said? Come on! Out with it.'

'Stop shaking me,' Alice wailed, trying still to speak steadily. Her words came in gulps. 'I said it was an accident. If he killed Jonathan, that is,' Alice said. 'Let me go.'

Sue started to yell obscenities.

'What have you done, you interfering old bitch?' she screeched, shaking Alice as if she were a rag doll.

For someone so small and slight she was extremely strong, Alice found, fighting now to keep her foothold on the paving stones beside the pool, where matted leaves had collected in damp, soggy clumps.

They struggled there together, both rendered primitive, the one by rage and the other by the urge for self-preservation. Sue's foot, in its smooth-soled boot, slid on the slimy ground and her balance went, but she still clutched at Alice, who dropped the primroses and caught at the girl to keep herself from falling.

They went into the pool together, at the deep end, but Alice, though she had not done so for years and was at first overcome by the rush of water into her nose and mouth, could swim. She fought, instinctively, to bring herself to the surface of the water and in doing so she thrust off Sue's clutching hands. Gasping, splashing, the weight of her clothing dragging her down, Alice struggled to the side and clung to the rail until she had regained enough strength to pull herself, hand over hand, to the shallow end and up the wide steps to the side.

She was far too shocked to think about Sue, whose floundering struggles and desperate cries had ceased by the time that Alice had pulled herself to safety. Long hair fanned out in the water, limbs extended, Sue lay, a black, spread-eagled figure at the bottom of the pool, with the murky water tranquil above her.

24

After the bar closed, Terry had gone off in the car for a haircut. One of the kitchen staff had recommended a unisex barber on the edge of Westborough. Leaving the barber's, he stopped for one or two things – toothpaste, a magazine about cars, a postcard for his mother whom he hadn't been in touch with since Christmas. Outside a newsagent's, a billboard yelled at him: LOCAL MAN DEAD IN QUARRY FOUL PLAY.

Discussing the crime with his bar customers, Terry had theorized that Jonathan had gone for a late-night drive and been mugged by someone who had stolen his car and dumped him. Most of his hearers thought this was the probable answer. So would the police. Terry was ebulliently confident that the car would never be found and there was nothing else to connect him with the affair. He went back to the Rigby, having delayed long enough for Sue to have given up waiting for him and gone for the bus.

He had a great shock when he drove back into the yard at the Rigby and was greeted by a plain clothes police officer who asked for his driving licence and insurance certificate. Terry produced the licence, but the VW was not insured. He said the certificate was in his room. He'd have to pretend it was lost. The officer escorted him there, large and unfriendly beside him.

Two more officers were already waiting in his room. The insurance offence gave them an excuse to take him into the station while they pieced together evidence of a much more serious matter.

It was the police who found Alice.

They had come for Sue, who had some explaining to do about what had really happened at the Court Grange Hotel, and had found the lodge deserted and the door unlocked. They had gone on to the main house where no one had answered the bell. Next, they had looked in the barn, where Alice's Metro was parked, the bonnet still warm. She had to be somewhere about, and they went into the garden to look for her.

Alice was just beginning to think about dragging herself towards the house when the two officers came the lawn. It was too late for Sue.

By the time Alice was in hospital, where the police insisted on sending her in an ambulance, and Giles had been told and was on his way home, police officers were guarding the lodge until the arrival of the scenes-of-crime team. Terry had talked, and quite quickly. They didn't believe his version of events, but there could be evidence at the lodge.

By nightfall, the living-room carpet had been removed. Fibres from it might match fragments on the dead man's clothing. Soiled sheets from the unmade bed might disclose the identity – or identities – of the source of their stains.

Alice, in her hospital bed, was well enough to tell the police that Sue had seemed very upset and angry, and had grabbed at her, causing them both to fall into the pool. Scuffed marks on the paving slabs and the scattered primroses confirmed her story.

They did not tell Terry that Sue was dead for some time. When they did, his protests grew hysterical. He had never gone in for violence, he cried; he had only been helping – an accessory, right, but not a killer.

It was useless.

A wad of money was found under Terry's mattress; Jonathan's raincoat hung in his cupboard. The woman he had met outside the church at Twistleton picked him out in an identity parade. His fingerprint was found on a page of Jonathan's diary and that was hard to explain. There was the mysterious telephone call made from the lodge on the Friday, and the fact of the uncleared line. Terry admitted that, and gave the true reason for it, but it made no difference. A witness was found who had seen Terry's VW at the building site in Great Minton during the crucial weekend. Staff at the Rigby Arms were questioned and a perplexed Mavis admitted to lending Terry her bike. It was borne off for testing, and yielded fragments of soil from the tyre treads which were similar to the soil around Twistleton – not proof in itself, but supportive. A Honda Accord stolen from Swindon and found later outside Twistleton was called in for forensic scientists to inspect. Tiny paint chips and more soil particles proved, beyond doubt, that Mavis's bicycle had been transported in it. The case was complete. Terry was charged with murder.

Alice followed the trial in the newspapers. Her part in the unmasking of Terry was never made public, for the trail that led to Sue would have led on to him without her intervention. She knew that, reading the account of each day's events in court, but if she had not done what she thought was her duty, Sue might still be alive.

Alice had been haunted, at first, by her memory of that struggle beside the pool: of the girl's evil expression, her violence. It meant that she knew what Terry had done and perhaps had even helped him afterwards. That was dreadful, but Terry was the chief culprit. It just showed what could happen when you set out on a path to deceive. Terry had twisted the truth and had ended a killer. Sue had died as a consequence. The effects of the murder had radically altered a number of lives; and Harcombe House had been sold.

From her paper, Alice learned that Hilary Cooper and her children were now living in a Suffolk village close to her parents. That was good, Alice thought; she would need support. Would she ever get over the hurt of being abandoned?

Sighing, Alice got up to put the kettle on. She paused at the window of her modern flat to look out at the sea, blue today, sparkling under the sun. She had moved back to Bournemouth before the sale of Harcombe House was completed, aided by her friend Audrey who had been away during Alice's winter visit. Audrey was helping Alice to pick up the threads of her life and thought it bad for her to brood on the case, now that it was in progress. Today she was coming to coffee. Alice wondered how much longer the trial would last. All along, Terry had protested his innocence, blaming Sue and saying that he had helped her because he was sorry for her. It was so like him to twist facts like that, Alice thought. She hoped it would all be over by Sunday, when Giles was coming to lunch. She looked forward to that. He was so much happier now; that was the best thing that had happened as a result of Jonathan's death. Of course, she reminded herself, he would probably have had to accept voluntary redundancy anyway, but he might not have made the break with Helen. As it was, he had used his severance pay to buy a small printing works in Winchester and a flat on the edge of the city. He would probably see almost as much of his daughters as before, Alice thought, since they were away at school for so much of the year. Alice had not seen him drink anything stronger than bitter lemon since the day Sue died.

Helen had finished renovating Harcombe House, including the installation of an effective heating system, as part of the deal over its sale to a television chat show host, and had moved into a small manor house in the Cotswolds. Her plan now was to keep on the move, doing up run-down houses for profitable re-sale.

While the kettle boiled, Alice picked up the paper again. On oath in the box, Terry had sworn that he had been appalled when Sue had shown him the body of Jonathan Cooper, struck down, in self-defence, by her hand.

'Struck down by your hand,' prosecution counsel had maintained, having already established that Terry, or someone with his blood group, which was not the same as Jonathan's, had enjoyed sexual relations with Sue in the big bed at the lodge.

No one had believed him when he said he had never been violent, apart from his mother, who remembered him salvaging a drowning rat as a child. There was something morbid in that, defence counsel had thought, and suppressed the story, but it had appeared in the popular press. Alice recalled Terry's wide, innocent-seeming grin. Who would have believed that he could be so wicked?

She often grieved for Sue.